AGAINST me

a Cedar Tree novel - book three

by

FREYA BARKER

AGAINST ME
(Cedar Tree, Book THREE)

ISBN: 9781682309094

Cover Design:

Rebel Edit & Design

Cover Model:

Chris Simons

Photographer:

Christopher Correia of CJC Photography

DEDICATION

For Dana Hook – A woman who really needs no introduction, since she is a universe all by herself.

Irreverent, loyal, loud and loving – You have a heart the size of South America and continuously try to fit everyone in it. If you had the power, you'd turn everyone into a bestselling author – hell, you try hard enough. Not only my partner in Rebel, but my bitch-buddy and task master; pimp queen and editor extraordinaire; you are so elemental and entwined with my books, I swear I'd be lost without you. Not to mention I'd miss my daily dose of hilarity either by your hand or at your expense!

Love you hard and always.

In Memory of:

Blue

TABLE OF CONTENTS

PROLOGUE

The first thing I notice when she walks into the room are her pale green eyes. It almost looks like they're lit from within.

"Hey Katie, meet Caleb. He'll be working with us on contract basis, same as you."

I hold out my hand and she slips in her smaller one. Soft - the feeling of her skin against mine causes an involuntary shiver up my spine, and I notice her sharp intake of breath. I try to get a read on her, but her eyes lower under my scrutiny. *Hmmm.* Interesting. The top of her head reaches my chin, and to my large frame, her entire body seems much smaller than my first impression of her.

"Good to meet you." Her voice has a smoky sound to it, a deeper pitch, a quality you wouldn't expect coming from the woman with a pixie face, flowing dark hair and those large expressive eyes. Despite her athletic build, she almost appears fragile to me.

"Same here."

Her eyes flick up to mine and then move to Gus, owner of Gus Flemming Investigations, and the man whose reputation finally convinced me to give in to his tenacious pursuit of my services.

I am a loner. I don't generally work with partners or under a boss. I like my independence and the freedom it provides me, but I haven't been able to resist the lure of working with the investigator who has one of the highest success rates in the state. It helps that the case he called me in on hits close to home. Literally. A child gone missing from the reservation I grew up on. I feel this one deep. I left the reservation under less than friendly circumstance. My fifteen year-old sister had died after a brutally short stint with cancer, leaving my family destroyed. My parents were never the same and both my brother and I carried the scars of our fucked up family life, on our souls, after she passed away.

Only seventeen at the time, almost eighteen, I was marked by the experience and pissed off at the world. I'm sure they were happy to see the back of me when I enlisted.

"I want you to work together on the disappearance of this twelve-year old. Stick your heads together and see what you can come up with. She's been gone for seventy-two hours and her family is frantic. Details are in the file."

Gus hands each of us a folder and his eyes linger on my hand, the one that still holds Katie's much smaller one. Reluctantly I let her go to grab the file Gus is holding out.

Great. My first partner and it has to be this woman. When I look at her, my displeasure must show on my face because her eyes are shooting fire. I can hear Gus chuckle, "Don't underestimate that tidy little package you see there, my friend. Katie has proven herself to be a great asset to my team when called upon."

"What the fuck, Gus? Tidy little package? Sexist much?" She punches him in the shoulder.

"Ah babe, you know I couldn't do without ya…" Gus throws his arm around her shoulder and smiles down.

10

The interaction between the two should've been a warning.

"Get behind me," I hiss at Katie as she tries to get ahead of me into the small shed.

We managed to get a lead on the girl from one of her friends in Shiprock. Or rather, Katie managed to. She was amazing at pulling the information from the twelve-year old friend. The missing girl had been talking to a guy online who had filled her head with promises and lies, finally convincing her to meet him in town. Her poor parents were drowning in self-recrimination for not keeping a closer eye on her internet activities. But we had a place to start and with the help of a young computer whiz kid Gus has working at the office, we managed to identify the guy. A local kid, only eighteen himself, had been talking to her online for the past two months. When we visit his home address, he's not there, but his mother is. She directs us to the small building at the back of this abandoned business that belongs to his dad.

"Don't fucking tell me what to do, Caleb." Katie hisses back, pushing ahead despite my caution. Following close behind her, I see some movement from the corner of my eye, just as we step inside. I instinctively throw myself on Katie, taking her down with force. The bullet that explodes from the shaking gun that had been pointed at her finds its way, unobstructed, into the wall on our other side. I roll off Katie and come up with my own weapon ready in my hand, aiming it at the figure in the corner. The acrid smell of urine hits my nose as the kid who's holed up there throws down the gun and wets his pants.

"Don't h-hurt me," he stutters, his hands stretched toward me with his palms out.

"Jesus," I run my free hand through my hair, scanning the small space while keeping my gun trained on the kid. "You okay, Katie?"

"Fine." Comes her terse reply.

"Can you check on her?" I nod my head in the direction of a pile of bedding, hiding what appears to be a very scared young girl. I get up and make sure the gun is far away from the kid's reach before pushing him face-down on the ground and securing his hands with a zip tie. "Is she ok?" I ask as I listen to Katie's soothing murmurs as she checks over the terrified little girl.

"You hurting anywhere, honey?"

"N-no, he didn't hurt me," a shaky little voice answers Katie's question. "He loves me."

Katie looks over at me with her eyebrows raised, feeling the same shock and frustration she obviously does. Fucking internet romance gone bad, and I almost killed the kid. Christ, I need a drink.

By the time we get most of their story, the sound of emergency vehicles begin filling the yard, so I grab my charge by the arm and pull him up.

"Come on, Romeo. Time to face the music."

Katie follows close behind with her arm around the young girl who's crying. "He didn't do anything wrong! We just wanted to be together."

"Sweetheart, he's an adult and you're a minor. That's wrong, and it's illegal. Not only that, he tried to shoot us with a gun he stole from his father's locker. That is all kinds of wrong."

Katie only succeeds in making the girl cry harder.

With both kids taken care of and her parents on their way to the hospital where she'll be checked out, Katie and I are left staring at each other.

"Look-"

"Listen up-" Katie interrupts, "I'm sorry."

I'm surprised; I was about to apologize to her for taking her down so hard. "What for?"

"I could've gotten us hurt. I was pissed and not focused on my surroundings."

"Well I was about to tell you sorry myself, for trying to order you around. I'm still trying to get used to this 'partner' thing."

She cracks a little smile and it does something to me. Even the brief minutes laying on top of her in the midst of chaos, I was fully aware of every curve of her body and the faint citrus smell of her in my nostrils.

"Want to go for a drink with me and discuss our partnership?"

Her eyes go wide and she's about to answer me when the slam of a car door and fast approaching footsteps grab our attention.

"Holy fuck, honey - you okay?" Gus wraps his arms around Katie and presses a kiss to the top of her head. Oh. So that's how it is.

I shake my head slightly and try to shake the unfamiliar burn of jealousy. Damn.

After a brief report to Gus, I make my excuses and am on my way to my car when Katie calls my name and I turn around. Trotting up to where I'm standing by my truck, she grabs onto my arm.

"Rain check?"

I look over to where Gus is standing, talking to one of the officers left on scene and contemplate my answer.

"You let me know when you're available and I might take you up on it."

A flash of guilt passes through her eyes and with a nod, she walks back over to his side.

CHAPTER ONE

"Morning, Katie." Sue, one of the day nurses walks into my room. "Ready for physio?"

"Sure," I tell her, less than enthusiastically. Still, she pushes my chair into the hall in the direction of the clinic area where the physiotherapist is likely already waiting for me with his weapons of torture.

Four fucking months I've been stuck in this damn wheelchair and my physiotherapy sessions are the only times I'm able to get out to move, which is the only reason I'm still going. They have me hung up in some contraption over a treadmill where I'm supposed to be exercising my leg muscles so they don't atrophy. I still can't carry my own weight and I'm not surprised— I've turned into a friggin' blimp in an alarmingly short period of time.

Ever since I sustained my brain injury almost half a year ago, I've had to relearn so much. It's been a long and tedious road, and still my legs can't seem to get it together. I'm pretty much fed up with this whole situation. For someone always on the go and quite strong and athletic, sitting in one place all day really does a number on me. As a result, I've really let myself go. I mean really.

I snort when I think about yesterday, the first time I went out in public. Arlene re-opened her diner after it burned down and Caleb had insisted I stop moping in my room and got me pissed off enough that I ended up joining him for the opening party. God, what a disaster. When he picked me up, he scowled when he saw what I had done with my hair.

"What the fuck, Katie? What'd you do to your hair? It's all gone."

True. I had it all cut off. My outgrown dark, thick pile of hair is gone. The hairdresser who came to my room asked me to confirm it at least four different times, confirming that that was what I really wanted. I told her to cut it super short; so short that I wouldn't even have to worry about brushing anything. I was tired of not being able to do much more than tying it back into a ponytail. This way it won't get in my way when I'm running through my exercises, or at least that's what I tell myself, which is partially true. If I were perfectly honest with myself, I'd have to admit that I was just desperate for a change–any change– something to give myself a kick-start, but if I admit that, I'd have to explain and I'm not exactly sure of what I'm looking for yet myself.

"I needed it gone. It gets in the way when I exercise. This is easier," I explain, hoping he'll take that at face value, but judging by the look on his face, he's not completely sold. He doesn't question it though; he simply looks at me with his light-brown, almost hazel eyes, that always somehow see right through me. From the first time we met, he seems to have the ability to read me like a book, and more than once, it's gotten us out of some sticky situations.

Finally one side of his mouth tilts up and he nods. "I like it," is all he says and rubs his hand over my head.

Without another word spoken, we drive the three and a half hours from Grand Junction to Cedar Tree. Caleb often goes through these phases of almost complete silence for long periods of time. At first they unnerved me, but now I'm getting used to them and to be honest, I don't mind it much at all. I just pull out my Kindle and read one of the many books that I've one-clicked in recent weeks. I spend a lot of time with my head in fantasyland. Let's face it; you can make life as simple or as complicated there and it takes your mind off whatever is going on in your life. In my case, there isn't a hell of a lot of anything going on.

When Caleb wheels me into the diner, I can tell by the looks of all the people I know in Cedar Tree, that they're shocked at my appearance. The first time I came here to help my boss, Gus, protect his girlfriend, who was being pursued by some shady organized crime characters, I'd looked much different. My hair had been long and healthy and I didn't have the extra thirty pounds that have settled on my body in the meantime. In part, the medication they give me is to blame, causing me to retain water and gain weight, but I also haven't been using my muscles the way I used to, and let's face it; eating is a way to cope with boredom. I've always struggled a bit with my weight, which is why I used to exercise vigorously every day and ate healthy. I guess I'm slacking off.

Emma is the first one to approach me, giving me a huge hug, telling me that I looked good. Sure. I like Emma, don't get me wrong, but it still stung when Gus had fallen head over teakettle for her in a matter of days.

Gus is next and ruffles my hair, just like Caleb had done.

"How's it going, Katie-girl?"

"I'm good. Fine really," I try to convince him as much as myself. Damn these investigator guys; both Caleb and Gus have an eerie knack for spotting a lie a mile away, and Gus is the second man to throw a doubtful look at me within hours of Caleb doing the same.

"If you say so," is Gus' response.

"Love the hair. It suits you." This from Seb, Arlene's cook and now lover, who has come walking out of the kitchen to greet me, but the next person isn't as complimentary.

"Fucking hell, woman. You almost look like a dyke!"

"Arlene, good to see you too," I manage to get out, laughing at all the shocked faces around me, "You like the cut that much, huh?"

Arlene isn't one with a ton of tact or diplomacy, but she is honest to the core and always tells it like it is. I can appreciate that.

"You becoming a smartass now too, Katie?" She teases me back with a little smile on her face.

Catching up with everyone is nice, but I still feel too self-conscious sitting in this damn chair. There are some vaguely familiar faces here and a few I'm sure I haven't met before. The drive and then the crowded party have me tired in no time, and before I know what's happening, Caleb has me outside on our way to his truck.

"Wait. Where are we going?" I ask him.

"You're tired, and we have a long drive back."

"Back already?"

"It's a three and a half hour drive, little one. You'll be asleep within 20 minutes, I bet," he says, smiling as he lifts me out of the chair and into the passenger seat.

"I can stand for a bit, you know," I remind him.

"Yeah, I know, but you're tired and had a few drinks. Not taking any chances."

I choose not to say anything, but simply allow myself to enjoy his fussing, just this once because he's right. I am tired and I'm not looking forward to the drive back.

Of course he's right. We're barely past Cortez before I doze off because I can't remember a damn thing after that, not until we get back to the centre where once again, Caleb lifts me out of the truck and into my chair before wheeling me inside.

Larchwood Inns is the rehabilitation centre where I have spent the past months relearning everything I lost as a result of my head injury. I remember clearly the first time I opened my eyes in the hospital in Durango and saw Caleb's face. It surprised me and I wanted to say something but my ears couldn't recognize the sounds that came from my mouth. I was terrified and not quite sure what was happening to me. When Caleb called for the nurse, he wouldn't let go of my hand. His calm voice told me not to try and speak yet, just to give it time. When the doctor showed up and told me the extent of my injuries, his thumb never stopped stroking the skin of my hand. The news was devastating for me. I was told I had to relearn everything, and that it wasn't clear what the long-term effects were going to be. In a flash, I saw my life as it was falling apart. My independence was gone. With no remaining family, at least none that I knew of at the time, the only option for me was to transferr to an inpatient rehabilitation facility, where my basic abilities would have to be relearned.

There were times I wished I hadn't survived. The idea of that kind of dependency went against everything I had worked for. Thirty-seven years old and back to having someone wipe my ass. It was humiliating and demeaning, but Caleb was a constant—encouraging me to claim my life back. He also seemed to be the only one who was able to interpret my incoherent mumblings, or perhaps it was his uncanny ability to read people in general. Regardless, I was glad whenever he was around. It almost felt like I was able to communicate after all. Although why he insisted on being at my bedside all the time was a mystery to me. I mean, we'd been friends for years, but I never would have expected of him to spend as much time with me as he did.

Moving from the hospital to the centre had jump-started my recovery. At first I was taken aback by the aggressive approach and intensive full days of therapy, but I was grateful for it the first time I managed to speak a fully formed and coherent sentence. My biggest obstacle remains my lower half. My hands I was able to use almost from the start, but the larger motor skills lagged. My arms were getting stronger, but my legs simply wouldn't move. To this day they don't move, not the way I want them to anyway. With support I can now stand, but walking is still difficult and I'm beginning to become discouraged.

I know this trip to Cedar Tree was an attempt by Caleb to shift my focus, to see if it would motivate me to keep working at it. It did, but most of the time I'm bored out of my brain, and despite asking both Gus and Caleb many times if I can do some computer research for GFI, they're hesitant to allow me to focus on anything but my recovery. Me? I'm starting to wonder if I'll ever walk again. Nevertheless, I still let the nurse wheel me to my physio sessions, where I know I'll come away frustrated again.

"Hey Katie. How's my pretty neighbor doing?"

Juan is sitting right outside the physio clinic where he sits every day, waiting for the 'pretty girls' to pass by, just so he can flirt with them. He's harmless and charming, and at eighty-two, he's still a handsome man. I bet he was a real catch in his younger days.

"Doing good, Casanova. You're looking smart today," I say with a wink.

He chuckles as he always does when I flirt back. It's amazing how it's the little things that have the ability to make or break a day. This daily interaction never fails to put a smile on my face and lift my spirits. Part of me suspects it's why Juan makes sure to sit in that spot, right at the start of my therapy session.

"Come have dinner with me tonight? I'll save you a spot in the dining room."

His hopeful expression has my determination of 'not to get too attached,' wavering. At least once or twice a week he asks me to have dinner with him in the dining hall, and I have a hard time refusing the man. He apparently has children, but I rarely see anyone come and visit him.

"I'll be there. Five o'clock okay?"

One of the things I'm still getting used to is the food service hours. Based mostly on the needs and desires of the seniors, who make up about eighty-five percent of the population here, it's unusually early for me. Not that I have a particular time for any meal, I've just been used to eating on the run most of my life. This type of structure is a bit confining for me, but when in Rome and all that.

The response I get from Juan is a big smile and two thumbs up.

Encouraged by the best physio session so far this afternoon, I make my way over to the table where Juan has reserved a spot for me.

"So what's on the menu for tonight?" I ask him, wheeling my chair up to the table.

"Grilled chicken or lasagna," he smiles, already knowing what my favorite will be.

"No-brainer. Lasagna of course," I confirm.

"Love to see a woman enjoying her food. I can't stand those people who fuss over every bite they put in their mouths. Have you noticed that most of those folks seem unhappy?"

I laugh, having heard this theory of his before.

"You know I have no problems enjoying food. Heck, look at me. I've indulged a bit too much lately," I motion to my uncooperative body that's been getting softer and softer over the past months.

Juan just shakes his head at me. "Men like to feel the softness of a woman, my dear. Don't doubt that for a minute."

I'm relieved at the interruption when a server comes to the table and asks our choice of meal. Both of us order lasagna and Juan gives me a conspiratory wink. Cheeky old geezer.

"So, tell me how the search for your birth family is coming along?" he prompts me.

When my father died three years ago, I was going through some boxes from his office and found adoption records. It completely threw me off; I'd never been told that I was adopted. I'd always figured I'd had shitty luck for parents, but until that moment, I hadn't realized I had shitty luck times two. Go figure. My first parents give me up for adoption, and the second set of parents made me feel like a burden. Part of me is relieved to find that the people who raised me did not in fact create me. I just hope my genetic donors are a bit more... let's say, palatable.

I haven't been in touch with my mother for years, not since she walked out when I was fourteen. I couldn't tell you if she's alive or not. I never did much with the discovery of my adoption, not until I came to Larchwoods. With nothing better to do, and Gus not letting me in on any cases, finding out more about my biological parents seems like the closest I'll get to an investigation. A bit of a diversion, I suppose, although I must admit that it's become more than just a passing of time. Juan is the only one I've told about my search for my family so far, and he's been very encouraging.

"I've narrowed the adoption lawyers' names down to a handful of candidates, but no one I talk to seems to want to provide answers, not as long as there's a possibility my adoptive mother is alive somewhere. First, I'll have to find her."

I know there's a quick way to get some answers, but I don't really want to involve Caleb or GFI at this point in time. Call it being stubborn, but this is something I want to do for myself, if only to prove that I'm not completely useless.

CHAPTER TWO

"How is she really doing?" Emma has me pinned down in the kitchen of her and Gus's newly renovated house.

"Hard to tell. She recovered most of her basic skills without much effort, but using her legs seems to be an unexpected challenge. I'm thinking she's losing faith."

"I would if I were stuck in a facility with mostly seniors. I don't care how good a reputation this place has, being surrounded by elderly people all day, every day, must become depressing at some point, don't you think?"

I can tell Emma is working up to something. She has this diplomatic way of laying out the groundwork in order to get her point across more effectively. Curious to see what she has up her sleeve, I nod my agreement.

"Excellent. I knew you'd be on board," she smiles brilliantly.

Wait. What did I miss here? I can't remember agreeing to anything, but the big grin on Emma's face tells me I'll find out soon enough.

"I have already talked to Faith's therapist, and she says she will even come work with her at home if needed."

Faith is Seb's younger sister who also suffered a head injury, but at a much younger age and frankly, with much more devastating results. Confined to not only her wheelchair, but with the capacity and mental maturity of an eight or nine-year-old. She lives in a nursing facility in Cortez.

"Wait a second. What home? Katie doesn't have a home anymore. She let go of her apartment in Grand Junction and hasn't explored any other options."

Emma smiles like the cat that got the canary. "Of course she has a home. Now that you're buying your own place in town, the guesthouse is free, and what more perfect place since it's completely accessible."

My boss's wife has rheumatoid arthritis, among other things, that has limited her physical abilities. Not that that would ever slow down Emma. Good lord, no. The woman can be like a bulldozer if you don't watch it.

"Uhm, Emma? Have you discussed this idea with Katie? Or even with Gus? I mean, the two do have a history. They might not be as comfortable with this idea of yours."

I hate bursting her bubble, but the reality is that Katie was hurt when Gus fell in love with Emma. I'm pretty sure there'd been some hope that her occasional entanglements with Gus might've turned into something more. Not that she ever told me, but I'm able to read that woman like a book. Katie might not be so eager to live with the daily view of something she missed out on, and I have a feeling Emma may not have considered all the emotional pitfalls that Katie's moving here might open up. Sounds like a potential minefield to me.

The brilliance has gone off Emma's smile, but she shrugs her shoulders and stands as tall as she can. "I know Gus wouldn't hesitate in welcoming Katie if it meant she'd have some friends around her to motivate her. And Katie, well, I had hoped you might broach the subject with her."

It's been three weeks since I forced Katie to come with me for the re-opening of Arlene's Diner, and although she finally conceded, it wasn't entirely convincing.

I'm a selfish bastard, I know. It was as much for my benefit as hers. I'm ready to make Cedar Tree my home. I even bought property, but I can't see moving here with Katie stuck in Grand Junction, keeping herself locked away in that damn hospital like a hermit. I'm not gonna let her hide out there licking her wounds for much longer. I want her to reconnect to people and know she has a safe place. The hospital isn't it.

Ever since she was attacked, while on protective detail last year, she's withdrawn from everyone she knows. I suspect in part because the person she was protecting was her boss's new girlfriend, but I wouldn't be surprised if she wasn't partially relieved not to have to see her ex-lover with his new woman on a regular basis. I know Gus felt pretty casual about their former relationship, but I'm not so sure about Katie. Add to that little fiasco a blow to the head – so fucking hard that she had to relearn even the most basic of things – and it's not surprising she wants to crawl in a hole. Not that I'd let her, but still.

I want her close. It's that simple. For years I've watched her keep everyone at a safe distance, even Gus, our boss with whom she had a relationship at the time, had not been able to penetrate the determined and independent barrier Katie pulls up around her, but I can see the secret longing there. Always have, and from day one, I've felt the urge to scale those walls, but I've bided my time.

Not like me to tread on someone else's territory for one, and for another, I don't think she was near ready for me.

The moment I saw her lying crumpled in that hallway, blood pooling away from the gash in her head and not knowing whether she was dead or alive, all that changed. Fuck ready. The thought I might have lost her before ever having had her still makes me break out in cold sweat. Not a chance in hell I was going to let her get too far from me, be it physically or emotionally.

"Hey Caleb. Been here long?" Gus walks into the kitchen with a chin lift to me, then turns to Emma to corner her against the counter for a kiss I probably shouldn't be witness to.

"Mmmmmm, followed the scent of baking in. Smells good in here, Peach."

Hard to miss the mouth-watering fragrance coming from Emma's oven. She provides her friend Arlene's diner in town with all their fresh baked pies and has quite a collection lined up on her counters already.

Emma smiles at him, "Don't worry, I have one of your favorites put aside."

"Great. Caleb, wanna pop in my office? I have a new case I wanna go over with you."

"Sure." I grab my coffee and follow him into the new addition that was recently built onto their bungalow. It houses the new offices of GFI, the security and investigative company that I have committed myself to working full-time for now. The decision hadn't been too hard. After my years as a Ranger, working free-lance suited my need to feel independent, but for the last while, I've been wanting to set down some roots. Funny, for the longest time all I wanted to do was to fucking rip out every last one of my roots, but a lot of anger and bitterness I nurtured when I was younger has long since dulled to a slight bruise. Leftovers from growing up on the reservation.

Now with Katie's future uncertain, I feel even more set to find some stability. For me, and hopefully for her.

"Sit," Gus indicates the chair on the other side of his desk, which is littered with maps and pictures.

"A small plane crashed just outside of Shiprock, New Mexico, about a week ago. Pilot died on impact. The single passenger was rushed to the hospital, but died a few hours later. Close to a hundred pounds of meth was recovered from the wreckage."

A whistle escapes my lips. "That's near a million and a half street value. Airplane? You thinking cartel?"

Gus nods. "That's what the feds are going with, especially since they believe the passenger to have been Hernan Duarte, the youngest of three brothers running the Agave cartel. Last three years, the cartel has been slowly making its way north from the Jalisco region of Mexico, up the West coast and across the border into the United States. They haven't been able to pin connections, but suspect crystal meth is being fed into the US through some reservations in the Four Corners region."

When he looks at me his eyes are solemn.

"You want me for my connections to Shiprock," I say, perhaps a bit short.

"The feds want you. You have a reputation as a tracker and you grew up on the reservation. I understand what I'm asking you is opportunistic and probably not easy for you but fuck, Caleb. Those kinds of numbers scare me. What it translates to on the streets scares me, and what it will do to the reservations scares me. All of it scares the crap out of me."

I drop my head in my hands. Jesus. For years, I've avoided going back as much as possible, not wanting the reminders of either the good times that won't come again, or the bad ones that are too fresh in my mind still. I can count the times I've returned home on one hand.

I grew up on the reservation near Shiprock, New Mexico - in a pretty regular family. My dad was a carpenter by trade, but did a lot of local general contracting work. Mom chose to stay close to home and take care of us kids—three of us. I was the oldest, my sister Nascha followed behind me, and my brother, Malachi, closed out the trio. A normal childhood, enriched by our culture and never crippled by it, not until in the short span of three months, cancer took out my sister and left devastation in its path. She was only fifteen. I was a year older and had seen my mom become a shadow of grief, no room left for anything more than the pain she carried. My pop found solace in a bottle and lost all care. I was angry and made some seriously fucked up choices I wish I could take back, but Malachi... poor Mal was only twelve years old at the time and had no one to steer him straight, so he sank to the bottom.

"Caleb?"

Gus interrupts my train of thought and I realize he's waiting for my response.

"Yes, of course. Of course I'll go. I just... can you give me a couple of days so I can check in with Katie in Grand Junction? There are some things I need to go over with her before I disappear for however long."

"Absolutely. I'll let them know."

I can feel his scrutiny, so I lift my eyes and face him.

"How is Katie?"

"She's... she's stuck. Her legs aren't coming along like the rest of her body did and she seems to be losing the fight a little. I plan on bringing her here."

Gus's eyebrows shoot up. "That so? Does she know about that?" he chuckles.

"Told you there were some things I needed to go over with her about," I tell him with a smirk.

"Gonna enjoy watching this one develop," Gus leans back in his chair and rubs his hands together. "Seen it coming for a while, but I can't wait for the show."

Smug bastard.

"Yeah, yeah. Fuck off, asshole. I'm sure it won't be half as entertaining as it was to see you get balled and chained."

"Those were just fireworks compared to the nuclear explosion I see a-comin'!"

CHAPTER THREE

"Her name is Cora Helen Acker, nee Simpson. Date of birth is December 14, 1948. My dad always said she was originally from Boulder, but I haven't been able to locate any known relatives there. Everything so far has been a dead end. Last known place of residence is Montrose, Colorado, and she walked out of there 23 years ago without a trace."

I scan over the paperwork to see if there was any more information that I could give Neil, but other than my adoptive father's name and the date of adoption, it's all I have.

"I'll run it through DMV and I'll see if there are any warrants outstanding. I'll include any other databases I can think of. Katie, are you sure you don't want Gus's help with this?"

"Keep it to yourself for now, but I don't want you to lie about it. If he finds out, he finds out. It's just something I want to do for myself. I really appreciate your help with this, Neil. With GFI now based from Cedar Tree, are you considering moving down as well?"

"Meh, not sure yet. Don't want to leave Dana alone in Grand Junction, and we still have the office to keep running. Caleb continues to use this as a base for some of his jobs as well. We'll see what the next year brings. I'm too young to give up on the Grand Junction nightlife already," he says with a chuckle.

Neil is such a sweetie; a young mid-twenties computer techie who has worked for Gus Flemming Investigations for a few years now and runs the satellite office in Grand Junction along with Dana, who is one hell of an office manager.

"Well, I really appreciate your help, Neil. I wasn't able to get very far on my own and the adoption lawyer was a dead end without my adoptive mother's consent."

"I'll let you know if I find something, Katie, and you take care of yourself. We miss you."

I have trouble swallowing the big lump that forms in my throat. I miss them all too. So much.

"Yeah, me too."

"Ah fuck *Yázhí*, come here."

I hadn't heard Caleb come in. The rumble of his voice penetrates and his big arms fold around me from behind.

The phone call with Neil had left me unsettled, and the flow of emotions, once started, seems endless. So I just let it come. Let it all fucking flow out of me, because frankly, I'm so tired of not feeling myself. I've always been alone, I guess, but I've never felt really lonely until now. It sucks. It really does, and it makes me weepy and emotional. I'm not good with that. I normally stay busy, but I feel idle; useless. *Arghhh!*

Now being held by in his strong arms, and his warm breath against my ear, I start bawling in earnest. What the fuck is wrong with me? I don't even resist when Caleb lifts me out of the chair and settles me on his lap on the bed, still firmly held in the circle of his arms. One of his hands slides up to press my head to his chest. Those fucking arms...

Feels like I've cried a bathtub full by the time the flow stems a little, and all this time, Caleb hasn't said a word. He just keeps massaging my scalp with the fingers of his hand and never lets up the tight hold on my body.

"Sorry," I mumble.

"For what? Been waiting for that."

I push back and look at him indignantly. "What do you mean, you've been waiting for that?"

A small pull at the corner of his mouth is a tell he's amused, which only pisses me off. Waiting for me to fall apart? I try to move off his lap, but his hands slide to my hips and hold me in place.

"Been waiting for you to do some processing instead of burying, which is what you've mostly been doing. Can't rebuild on loose ground, Katie. You bury too much, the ground's gonna be pretty loose," Caleb cups my chin in his hand and lifts it so I'm looking into his dark, hazel eyes. "You know you gotta get rid of the build-up in order to move forward."

I hate it when he talks in that obscure language, but I still know exactly what he means. I hate it even more when he's right. *Frig*. Leaning forward, I let my forehead drop against his chest and I can feel the vibrations of his deep chuckle.

"You annoy me."

This only makes him chuckle louder.

"I know. Now, you wanna tell me what brought that on?"

"Nope, 'cause that's probably gonna have me blubbering again and I *really* don't wanna go there." I shake my head but don't lift my head off Caleb's chest. It feels nice. His large hand slowly strokes up and down my spine, giving my exposed neck a small squeeze every time he reaches it, sending vague shivers of awareness over the surface of my skin.

"Fair enough. We'll save it, but I'm not gonna drop it. We'll tackle it when I get back."

"Back?" I sit back to create a bit of distance. The close contact is confusing me, but I'm struck by the dark look on Caleb's face.

"Yeah, I've gotta head out on a job in New Mexico; heading back to the old stomping grounds it looks like. It's where I grew up on the reservation. Not sure how long it will be, but I won't be too far so you need me for anything, you call."

"Okay. Well, no need to worry 'cause I'm fine. Taken care of, and all that."

I know I'm being dismissive, but my emotions are still a bit raw and I don't know what the hell to say.

Then Caleb frames my face in his hands and leans his forehead against mine.

"No, little one. You don't get it. I wanted to be around to hold you when you let go a little, and I'm fucking thrilled I could do that. It's a start. There is so much more we need to talk about but it's getting late and I have to get a move on. When I'm back, I really want to spend some time talking, but in the meantime, you need me for *anything,* you call me. You hear me now?"

I heard. I'm still not quite sure I'm computing, but I nod.

"Good."

After he lifts me back into my chair, he gives me a peck on the cheek and ensures me he'll be in touch. Caleb is out the door, leaving me to check out his fine physique as he walks away, which is nearly as fine as it is coming. *Holy shit.*

The rest of the afternoon, I spend scanning archives and back issues of the Montrose Daily Press and the Boulder Daily Camera to look for any reference to Cora Acker, without much success. That, and replaying Caleb's slightly cryptic words over and over again in my head. For the past six months, he's gone from a good friend at the periphery of my life, to someone who seems to be in the thick of things. Every time I open my eyes, and as with everything else, I have successfully avoided looking too closely. I've never been comfortable being anyone's focus. It makes me very uneasy. The more their attention is on you, the more you feel the loss when they tire of you. No, I've been quite happy keeping everyone outside a certain perimeter, and making sure I stay there as well.

Somehow though, Caleb snuck in closer than anyone has before, and I honestly don't know how to feel about that. Part of me wants that safe space back, but shit. There's a huge part that really, really likes *this*—This closeness, or whatever it is. I just know that it feels nice, yet scary, too. Damn. These feelings I get, they're not 'friendly' feelings, not at all. Especially not when he calls me 'little one.' I want to purr and rub up against him. *Gah!*

My eyes are gritty from rubbing and staring at the screen for hours, when there's a knock at my door.

"Yup, door's open." I call out, expecting one of the nursing staff. What I didn't expect was Juan pushing the door open gingerly, a tentative smile on his face.

"Afternoon Juan. Are you alright?"

I wheel myself over to him when he doesn't come into the room any further and lingers in the doorway. Close up, I can see his eyes are red-rimmed and watery.

"You want to come in and sit down?"

Concerned with his continued silence, I gently grab his hand and encourage him to come inside, considering whether I should ring the bell for nursing staff or not. The poor man looks desolate as he makes his way over to the lone chair and sits down, his eyes down on his hands he holds, folded in his lap.

"Juan, you're worrying me. What's wrong?" I try again, and this time when his eyes scan up to meet mine, a lone tear trickles down his cheek and a shuddering breath leaves him.

"I... I received some bad news." With that, his head drops down again.

Rolling as close as I can get, I lean forward and put my hands over his.

"Do you want to tell me about it?" I ask him, but he immediately starts shaking his head.

"Can't... They won't like that. I'm not supposed to talk, it makes them angry." Juan pulls his hands out from under mine and pushes himself up from the chair.

I'm at a loss. Angry? Who would get mad at a harmless old man?

Who gets angry, Juan?"

But he's already moving toward the door, mumbling to himself in Spanish before he opens the door, almost falling through when it's pulled open from the outside.

"*Qué estás haciendo aquí, viejo?*"

The bitten-off Spanish words don't match the sharply dressed, handsome man standing in the hallway. Neither does the furious look he throws poor Juan who seems to shrink even further under his glare.

"Excuse me," I offer, trying to get some control of a situation that feels out of control. "Are you looking for someone?"

The man's eyes whip to me and his face does an instant transformation.

"Ah, *discúlpeme*. I'm sorry for the disturbance. My uncle... he is confused. I hope he didn't bother you?"

The toothy smile he throws me is blinding, or at least it would be if I were looking directly at him, which I'm not. I'm keeping an eye on Juan who's tried to slip out into the hallway, but his nephew seems to have quite a firm grasp on his arm. Something feels off, so I tread carefully.

"No bother at all. Your uncle came to check on me. I haven't been feeling well and he's always kind enough to look in on me."

Fuck. I can't lie for shit, and it is abundantly clear when I see the slight narrowing of the man's eyes—he's not buying it for one second. The brilliant white smile has all but disappeared and all that's left on his dark face is the slight sneer of his lips.

"Wonderful! I see you found your uncle," Sue, who is apparently on shift again, walks right up behind him and breaks a rather awkward stare down between us.

With a terse nod in my direction, he turns and walks out, taking his uncle with him. Just before the door to Juan's room closes behind them, shutting off all sound, I hear the old man's voice say, "*Por favor, mi hijo,*"

"That guy gives me the creeps," Sue whispers to me. "This is the second time I've seen him and it's not getting better." With a grimace and a faux shiver, she pulls the door shut and leaves me alone with my thoughts.

Mi hijo?

I remember enough high school Spanish to know that means, *my son.*

CHAPTER FOUR

My phone rings shortly after I cross state lines into New Mexico.

"Whereabouts are you?" Gus wants to know.

"Just coming up to Aztec, New Mexico. The drive through the mountains was pretty bad. I should've come the other way and cut through Utah, but since the weather forecast was clear, I thought I'd be ok. Didn't expect parts of the 550 would be closed off because of mudslides."

"Where was this?"

"Just north of Durango, but there were slides as far back as Ouray, they just weren't blocking the road all the way, but it made driving treacherous even so."

"Must be the early spring runoff we're having. I know they've had some flooding in the lower lying areas here. Mancos has had a few issues. So what are your plans? It's almost eight o'clock now."

"I'll stop in Farmington, grab a bite and check into the Travelodge. Too late to do anything useful tonight, so I might as well set up camp there. No half-decent motels any closer to Shiprock anyway, and I don't mind a little bit of distance for when I need it."

"Sounds good. Check in tomorrow night when you've had a chance to look around."

Gus seems ready to hang up, but before he does, I decide to address the unsettled feeling that's been with me ever since I left Katie about six hours ago.

"Will do, but can you do me a favor and keep tabs on Katie? Saw her this afternoon and she knows I'm on a job, but I don't feel settled."

"Did she say anything? Something come up?" he wants to know.

"No. Just don't feel good about being half a day away from her."

I hear a low chuckle over the line and curse under my breath.

"You are so fucked," Gus feels the need to point out.

"Pointing out the obvious, my friend. Quit yanking my chain."

"No worries. I'll keep tabs. I'll give Neil a call in a bit. He's almost around the corner from Larchwood Inns, that close enough for you?"

"That's about as effective as buying her a watch-bunny. Jesus, Gus..." I run my hand through my hair, not feeling any better at all when Gus starts laughing.

"One of these days, I'm gonna let you in on a little secret about our quiet Neil. His waters run deeper than even you have obviously detected, and I can't tell you how much that tickles me. Trust me when I say Katie will be well taken care of. You have my word."

Not left with much choice, I reluctantly agree and sign off, ready for something hot in my stomach and a place to bed down.

A decent meal and a good night's sleep have done me good, and I find I'm not dreading the upcoming reunion with my family and childhood home as much as I thought I might. The drive into Shiprock is pretty uneventful, and it isn't long before I find myself turning onto the dirt road that leads to my parents' place.

The old house is surrounded by farm fields—had been for as long as I can remember. We used to walk to and from school, which is close to the centre of town. Wouldn't take us more than ten or fifteen minutes and we'd snatch whatever was growing on the fields to munch on, coming or going.

Pulling up to the neglected house, I notice a brand-new Dodge Ram parked right beside my dad's old rusty Ford pickup. Before I'm even out of my SUV, the front door slams open and the angry form of my brother appears in the doorway; arms crossed over his chest and a dark scowl on his face. Fan-fucking-tastic. We have a welcoming committee. I simply wanted to alert my mother I would be around for a bit, doing some work from Farmington without going into detail, but apparently Malachi has already gotten wind of my presence. I'd hoped my father wouldn't be around, but I guess I'm out of luck on that front too, since his truck is there.

"The fuck do you want?"

"Mal, Good to see you too. I'm here to see *nihimá*, to say hello. Gonna be around for a bit for work."

"And *nihizhé'é*, Caleb? Aren't you forgetting your father?"

"Not forgetting a soul, Mal. I'll say hello to everyone."

I don't want to get into an immediate confrontation with my brother, who also happens to be the leader of the Klesh: a gang based out of Shiprock, suspected of involvement in drug trafficking. Yeah, I'm the lucky guy assigned to investigate his own fucking family members.

Managing to get by Malachi, who insists on staying in the doorway like some sentry, I walk into the small living room, which hasn't changed in the past twenty-five years. I'm not even sure if it's been cleaned. A rank smell of unwashed bodies and decaying food assaults my nostrils. I have to fight the urge to turn on my heels and walk right back out that door, but family loyalty, a sense of responsibility, and a love that's undeniable has me standing my ground.

"Mom. Pops."

I'm met with the blank look of my mother, who continues to rock herself on the edge of her seat, lost to her pain and the memories of happiness. She still clings to the old horseshoe frame with the baby picture of my sister, Nascha. Pops doesn't respond either, but he isn't even conscious. Passed out in his old Lazy Boy recliner, the only sound he makes is the gentle snoring of oblivion. Just the way he likes it. Claustrophobia tugs at my senses, but I shake it off as I turn to Mal, who still lingers in the doorway.

"Have they eaten?"

His eyes register surprise, his anger momentarily forgotten.

"Nothing in the house. I was gonna grab some stuff. Just got here."

So maybe my arrival had been as much of a surprise to him as his presence was to me.

"Why don't you go do that, and I'll go clean out the kitchen. It fucking smells like a dumpster in here," I suggest, looking over my shoulder into the kitchen where every surface is covered in dirty dishes and empty containers. *Christ!*

"And get some bleach while you're out. We're gonna need it."

Turning my back, I can hear Mal's involuntary chuckle behind me and it about freezes me in my tracks. It's a sound I haven't heard since he was a teenager. It's been fucking years.

"On it, El Jefe," he taunts me with my childhood nickname.

It hadn't been my plan to clean out my parents' place. I had intended just to go in, say hi and start nosing around, but given that my potential biggest lead was standing on their doorstep had me shifting gears quickly.

That's how I find myself three hours later, with my fingers pruning from the hot water and bleach concoction that I'm using to disinfect the grimy surfaces of my parents' bathroom. Holy hell, it must've been some time since this place has seen a sponge or water. The kitchen has already been sanitized and I've tossed the entire contents of the refrigerator. There was nothing in there that hadn't expired over two months ago. To think that this place was once a source of great pride for my mother, who was like a Native version of June Cleaver.

Mal came back loaded down with boxes of groceries and had the foresight to stock up on the basics as well. Good thing too, since everything that was there before is now in the trash. He's still here, not talking much mind you, but I figure this silent standoff we have going on here, on home ground, might provide me with a better chance to get some information than when I try and chase him down on his turf. Still, it fills me with guilt. All of it does. The conditions my parents live under, lying about the reason for being here, lulling my brother into some kind of companionship just to fuck him over. Sure, I stand on the right side of the law, but Christ. These are my people; my family. They're all I have left and it shames me. They shame me. Fuck.

Pops woke up briefly when Mal came in with the groceries and barely coherently started yelling at us being in his house. Something about respect for your elders. Right.

"Shut up, Pops," Mal snarled at him, when he kept on rambling.

I promised myself long ago not to get sucked into the negativity any longer, so I didn't say a word. My parents and brother chose their path; it didn't mean I had to be dragged along. I would stand by my choices, on my own if I had to, and I had for over twenty years now.

"Your fucking phone's ringing!" Mal's voice comes bellowing up the stairway. I must've left it in the kitchen when I was cleaning there. Taking two steps at a time, I make a beeline for the kitchen, hoping the ringing hasn't woken my father again. Don't need another repeat performance.

I find Mal standing by the kitchen counter, my cell in his hand. He's looking at the screen with his eyes squinted tight, listening to it ring in his hand.

"Phone?" I hold out my hand expectantly.

He tears his eyes from the screen and without a word, tosses my cell on the counter and walks out of the kitchen. What the hell?

I snatch it up and hit talk, "Yeah?"

"Know you're busy, my friend, but we have a situation. It's Katie."

My son...

Why would Juan call the creepy Latino guy 'son' when that's supposed to be his nephew? For all the time I've spent with him over the past month or so, I've never seen him this upset, or known him to be that confused. Would this be one of his children? The ones who never show their faces? The investigator in me has bells going off all over the place. I don't have a very good feeling about this, but have nothing to really base it on.

The incident with Juan made me forget all about dinner, and with a quick glance at the clock, I see I have to hustle if I want to make it to the dining room in time for the last sitting. Grabbing a light sweater and my room keys, I head out, keeping an eye on my neighbor's door, but there's no sign of life.

Downstairs, I find the dining room almost empty, most folks here preferring to eat earlier. Juan often joins me later. Looking to our usual spot, I'm a little disappointed to find the table empty, but I grab a tray and make my selection, then I sit by myself.

Halfway through a tasteless chunk of tilapia and some steamed vegetables in an attempt to battle my growing bulge, I notice Sue on the other side of the dining room and wave to get her attention.

"Hey girl, watcha doing sitting here all by your lonesome?" She asks as she pulls out a chair to sit down beside me.

"Almost forgot to eat after that little scene outside my door earlier. You on break?"

"Nah, I'm done for the day. I was on my way to grab a coffee for the drive home, but I'll sit with you for a bit." She plops her bag on an empty chair next to her and settles in.

"So what's with the slinky smooth dude? You've seen him before?"

"Ugh," she says, making a face, "Ernesto. He's as fake as a two-dollar bill. All smiles and teeth until you look into his eyes. They're black holes; dead and soulless. No emotion in them whatsoever. He freaks me out. First time I saw him was last year when Juan moved in, which was just after you did. I was dispensing his evening meds when the guy just barges into the room without knocking and seemed angry to see me there. When he realized I was staff, he introduced himself as Juan's nephew and tried to assure me he was just looking to make sure Juan had settled into his new home. He actually flirted with me."

The look of disgust on Sue's face and her involuntary shiver make me laugh.

"That bad, huh?"

"Ewww. Gives me the creeps, and in the few times I've seen him since, he hasn't let up on the flirting thing. Makes my hair stand on end."

"So what happened this afternoon?"

"I hadn't seen him come in, but he came barging into the nurse's station earlier, demanding to know where his uncle was. I assumed he was in his room, but when I suggested it he almost bit off my head. He said he'd checked there first. Then he went storming off and I guess he found him outside your door."

"Actually no, now that I think about it, he didn't. Juan was visiting with me, upset about something and when he tried to open the door to leave, it was being pulled on from the outside already. The slinky dude, Ernesto? He was right outside and yelled at Juan when he saw him. I think Juan is afraid of him."

I don't want to share that I suspect Juan may actually be his father, not just yet. Not until I have a better idea of what is going on.

"Sue, do you know anything more about Juan? About his family? Where he's from or how he came here?" I quietly ask her, keeping an eye on our surroundings to make sure we won't be overheard. She seems hesitant, focusing on her fingers and fiddling with the rings on her hands rather than looking at me. When she finally does, it's, with nothing short of fear in her eyes.

"I'm not sure it's a good idea for you to get into this, Katie. Actually, I'm pretty sure it isn't. When I tried to ask questions about him after my first confrontation with Ernesto, I was told in no uncertain terms that I was not to stick my nose where it had no business being." Her normally lively demeanour has completely disappeared. I cover her hand with mine, stopping her twirling fingers.

"Who told you that?"

"Our director, Holman. Now please, let's just drop the subject, ok?"

"Listen. I don't want to cause trouble for you, but I'm worried about the old man. He's been nothing but nice to me since I got here, but I'm not going to make you say or do anything you're uncomfortable with. Go home; relax. Forget I mentioned anything."

Without saying a word, but offering a little smile, Sue picks up her stuff and leaves. I'm already contemplating what my next move is going to be. Do I risk trying to hack into one of the facilities' computers to see what I can find out, or should I just concede to the whiz kid right off the bat? Hmm. Neil it is.

Just as I roll my chair back to go drop off the tray at the counter, I catch a shadow in the dining room's entry way. Mr. Sleek and Slinky, Ernesto, is leaning against the wall, not even trying to hide the fact that he's glaring at me. *What the fuck?* I quickly drop the tray on the counter and turn back around, only to find him gone.

I don't think I've ever hated being confined to this fucking wheelchair more than right at this moment, and without hesitation, I make for the elevators to get up to my room where I can lock myself in and think calmly and rationally. Preferably with the bottle of Glenfiddich I keep for when Caleb comes.

Caleb. How ironic he just left for a job that afternoon and is the first person that comes to mind when I need to talk. and I *need* to talk to someone.

The elevator is empty, thank God, and I find no one roaming the halls when I get to my room. I'm momentarily tempted to try and knock on Juan's door to see how he's doing, but that might not be wise, so I lock my door, find the bottle of Glenfiddich, a glass and proceed to contemplate my strategy.

A sharp rapping on my door breaks through my fog. When I peel my eyes open, I can see it's daylight out and I'm still in my chair. Lovely. I'm going to have a crick in my neck today, although I have a feeling that might be the least of my problems. My fucking head is about to explode. Another sharp knock reminds me there is someone waiting.

"Hold on!" I try to yell, but it comes out no more than a croak. What the hell did I do to myself last night? But the struggle to remember has me lightheaded and nauseous.

Flicking the lock on the door – I seem to have had the presence of mind to throw that on last night at least – I pull it open to find a uniformed police officer and plain-clothed cop with the facility's director Holman, all with serious looks on their faces. *Shit.*

CHAPTER FIVE

"She's what!"

My raised voice must have woken up my pops, because he appears in the doorway to the kitchen with a confused look on his face. I turn my back on him and my attention back on Gus, who's on the line.

"Taken in for questioning this morning. At least that's the official word out there. She had the presence of mind to contact the office before they took her. Dana answered, got Neil on the other line, and he got through to me. He's been digging away ever since, trying to get hold of a contact of ours with the GJPD, but so far, no luck. Sit tight, I'm on the road now and I'll let you know what the scoop is."

"Sit tight, my ass! I'm on my way." I bite out, not doing well being told to stay back when he's talking about *my* girl.

"Caleb, you have a job to do. You just got there, and leaving now could seriously fuck that up," Gus tried to convince me.

I actually laughed at that.

"You for real? This was Emma in trouble, would you sit back and wait for someone else to fix it? You'd keep doing your job and wait for me to tell you which way is up? Fuck that, Gus. I'm on the road in five." I hit end, tuck the phone in my pocket and I'm about to head out when I see my dad standing by the door. His unusual hazel eyes focused this time, straight on me.

"Leaving so soon?"

"A friend ran into some trouble, so I have to head back to Grand Junction."

"More important than your *álchíní*, your family?" He mocks me as I pass by him. It's something I would otherwise ignore, but I'm wound up and anxious to get to the hotel, grab my stuff and get moving, so I stop and turn to face him, bring my face close and bite out, "She *is* my family."

I can hear his deriding chuckle behind me as I climb in the SUV, but I've said as much as I'm gonna say. There isn't anything positive to be pulled out of this situation and there's no reasoning with a man who lost his soul decades ago. I know, I've tried enough, and since then, I've tried to make sure that the only thing I've inherited from him is the unusual hazel color of my eyes, and nothing else.

My brother isn't anywhere in sight when I leave the house, but I'm sure one glimpse at the call display on my phone killed any tentative inroads I might have had with him over the few hours we'd spent 'bonding' over our parents' mess. He can figure out what the tag '*Boss*' on the screen stands for, I've never kept my business a secret – unlike Malachi – but I'm sure the reminder we are on opposite sides of the law was like a cold shower. Regardless, by the time I get outside, his truck is already gone.

It doesn't take me long to pick up my stuff from the Travelodge and get back on the road. This time I'm avoiding the mountains. I'm not taking any chances being waylaid by slides and road closures. I gotta get to Katie. Don't have a good feeling about this.

I've been stuck in this room for going on three hours now and I still can't get a grasp on what they want from me. The fucking hangover doesn't help much, either. I can remember being scared when I caught that creep watching me in the dining room, and being pissed off I actually felt vulnerable enough to get scared. I also remember clearly getting to my room, locking the door and hauling out Caleb's prized bottle of Scotch, thinking I'd calm myself down before calling in the troops, but it all gets fuzzy after that. Actually, I got nothing after that until these yo-yo's woke me up this morning, still comatose in my chair. Apparently, I never even made it to bed. All they said was there had been a problem that occurred overnight and they needed me to come in for questioning. Since they weren't being very forthcoming, I insisted on calling my lawyer before I went anywhere, and called the GFI offices instead, hoping to get Neil or Dana. They would find out what the hell is going on.

Yet here I am, still sitting in this damn room where Detective DiRoberto and officer Beck left me after a brief round of questions about my whereabouts last evening and night, which I answered to the best of my knowledge. When I asked what had happened, all I got was a "we'll be right back," and they were out the door. That was about two hours ago according to the clock on the wall.

I'm wearing the clothes I fell asleep in last night. I haven't even brushed my teeth or run a washcloth over my face, let alone had anything to eat or drink and I really, really need to piss. Twice already I knocked on the door I found they had locked, to get someone's attention, but no luck. They keep me waiting much longer and I'll piss on the floor. Let them clean up the mess and *then* I'll launch a fucking complaint afterwards. Morons.

I was getting good and steamed up when the click of the lock being released had me look up and see DiRoberto come in the room, followed by Gus.

"Katie," he nods in my direction, "You okay?"

"Am I okay? No, I am not fucking okay. I've been stuck here for three goddamn hours without food or drink, or – and let me point out that this is of utmost importance – a goddamn washroom break! I'm about to piss my pants and I don't give a rat's ass if it's all over your damn floors!"

Most of my tirade's been directed at the detective whose previous blank look is replaced with a barely detectable frown, but when Gus turns his ire on the detective as well, the change in DiRoberto is instant.

"Are you fucking telling me my disabled employee, whose ass was dragged in here as a potential witness to a murder, has been left without basic needs? I could have your fucking badge for this!" He thunders two inches from the detective's face.

But I've stopped listening. I stopped listening when I heard 'potential witness to a murder,' and a sick feeling settles in my stomach. *What*? I lift my hand to stop the tirade, but it isn't until I yell his name that Gus turns to me.

"Gus! What murder? Who's dead?"

"They found the body of a woman in the dumpster on the edge of the nursing home's parking lot this morning. All indicators are she died sometime last night. She was a nurse at Larchwood."

My hand slapped over my mouth to hold back the bile that was coming up. I'm afraid to ask, but I need to know for sure.

"Who? What was her name?" I whisper.

"Woman by the name of Susan Conklin." Detective DiRoberto has to look at his notebook to get the name right.

"Sue. She goes by Sue," I manage, before I start heaving.

Another small room with another small window, but this time it's a bathroom in the police station where I'm trying to clean myself up after spitting up bile all over myself. I wasn't very clean to start with, but now I reek like a homeless alcoholic after a 5 day binge. One of the female officers was kind enough to give me a spare set of sweats she had in her locker, or else I'd have to go back in there stinking to high heaven, but I'm going back in there. I have so many questions.

A commotion outside the bathroom is penetrating my thoughts, and I'm about to stick my head out to see what's going on when I hear Caleb's voice.

"Where is she? I need to see her right the fuck now. Tell me where she is or I'll tear this whole goddamn place down. I took three and a half hours to make a four and a half hour drive to get here, with nothing but my thoughts. I just need to see her."

When I pull open the door, he's standing right there in the hallway, all six foot five inches of him. His normally calm hazel eyes are looking wild, and Gus is standing just steps away with his hands up defensively. Oh boy. Not sure what I just stepped into, but let's calm this sucker down.

"Caleb," I call out to him, "in here."

Two steps it takes for him to reach me. Two steps and his hands are on my face, his eyes scanning every inch of me.

"You okay? You all right? What happened?"

I grab his wrists to still him.

"Come with me."

In the small bathroom, I close the door on us and turn to face him.

"I'm sorry I smell like the morning after a frat party gone bad, but I'm trying to clean up."

"Don't care," Caleb mutters as he sinks on his knees in front of me and buries his face in my neck. It doesn't take a minute for him to pull back with a chuckle, "Okay, I give. You do smell. Let's clean you up."

Without another word, he strips my shirt off and moves to take off my soiled yoga pants as well when I stop him.

"Erm, excuse me, but I can handle this, Caleb. Ever since about three years old, and I've been quite good at it."

He looks at me confused, and then slightly embarrassed when he clues in.

"Right. Want me to wait outside?"

"I promise I won't be long," I assure him.

I need a few minutes to process what just happened. At the best of times, Caleb is intense, but having all that intensity directed squarely at me was, well, rather overwhelming.

I didn't totally mind it, though.

Flanked by Gus and Caleb this time, I find myself back in the same room I started in, except someone thankfully cleaned up the mess I made and put out some coffee. Thank the Lord. I was ready for some caffeine, some details, and then for this day to be over, and in that order.

Detective DiRoberto, accompanied by his boss, Sergeant Teva, a short buxom and fierce black woman who clearly wasn't impressed with her department's handling of the matter thus far, as witnessed by her repeated apologies to me and scathing sideways glances at DiRoberto, who sat squirming in his seat across from me.

"It appears my detective here received a phone call this morning from one of his regular informants with a tip about a body in the dumpster at the Larchwood Inns and your name was mentioned as a person of interest, Ms. Acker-"

"Katie, please," I interrupt.

"Very well. Katie. Upon arrival at the home, DiRoberto and his assigned officer discovered the deceased body of Ms. Susan Conklin, an employee. He secured the scene, called in the appropriate enforcements and proceeded to contact Larchwood's director, Mr. Holman, who met with our officers in the lobby. With Mr. Holman's assistance, they obtained security footage of the previous night to see if Ms. Conklin's movements could be traced. After observing an interaction between yourself and the victim in the dining room and the victim leaving in an apparent agitated state, Detective DiRoberto felt that was sufficient evidence, combined with the telephone tip, to haul you into the precinct for some hard-core GJPD hospitality. Isn't that right, DiRoberto?"

The venom in the small woman's voice, combined with the sheepish look on the detective's face, was enough to draw a chuckle from Gus.

"Now we've had a few developments since then that have convinced even Detective DiRoberto here, that perhaps his conclusions may have been a tad hasty."

"What kind of developments? I'm not even sure what's happening in the first place," I put out there carefully, keeping my thoughts to myself for now.

"Your neighbor, a Juan Duarte, has gone missing sometime this morning."

"Juan?"

"Duarte?" This from Gus and Caleb almost simultaneously.

We all exchange looks before Sergeant Teva takes the lead again.

"I get the feeling we'll be here a while. DiRoberto, do you want to order up some sandwiches?"

CHAPTER SIX

"Why am I going to Cedar Tree?"

Ever since the clusterfuck of major proportions unfolded in the offices of the GJPD, I've thought of nothing else but to get Katie to the safest place I know, where she is surrounded by people who will look after her.

"Katie, think. You're not safe going back to Larchwood. You were the last known person to speak to Susan Conklin *and* Juan Duarte, let alone the fact that you are the only person who suspects a possible connection between the two from personal observations. And last, but not least, the fact that you were living next door to a possible family member of the Duarte brothers, leaders of one of the most worrisome Mexican cartels, if we are to believe the feds. Don't even want to think about the freaky coincidence that I happened to be investigating these guys a state away while they were within breathing distance of you."

My hands clench the steering wheel as I try to calm the agitation boiling my blood by slowing down my breathing. Katie must have sensed my struggle for calm, because she quietly puts her hand on my leg and her head on my shoulder, which makes my blood boil for different reasons altogether.

"Okay."

Katie's quiet response to my rant surprises me, and I glance over at her.

"Okay? That's it? You're not gonna argue with me?"

She peeks at me from under her long, dark eyelashes with a sparkle in her eyes and a teasing smile on her lips.

"Well, if you'd rather I give you a hard time?"

I can't hold back a chuckle. "No, thanks. Enough excitement for one day, thank you very much."

"Thought so," she mumbles as she snuggles in to my side.

Fuck, she's gonna be the death of me.

"I'm in serious need of a shower, just so you know. Didn't get a chance this morning. I'm also still wearing that officer's sweats, and I also wouldn't be adverse to putting something in my stomach at some point in junction."

"You haven't eaten? It's fucking six o'clock at night, Katie. Did you not grab a sandwich earlier?"

"Holy crud, Caleb, take a chill pill. Seriously. It's not like food was foremost on my mind today and those sandwiches were gross. Who eats sandwiches from a machine? Yuck."

I bite my tongue. No use getting into a discussion with her about looking after herself. She's got a point anyway; I am wound tighter than a drum; A remainder of the long hours of tension and fear I spent driving up here. Not knowing what was happening, not clear on Katie's state of mind or her condition. I'd been crawling out of my skin and apparently the feeling lingered.

Lifting one hand off the steering wheel, I slip my arm around her shoulders and tuck her in a little closer, leaning in so I can kiss the top of her head. Her familiar scent goes a long way to finally calming me.

"I'll stop the next chance I get and we'll pick something up."

A Subway in Monticello supplies us with a quick bite to eat in the parking lot, so we can get back on the road in short order, and the rest of the drive is made in near silence until we turn into the turn off to Emma and Gus's place, when Katie suddenly pushes off me and scoots way over to the other side.

"You're bringing me to Emma's house? Seriously? Jesus, Caleb, can't I go stay at the motel? I didn't think you'd be bringing me here."

Katie sits ramrod straight in the passenger seat beside me with her arms crossed, obviously not happy with our destination. Tired, irritated, and a bit blindsided by her reaction, I snap at her.

"You're not staying at the motel where you won't be as secure. I get your reservations, but you need to get over the fact that Emma is in Gus's life and start thinking like the security expert you are. You'll stay with me in the guesthouse."

The thought that being around Emma and Gus would still be difficult for her irks me, and has me acting like a fucking bull in a china shop. I know I fucked up right away; I don't even have to hear the sharp drawn-in breath beside me to figure that one out. *Jesus.* I run my fingers through my hair, trying to find the appropriate words to apologize when Katie suddenly throws me a helluva punch to the shoulder, causing me to lose my grip on the wheel.

"Ouch! Damn, woman. You almost had me go in the ditch."

I quickly pull around Emma's bungalow and up to the small guesthouse they had built months ago for when Kara, Emma's daughter, or one of the GFI crew, would need a place to crash. The bungalow itself has no spare bedrooms and the space they added on is solely used as offices for GFI. The guesthouse was fully wheelchair accessible, which was one of Emma's requests since she has some mobility issues of her own. That, and the fact that Katie would be close to caring people, had all been taken into consideration when Gus and I discussed where best to take her. Neither of us had stopped to think it might be awkward for her, or had bothered to include her in the discussions. Damn.

When I turn off the ignition and turn to her, I take her in. Katie at full strength was a sight to behold; but her once sharply cut muscles have made way for softer, rounder curves now her mobility is challenged, and I like the softer look on her. You won't hear me complain about the added roundness. The defensive posture she has taken, with her arms crossed over chest and her full pink lips pursed in her angry face is cute, and almost makes me chuckle, but I'd be in even hotter water if I let it escape. I've scrapped with this woman before in friendly bouts, and even without the use of her legs, I know she can still be quite lethal with her hands. Not gonna poke that bear. Instead, I take her face in my palms and turn it to me, fully expecting the instant snap of her hands grabbing onto my wrists. She won't budge me though, not even the fire shooting from her eyes will sway me.

"I'm sorry, little one. I'm a dick. I messed up all over the place, starting with not discussing any of this with you beforehand. That was not cool."

Katie is doing her best to avoid my eyes and won't stop yanking on my wrists.

"Hey. Look at me. I'm trying to apologize to you. Would you stop for a minute?"

When she drops her hands, I can feel the resistance going out of her, but she still won't lift her eyes, so I dip my head low and am shocked to find tears pooling in her eyes. I can count the times I've seen Katie cry on one hand easily, and the thought that I'm responsible for her tears makes me feel like crap.

"Ahh fuck, sweetie. Come on." I unclip her seatbelt and my own. "We're going to continue this inside."

It doesn't take long for me to have Katie in her chair and inside where she has a look around while I grab our bags. When I walk down the short hall to the bedroom to drop off the bags, Katie is in the doorway looking at the large, king-sized bed. She hears me walk up behind her and turns around, one eyebrow raised.

"One bedroom?"

Yes, there is that. Not something I allowed myself to think of too much, only because I was already having a hard time controlling my baser urges.

"Yes," I say as casually as I can, passing by her into the room and placing the bags on the bed, "where *you* will sleep. There's a perfectly comfortable couch out there where I'll crash." I cringe when I think of the couch, which is at least a foot too short for my six foot five frame.

"I'll sleep on the couch. You're way too big."

And there it is, the combative side of Katie I'd been expecting much earlier. I rub my hands over my face before answering.

"I'll be fine on the couch, Katie," I sigh. I'm tired. It's been a long day and I've spent most of it in a car and on pins and needles, and I'm sure Katie hasn't fared any better. I can feel her eyes on me and turn to face her.

"I just don't like the feeling of putting you out. Don't like the feeling of putting anyone out, that's why I didn't want to come here in the first place. Do you know how absolutely demeaning it is to have to come back here for *my* safekeeping? To this place?" Obviously frustrated at the blank look on my face, she rolls her eyes.

"Jesus. I know that you think my issues are with Emma and you're wrong. Dead wrong. Think, Caleb. I was supposed to protect that woman and ended up getting myself hurt and she ended up pulled from her own house; this house. You think she needs me around as a daily reminder of that?"

For someone who's known for his insight, I'm doing a piss poor job with Katie. Walking over to her chair, I sink to my knees in front of her and grab her hands.

"First off, you know damn well you don't carry the burden of what happened here last year, and if not, let me remind you that no one., and I mean *no one*, holds you responsible, so those thoughts better end right now. Secondly, it's pretty obvious I'm blind when it comes to you. All day I've been out of sorts, saying and doing the wrong things; putting my foot in and misjudging you. Then when I try to make it right, it just seems to have the opposite outcome."

Katie pulls her hands from mine and rolls her chair back to create some distance

"You don't have to do anything, Caleb, don't you see? I appreciate it, I really do, but I should be taking care of myself. Instead, I've been lugged around like a piece of baggage no one's sure where to put so it's not in the way. I don't want to rely on you, Gus, and certainly not Emma!"

The woman in equal parts infuriates and excites me; it's always been this way. Single-minded, argumentative, and so damn self-reliant, with that hint of vulnerability that brings out the urge to protect in me. I get up off the floor, taking in the fire in her green eyes, a blush high on her otherwise pale cheeks, and her pointy little chin lifted in defiance. The fact that her short feathery dark hair and soft body make her look like a pin up version of Peter Pan doesn't make her less formidable or challenging.

"Fuck Katie, no one is asking you to rely on me or anyone else. I know you're quite capable of taking care of yourself, but looking out for you is simply something I have to do."

"Arghh. You can be such a caveman! I don't want to be this obligation you have to fulfill," she throws up her hands in frustration.

A fucking obligation? That's what she thinks she is to me? Aggravated beyond reason, and determined to get my point across, I hold her eyes with mine while I unbutton my jeans and shove them down my hips.

"Does this look like something caused by an 'obligation'?" I grab my hard cock and pump a few times, feeling myself harden more as her eyes slowly slide down and look at my obvious arousal.

"Jesus, Caleb." She mutters.

"Well?" I press, but when I still don't get a satisfying answer, I take a few steps to where she sits in her wheelchair, grab her hand and wrap it around my dick. I almost go weak at the knees feeling her small, soft hand against my hot flesh.

"Feel that? Does it feel like I'm doing you a favor here, Katie? Does it feel to you I'm here for pity? Does it?" My anger now slipping out, I barely notice Katie moving forward in her chair and I suddenly feel the wet heat of her tongue tasting the head of my cock.

"Holy shit, ahhh... little one. I haven't even kissed you yet."

Holy crap! What just happened?

One minute we're in a heated argument and the next, we're in the middle of a heated... something else altogether. The sight of that man is stirring, the thick midnight black hair he keeps closely cropped to his head with hints of silver over his ears, the sizeable straight nose and fine wrinkles that fan out from his uniquely hazel eyes, the strong long body, but seeing him with his pants down and his big hand wrapped around that magnificent cock shifts something inside me. Moisture pools in my mouth and between my legs almost instantly, and I don't resist when he wraps my hand around his rock-hard heat. Fuck me, but it's been too long. The man in front of me, the temptation in all that he is – his beauty, his unique scent – already so safe and familiar has me leaning in for a taste. Ah, yes. As soon as my tongue touches the crown of his proud cock, his flavor invades my senses and a small groan escapes me. He tastes so good, so rich, so... right.

But before I have a chance to wrap my lips fully around his length, I hear him mumble something about a kiss and he pulls back from my mouth and my hand. I can feel the loss. The sound of his jeans pulling up and his heavy footfalls leaving the room without a word snap me out of my daze and full into embarrassment. Hearing the front door close, I finally lift my eyes. *Son of a bitch.*

I don't want to cry. I feel like it, but I don't want to because after the day I've had, I don't know if I'll be able to stop once I start. I pull the bags off the bed, grab my PJ's and toothbrush and head into the bathroom for a quick clean up before I pull myself up and into the bed, where I roll on my side, hoping for sleep to come.

CHAPTER SEVEN

It's not long before a light knock on the door is immediately followed by a soft, "Hello? Katie?"

I stifle the urge to hide my head under the pillow on hearing Emma's voice filter into the bedroom. Her wild head of curls appears in the doorway shortly after.

"Hey, sorry. Didn't realize you'd gone to bed already. I just wanted to check in and say hi." Turning around to leave, I quickly stop her with a raised hand.

"No, no. I wasn't sleeping, just... caving," I confess with a grimace.

"Caving?" Emma questions, a small smile on her face, "Yes, I guess that's a good term for it. I've been known to do that once or twice, holing up in a dark corner until the world stops spinning and leaves you the fuck alone. Something like that?"

A laugh bubbles up in my chest, and with it a tiny corner of the tight hold on my day's emotions peels up. Shit. With the first tear only halfway down my cheek, Emma has already somehow managed to get herself halfway on the bed beside me, hugging me close. I should be completely weirded out by this, but I'm too tired and wrought out at this point to feel anything but relief at the comforting arms around me. So the floodgates break open. For the next ten minutes or so, I let it all out, broken open by the unfamiliar feel of a nurturing hand stroking my back and the soft words of comfort murmured in my ear. When I finally pull back, I'm shocked to see Emma's face as wet as mine is with tears of her own.

"I think we needed that. Yeah?" She smiles through her tears, leaning over to grab a box of tissues off the nightstand.

"Guess so," I mumble, still a bit embarrassed at my breakdown and stunned at Emma's show of emotion. "I'm not usually one for crying."

Emma snorts out a laugh, "Yeah, I gathered as much, girl. Doesn't mean it isn't good to let 'er rip every now and then. Think of it as a cleansing."

Hmm, a cleansing. I have to admit I do feel lighter somehow.

"When Caleb came storming in the backdoor and made a beeline for the office, I figured something might be off, so I came to check. Guess it's been an intense kinda day all around."

This time it's my turn to snort. "Understatement of the year."

"Yeah. I figured that when Gus showed up shortly after you guys pulled up to the guesthouse and could barely throw me a hello and a kiss before he thundered through to the back office. Both guys are locked in there now, plotting God knows what and letting all that testosterone fly. I thought I'd come see what damage Caleb had done here before he came tearing in."

God that woman is funny; she has me laughing out loud now, her eyes sparkling with a remainder of earlier tears and a healthy dose of humor. I'm finding a whole new understanding of what makes her so special, and I have to admit that she's perfect for Gus. On impulse, I give her a hug.

"Thank you," I tell her quietly, before letting her go.

"Well now that we have the sappy stuff out of the way, let's get to the dirt. What *did* that idiot do, before he came over?"

"Erm, well, we kinda had a fight."

"Figured that one out myself. I need more."

"Okay," I hesitate. I don't know how to 'do' girl talk. Haven't had much experience.

"Just spit it out. Rip it off like a band aid, it's not that hard." She's laughing at me now.

"Fine. I may have said something about it not being a good idea to bring me here because of what it might remind you of, and I also may have told him he wasn't responsible for looking after me."

"Alright, the first is a load of crap, and the second isn't smelling that pretty, either. What is wrong with you?" She gives me a playful shove that almost sends me tumbling off the bed. "Oops, sorry. That was a little harder than intended," she chuckles sheepishly.

I shrug my shoulders, "Just used to being a bit of a loner, I guess. Not good with people just being nice for the sake of being nice."

"You are a ditz, Katie. Seriously. They're not being nice for the sake of being nice; they're being nice because of you. They *want* to be nice to you. Hell, we want to be nice to you because you're a likeable person, believe it or not," she snickers, "but I get the feeling maybe you haven't been told a whole lot. That's ok, we'll work on that," she says with a firm nod. "But fill me in on the day. All Gus would say was that you were in trouble when he left in a hurry this morning, and just now he barely said anything when he got home, so I'm flailing in the dark here."

Thinking about how my day started filled me with the instant weight of guilt over poor Sue. I'd only known her for a few months and only superficially at that, but she never failed to stop and chat for a bit about all kinds of stuff. The closest I'd really ever come to having a female friend since I was a teenager. The thought that I was upstairs very uncharacteristically drowning myself into a bottle of Scotch because I was feeling scared and sorry for myself while someone killed her just outside my window, didn't sit particularly well. Then there is missing Juan, who I'm positive was scared out of his wits and I did nothing for him. Me, top notch security expert, sat right next door, sucking back the Glenfiddich while someone took him from his room.

Haltingly at first, but then spilling out the sequence of events to Emma is like a purging of a different kind. She just looks at me, her mouth falling a bit wider as my story comes tumbling out.

"My," she croaks out after she swallows deeply, "Even in a care facility you manage to lead an exciting life," causing me to snicker this time.

"Not something I was looking for, I promise."

"I figure that. So what happens now? Gus just called from the road this afternoon saying you'd be staying here, which is wonderful by the way. It's exactly what I was talking to Caleb about the other day, anyway."

I must have had confusion written all over my face, because she mutters '*oh shit,*' under her breath.

"Guess he didn't have much of a chance to talk with you yet, huh? Fuck me. Mouth is running away on me again."

"Yeah. Not sure what you're talking about, but it sounds just like Caleb not to clue me in. He didn't on the discussions about where I was going to be going or staying."

Working up a good head of steam, I don't hold back.

"He's moving me around like a pesky piece of furniture that doesn't really fit but he can't get rid of. I'm sick of it. He makes these obligatory visits to Larchwood to see if I'm still breathing and then he's off to save the world again, and I don't even understand why he's taken on the responsibility. I hate feeling like someone's responsibility. Most of the time I don't know what the man is thinking, except the one time when I think it is obvious; when he does something so outside of his self-controlled norm, so glaringly provocative that I act on it, he fucking walks away! Arghh!"

My hands grip my short locks and I pull, wanting to feel the sting in my scalp, I'm so frustrated. All I hear beside me is a soft chuckle.

"Don't laugh, it's not funny. He seriously makes me lose control. I'm not this person; this crazy, emotional mess! I don't even know myself like this," I tell her, exasperated.

"You have feelings for him," Emma smiles at me.

Wait. What?

"You kidding me? I've known Caleb for years, he's a friend—at least I thought he was," I mumble. "Besides, I don't see him like that, I–" But as soon as the words leave my mouth, I recognize the lie in them and shut my mouth with a snap. Something is happening to me and I don't know if I like it. I can't deny my body's instant response to him, the need to touch him, taste him, and the surge of feelings that evoked in me, but it also makes me feel unusually vulnerable, and *that* I do not like at all.

Emma is quietly observing as I process the little bit of insight I've just gleaned, and I finally turn to her, not quite ready to drop all my defenses.

"Whatever messed up thing I might be feeling, Emma, it's probably a result of my scrambled brain. I hardly recognize myself these days, and what I do see, I can barely stand. I can pretty much guarantee that whatever misplaced emotions I might have, Caleb has zero feelings for me."

"That man feels for you. I don't care what excuses you pull out of your hat. If you gave yourself a minute to think clearly, you'd see that no one would be so attentive and protective of someone they saw as a responsibility. Smarten up."

The sharp retort hit its mark as I'm once again put in my place. I take a minute to consider Emma's words before I answer carefully.

"Not so sure you're right about Caleb, though. He tore out of here pretty fast when I... when he... oh, never mind."

"Oh pray tell. I just know this is too good to ignore," Emma begs, a lighter tone to her voice.

"Let's just say for a minute it got intimate and I guess he immediately regretted it because he was gone so fast, I didn't even see him leave"

"You didn't see me leave because your head was still down. I know, because I looked over my shoulder."

My heart skips up in my throat when hear the familiar smooth voice coming from the doorway. I look up to see Caleb standing there. How in hell did he get in here? I didn't hear a thing.

"And for the record, there are many things I regret, but that 'intimate moment', as you so eloquently put it, is not one of them."

As Caleb's hazel eyes drill into mine, the intensity turning them almost dark brown, I can sense Emma sliding off the bed.

"Well now," she announces, "I have a feeling my presence is no longer needed here." And jauntily maneuvers her walker through the doorway where she stops to give Caleb a pat on his chest. "About fucking time, buddy," she says, before leaving through the front door.

CHAPTER EIGHT

The sight of her dark head bending forward, long lashes feathered on her cheekbones and her wet, pink tongue sliding out to taste my cock is like a 150,000 volt electric jolt to my system that instantly sets all my body hair on end. The urge to grab her head and force myself deep into the hot recesses of her mouth is making me shake. *Have her suck me hard and make me spill myself down her throat.* With my last thread of control, before I molest her where she sits, I force myself to step back, tuck my painfully hard erection in my jeans and walk out the door. One look over my shoulder before leaving the bedroom gives me a glimpse of a confused, rejected, and embarrassed Katie. Fuck. I've come to care for this woman so much, which is why I'm determined to get a grip before I trust myself near her again, so without another word, I head over to the main house.

"I'm screwed." Is what I tell Gus when I barge into his office.

He's sitting with his back to the door, working on one of the various computers on his desk. Without turning around, he deadpans, "Yeah? What else is new?"

"Serious here, man. I'm on eggshells, constantly fucking up. Can't say the right thing if my life depended on it." My fingers are furiously tapping the edge of the desk with barely contained energy.

"Stop that."

"What?"

Gus swivels his chair around and grabs my wrist, "*That*," he says firmly, shooting me a 'don't-fuck-with-me' look, so I tuck my hands in my pockets.

"Now, I know what the problem is and I suspect you know what the problem is too. Don't need me to tell you that that woman in there has you in knots. I've known it since I walked in on you holding her bleeding head together in your lap. Wasn't hard to tell you were holding your life in your hands." He pauses, giving me a minute to recognize the truth of his words and relive the horrific memory of those moments. "But my friend, how long are you gonna sit idle? If not for this shit happening at Larchwood, you'd be satisfied to wait for years for her to show a sign of life so you could make a move. Your stoic patience is one of your strengths, Caleb, but in this case, it may well be the one thing that hangs you. Moving Katie here and under your nose may not be ideal, but fuck it. You need to pull your finger out and get with the program."

He's right. Of course he's right, but moving forward also means taking a risk. Truth? I'm scared. I've waited for Katie for years, learned to be satisfied with even a peripheral presence in her life, but if I push for more, I run the chance of ending up with nada. Zilch.

"Two days, Caleb. Take two days with Katie to talk or do whatever the fuck is needed to settle you down. We'll spend some time tomorrow going over this case and the weird fluke that has ended Katie up to her neck into an already complex investigation that just got a hell of a lot more complicated. After that, you head back to Shiprock and see what can be salvaged from your assignment there."

"Sounds good."

I have nothing more to say. In fact, I've said very little at all, but I heard every word Gus said. Trust his judgement above my own at this moment, which is why I came here.

"We good?" he wants to know; ready to dive back into whatever it was he was working on.

"We're good."

"Excellent. Now send that mouthy redhead back over this way, will ya? I think I have some grovelling of my own to do," he says with a smirk.

I rap my knuckles on the doorpost in confirmation on my way out.

The sound of voices gets louder as I make my way through the now dark guesthouse to the bedroom. Leaning against the doorway into the room, I can just catch the last few sentences exchanged between the women sitting on the big bed. It's obvious from the tearstained faces that some emotional stuff has gone down and I feel guilt eating at my insides, but then I hear Katie say that me walking out earlier meant I must have regretted what happened between us. I have to set her straight. She can't be further from the truth and it's time she knows it.

The moment her eyes meet mine, everything disappears. I barely notice Emma leaving. In a few steps I reach the bed, lean in and pick Katie up.

"Whoa!" she calls out, scrambling to hold onto my neck. "What are you doing?"

"You in my bed means I can't think, and I'm having a hard enough time thinking around you. We need to set some things straight." I tell her, trying not to get lost in the feel of her soft body against mine, her subtle scent teasing me, and her restless fingers playing against the short bristles on my neck. My dick, however, is a goner, and there's no way to hide it when I sit down on the couch with Katie in my lap.

"Stop squirming, you're making it worse."

When she throws me an irritated look, I'm glad to see the fire back in her eyes. There she is.

"Okay, enough of the manhandling, Caleb," Katie bats at my hands as I shift her around so she faces me. The old tank top and shorts she wears as PJ's aren't doing much to cover her and I can't help the tortured groan that slips from me. Fucking hell, this is gonna be torture with her nipples poking through the threadbare material, and right in my face.

"What the hell is this? I honestly don't know whether I'm coming or going with you."

"Shh, don't get upset," I try to settle her before the tears I hear wobbling in her voice start flowing. "I just needed a minute."

Cupping her face between my hands, I tilt her head so I can look her in the eye. "I have wanted and waited to do this for so long, I need to make sure I don't miss a thing."

Her eyes are big and a little uncertain, and her lips are perfectly parted when I brush my nose along hers, breathing in the soft pants of her breath. A light brush of my mouth over hers, barely skimming, and then I taste the length of her full bottom lip with my tongue before sucking its plumpness into my mouth. Fucking heaven. Her taste is heaven and I need more. Katie's finger, rubbing against my scalp is all the encouragement I need and I finally let go of my hunger for her and take her mouth. *Jesus.* Delicious, wet heat meets me when my tongue plunges between her lips. Someone groans, and in the now furious tangle of lips and tongues, I can't tell anymore. I want inside her. In one twist and without my mouth ever leaving hers, I have her below me on the couch, grinding my painfully throbbing cock between her legs. It isn't until she wrenches her lips from mine and murmurs, "Caleb," that I realize I'm fucking humping her like some deranged rutting animal. I shoot back upright and move to sit on the coffee table, my head in my hands.

"Fuck!"

Why? Why does she make me lose all control when control has always come so easy?

"Are you gonna walk out of here again?" The amused tone of Katie's voice tells me she may be a little more attuned to the struggle I'm waging than she was before. "Because, that would seriously mess with my self-esteem. You know; getting rejected based on my abilities for giving head *and* kissing?"

I throw my head back and laugh. "Oh sweetheart, you couldn't be further from the truth if you tried."

She shifts to where she's sitting in front of me on the couch with a twinkle in her eye, and I have a feeling we may actually have crossed a barrier. I reach out and frame her face.

"You know I couldn't let you worship me without me worshipping you first, right? I'm having a hell of a time hanging onto my control around you, Katie. More so now than ever before, and it's so foreign to me. I don't know where you're coming from, not really. I'm usually very good at reading people, but as you've noticed, I haven't done a very good job reading you lately."

I'm pretty sure she's hearing me when her face softly rubs against the palm of my hand and the slightest of smiles hints at the corner of her mouth.

I think I've finally discovered what it means to get your socks knocked off. Hell, that kiss about stripped all my clothes right off my body. I don't think I've ever felt that kind of hunger before and I'm liking it.

This time when Caleb pulls away from me, I can sense his struggle for control, so I try to break the tension which seems to work, because he throws back his head and let's go of that phenomenal laugh of his. Not something he does often, but when he does, it's a beautiful thing. His words go a long way to confirming what Emma had carefully suggested; that Caleb might be seeing me as more than an added responsibility. I'm thinking that panty-incinerating kiss made that glaringly obvious, and I'm kicking myself now for not seeing it clearer before. So wrapped up in my self-pity at times that it rubbed off on my view of everything and everyone else. That's gotta stop, and to be honest, finally acknowledging the feelings he gave me as something more than just 'brotherly' is refreshingly liberating.

We spend some time talking, with him sitting safely on the coffee table lightly touching me, and me still on the couch. He tells me a bit about the job that took him to Shiprock and gives me some family insight, then I finally tell him about my attempts at searching for my biological parents.

"Wish you'd have told me. I'd have been happy to help out, you know."

"I know. I've just never been great at sharing," I confess with what I know is a sheepish grin on my face.

"Right. Just know you can—no judgement," he says with such a serious face, it makes me chuckle.

"Pretty sure that was never my concern, Caleb. More my own messy hang-ups, but I'm working on it."

"Good enough."

The sweet kiss he gives me is spoiled by a gigantic yawn I've been fighting to suppress for a while.

"Tired?"

"Mmm. It's late and this has been a day of so many emotional twists and turns, I'm surprised my head's still attached to my body," I say as I stretch my arms over my head. A pained groan from Caleb has me look his way. "What?"

"You keep doing shit like that and it'll be impossible for me not to want to strip you naked and lose myself in you, but today is not the day, and I really want to sleep with you in my arms tonight."

With an almost angry scowl he stands up, adjusts himself and lifts me up in his arms, heading for the bedroom.

After a quick wash and rinse in the bathroom, and warmly tucked under the covers, I feel Caleb slide into the bed behind me, wrapping his arms around my waist and tucking his face in my neck.

"Best feeling, *Yázhí*," he mumbles, giving me tingles all over.

"What are you calling me? *Yázhí*?" I whisper.

"Little one, you've always been my little one. Now go to sleep."

"Night."

I pull up one of his big hands, kiss his palm and hold it pressed against my heart as I quickly drift off to sleep.

CHAPTER NINE

I never had a chance last night to take in all the renovations that have taken place here over the last months, but now with the warm sun brightening up the morning, I let my eyes wander over the substantial changes made to what was once Emma's little one bedroom bungalow. You can't really tell from the front, it still looks like the same quaint porch-fronted, one-level house, but it was opened up and widened in the back with a larger kitchen and dining area, boasting large sliding glass doors that showcase the great view of the mountains. Off to one side it extends into a large office space with a separate entrance for GFI, a separate office for Gus, and a sizeable conference room. Then there's the guesthouse, set back from the main house, completely self-sufficient and bordering on luxurious, at least the shower is.

"I'm gonna want a shower like that," I tell Caleb as we take the interlock pathway to the back entrance of the main house.

"That so?" he chuckles.

"God, *yes.* It has showerheads frigging everywhere. Even down low, aiming up and reaching all those spots that never get any attention 'cause they're hard to get to? That felt so good." I stretch my arms up, letting the sun warm my body when I feel him bending over me from behind, his mouth by my ear.

"Word of caution, little one. I was being a gentleman this morning, giving you some space and letting you have a shower alone, but now I'm done with that. We're about twenty steps away from meeting up with the boss and I have a hard-on the size of the Washington Monument. Already know my control is worth shit around you, but unless you want me to turn you straight back around to fix that, with Gus already watching through the windows, I suggest you stop teasing me."

My eyes snap up and sure enough, Gus is visible behind the glass doors of the kitchen, a mug of coffee in hand.

"But I wasn't..." I try before Caleb's deep growl from behind me cuts me off. Better not.

It'd been pretty clear this morning that he was trying to keep some distance. I was disappointed to find the bed empty when I woke up. He walked in a few minutes later with coffee and suggested I have a shower so we could have some breakfast and a powwow at the house. The only reminder of the events of the night before was a gentle kiss on my lips.

"Morning. Better sit yourselves down, 'cause Emma's cooked for an orphanage," Gus says as he holds the door open for us.

"Shut your mouth, Gus, or you're not gonna get any." Emma pipes up from the kitchen, "And when I say 'any', I mean *any!*"

The faux-shocked expression on Gus' face inadvertently makes me chuckle, "Show me the way to the food, but I'm warning you, if I get any fatter, I'll need a sumo wrestler to wheel me around."

The dead silence should've been an indicator that my joke doesn't go over too well.

"I need a word, Katie," is my only warning before my chair gets pulled around and pushed back outside. Okay then. Next thing I know, Caleb is in my face with his eyebrows scrunched up.

"Please don't do that."

"What did I do?" I know, I just don't want to admit it.

"Tell me honestly," he asks, "is who you are so wrapped up in what you look like that you think it's all anyone sees? 'Cause I'm not buying it."

I shake my head because it's not. It really isn't, but insecurities pop up and spill out all over the place, unattractive as they may be.

"Aside from the fact that 'fat' is not an adjective that should ever be used in a description of you, it's a load of crap. You want it straight? You have gained weight, rounded out and softened up. You have flesh my fingers want to sink in and my body wants to rest on, but I'd have taken you any way – thin, firm, soft – 'cause the only place you can find ugly is on the inside."

I nod. Shit, what else am I supposed to do? It's beautiful, what he says. I don't want to take anything away from that.

"Let's go eat."

I'm eager to show Katie the place I've bought. It's not looking like much yet, but the location is beautiful and the building is large and full of potential. The contractor is starting with reinforcing the structure next week, and then we'll slowly start building from the outside in. The drawings have been approved, I just need some of the details worked out. I would love to do as much as possible myself, I did grow up the son of a contractor and know my way around a building site, but it all depends on this current case, and Gus is eager to have me back to Shiprock the day after tomorrow. I want to make sure I have Katie involved in my plans for the house first; want to give her something to believe in, even if she's not quite ready to believe in me yet.

We just left Gus and Emma's after a mind-boggling breakfast spread over which we discussed plans for the immediate future, including Katie's move to Cedar Tree and all that entails. Katie's residual irritation at having been excluded from the initial planning quickly dissipates when she hears the lengths to which we have gone to prepare for her arrival. When I explain we had wanted to give her options instead of uprooting her without discussion, as I was forced to do, she seems to finally embrace the thought of Cedar Tree as a more permanent solution. Especially when Emma eagerly informs her that the therapist who has made great headway with Faith, Seb's disabled sister, is available to come and work with Katie, and Gus lets her know he really needs some help running GFI from here. That leaves my plans for the future still under wraps, but those are not something you discuss over breakfast and in company, which is why we are taking a drive right now.

"Where are we? I don't think I've been this way before," Katie inquires, her eyes scanning the quiet surroundings on this side road about two miles out of town.

"You'll see in a minute."

Beyond the next turn in the road, on the left side is the obscured driveway onto the property. Lined with trees, you only get a glimpse of what lies ahead; standing alone, with trees flanking the right side, is a huge, old beautiful barn. The wood is still in excellent condition and it was built on a solid concrete foundation. The inside is a structure of massive beams and posts that have all been incorporated into my plans. I feel a small pang of pride of ownership every time I drive up here, not quite believing I am this close to realizing a dream I've had since childhood.

"Oh my God! This is gorgeous! What is this place?" Katie has rolled down her window and is hanging out, taking in the building and the surrounding fields and woods.

An unconscious weight slides off my shoulders and is replaced with an intense feeling of relief at Katie's reaction, and a smile steals over my face.

"Caleb? Where are we?"

"It's mine. Come on, I want to show you." Without waiting for an answer, I get out and walk over to the passenger side to help Katie out of the truck.

The driveway is packed dirt and it isn't easy to maneuver her chair across the potholes.

"The first thing that'll get done is a proper paved drive so you can get around."

Katie's surprised eyes land on mine, but she doesn't say anything. Once inside the huge barn doors, she gets a first look at the vast expanse of space.

"This is amazing, Caleb. Absolutely amazing. This is going to be so beautiful. You're making it into a home, right? It fits you perfectly. I'm so excited for you." She turns to me with a giant smile on her face.

I want to tell her I'm making it into a home for *us*, but I decide to show her instead. Walking over to the large drawing table off to the side, I start unrolling the plans that are stacked on there.

"I'm keeping the big barn doors, but they'll be left and fixed open. In the frame, I'll have large windows installed, floor to ceiling. Same on the back. You can see there are barn doors directly opposite and those go out into the fields. There I want glass as well, but sliding so it can open up to a deck. Everything has to stay one level, except where the hayloft is up above. It'll be the sleeping quarters with a large master and bathroom in the back, and two smaller bedrooms with a bathroom in the front. I'm also keeping a separate room on the main level, which can be converted into an office or a den. Those will be the only rooms with doors, aside from a powder room. The front door will be right beside the barn doors in the front and a mudroom with laundry will be right off the side with a laundry shoot from the upstairs hallway. Beside the mudroom are the stairs and a small elevator. Beyond that, the entire back right side of the house is a large eat- in kitchen, most of which will face out the side and back with large windows. All the space between the front and back barn doors will remain open space for living areas."

I've been leaning over the blueprints, pointing everything out as I've explained them, feeling Katie beside me following along. Turning to her now to gauge her reaction, I see surprise and confusion warring on her face. I run my fingers over the slight frown in her forehead along her cheeks and lightly over her lips, before cupping her chin in my hand.

"What's that look for?"

She swallows deeply, "You're installing an elevator?"

"Yes, I'm installing an elevator. A small one-person one. With friends who have limited mobility, I'm learning to never take anything for granted, so since I'm building up from scratch anyway, I figure I might as well be prepared for everything."

"Right, makes sense, I guess." Katie turns her face away.

"But mostly it's because I want to make sure a certain someone can get around independently and effortlessly in this house, regardless of what the future holds for her," I add, knowing it was mean to keep her hanging, but needing that little sign of dejection to know she wanted this.

I step around her just in time to see her wipe a tear before it has a chance to roll down her cheek.

"You okay?"

"Fast. I feel like Alice down the rabbit hole a little, with all that is happening. Overwhelmed, but in a good way, I think." She puts her hand on her chest to emphasize and chuckles. "My heart is almost beating out of my chest."

"Gus gave me two days to settle things between you and me. Not a lot of time when I've been on the sidelines for four years, little one. Two days to ease you into considering I might envision you in my future. Two days to see if there is any hope for you to see me as part of yours. It's not enough, but it's all I have and what I need to get my head back in the game, so I'm laying it all on the table. No more hiding in the shadows, I'm going balls to the wall on this and fuck knows, I don't want to put that kind of pressure on you, but I figure with the blows you've been dealt, you're probably better off knowing where I stand than dealing with another set of uncertainties."

"Wow. I'm scared, and excited, and very freaked out right now because I don't know what to say. But I really, really wish I could fucking stand so I could get a hug. I really need one."

I have her up and out of her chair and clinging onto me like a monkey in two seconds flat. Her arms around my neck, mine around her back and under her butt, holding her off the ground and tightly against me.

"If I could get these frickin' legs to move, I'd wrap those around you too," she mumbles in my neck, making me chuckle.

"Tease," I whisper back, lowering her body slightly so she can feel the instant and very hard effect she has on me, pressing against her stomach. A low groaning comes from my neck area.

"Mmmm, who's the tease now," she purrs in my ear.

I'm already scanning for a place where I can get us horizontal and fast, when a loud crash comes from just outside.

Dropping Katie down in her chair, we both approach the barn door from opposite sides. I have to bite my lip not to motion Katie back to safety, but the truth is, she's as much a trained operative as I am. I have a small handgun from my ankle holster at the ready, and Katie somehow found a discarded broomstick she has across her lap. She holds up just inside the closed door, brandishing the stick in a way that would take out the knees of anyone coming through that door. With her eyes on me, she simply nods for me to make a move and I slip through scanning the surroundings immediately for movement, which I see, but I don't shoot.

In front of me stands the mangiest, biggest dog I've ever seen. The thing is ugly, but seems to be harmless and clumsy since he knocked over an old wheelbarrow that'd been resting against the side of the barn. Not scared either, it just stands there and looks at me.

The light crunching of wheels on the ground alerts the dog to Katie's approach and his eyes zoom in on her approach.

"It's a puppy!" Katie squeals behind me, startling the dog into taking a step back.

"That rangy dog can hardly be called a puppy, sweets. I'm thinking mutt is a more appropriate description."

"Don't be mean. He's a puppy, aren't you boy? Such a good boy." She patting her knees and damn if the dog's tail isn't slowly starting to sway from side to side.

"Where'd you come from? Is there a tag on him, Caleb?"

I just finished tucking my gun back in my ankle holster and look up to see if there's anything dangling around his neck.

"Can't see anything, and I'm not too sure he'll be happy if I walk up to check closely. Probably just a stray or a reservation dog."

"Reservation?"

"We're not too far from the Ute reservation here. In fact, most of what you can see out the back doors is reservation land."

The dog seems to have forgotten all about me and is tentatively inching his way over to Katie, tail furiously wagging.

"Careful. He's a big boy and we don't really know him."

Katie rolls her eyes at me and continues to coo at the pooch.

With the earlier heated scene a vague memory by virtue of our unscheduled visitor, I figure I might as well close up so we can head back to town.

Doesn't take long for me to tidy up the plans and shut the back doors. When I come out, the sight before me stops me in my tracks. A big smile on her face and her head bent down is Katie, softly talking to the big mutt whose head is resting in her lap, obviously enjoying the ear scratching he's receiving. I'll be damned.

CHAPTER TEN

"So your neighbor never mentioned anything about his family? No indication of his life before he came to Larchwood?" Gus is asking for the third time.

"Like I said before, I knew he had family because it was mentioned to me, but he never elaborated about his life before, and he just seemed like a sad old man. Confused most of the time, except that last day when he came into my room. He was scared and it was the first time I'd seen anyone come to visit him."

We've been at this for a couple of hours now in the conference room at the GFI office. Gus had called Caleb in earlier to 'go over things' and seemed a bit taken aback when I showed up in tow. Before I could justify being there, Caleb calmly stated that since I was already involved, possibly had information to add, and given I'm a fully qualified investigator working for GFI, he failed to see why I shouldn't be present. The men locked eyes for a moment in what seemed to be a silent power struggle, but Gus broke it by giving Caleb a nod and turning to me with an apologetic grin. Men.

So for a couple of hours, I've been immersed in all things cartel; learning about the downed airplane and the possible connection with the Klesh, a known gang based out of Shiprock, and apparently headed by none other than Caleb's brother. One of the men killed in the crash in Shiprock was the younger brother of this guy, Ernesto—the creep who was hanging around Larchwood. Jesus, sometimes the world is too small. The picture

Gus showed me confirms it though. Although grainy, there's no doubt in my mind it's the same guy, and that leads to this current line of questions.

"Why have their father, if Juan really is their father, in a home in Grand Junction? Why not closer to home?" I want to know.

"Few reasons I could think of; one being that the likelihood of anyone knowing who he is in Colorado is far less than back home in Mexico. Another possibility is that having their father set up in Grand Junction gave them an excuse to travel into the country on a regular basis. Providing him with the best possible care would've been a valid point to having him placed in the States as opposed to back home. Could be a combination of the two, I don't know, but I do know that they wouldn't want someone privy to the ins and outs of cartel business to start slipping up on information due to a mind that is failing."

I'm stunned when I look at Gus.

"What do you mean 'someone privy to the ins and outs of cartel business'? Juan? That sweet little old man? You're shitting me. He wouldn't hurt a fly. For fuck's sake, he was flirting with me every day. I even talked about my daily progress on finding my biological parents with him."

"That 'sweet little old man' is the one who built the cartel up almost from the ground, and on the bodies of hundreds, Katie."

An involuntary shiver runs down my back. *Holy shit.* Never looking at seniors the same way again, I can tell you that.

"Okay," Caleb interjects, "so we know who all the players are on the cartel side, and it's up to me to figure out if and how it ties in with the Klesh and Shiprock. We also need to make sure

98

you stay safe, Katie. The killing of the nurse worries me. Was she a witness to something?"

"She was actually the one that warned me to stay away from Ernesto; told me he was a creep and she didn't trust him. Apparently, she had tried looking at Juan's files before but was caught by Larchwood's director and threatened. She was pretty scared that night. When I heard she was dead, I thought of him right away."

I can feel the reassuring squeeze of Caleb's hand on my leg. It helps. Thinking about Sue pulls me down. Finding out Juan was a brutal cartel boss gone soft in the head almost completely crushed my faith in humanity, and in my judgement.

"Saturday you're heading back down, Caleb?" At Caleb's nod, Gus continues, "Okay, I'll see if I can get Neil to come down here by then. The place above the diner is available. I'll have a talk with Arlene; make sure I can put him up there. I think we may need a bit more manpower. I'm not liking the feel of this case, it has too many inroads into our lives. I also suggest you hit the shooting range, Katie. Don't know how your accuracy is since the injury, but better you find out before rather than after you need it."

"I'd love to go." I probably sound a bit more enthusiastic than I should, but it's been too long since I've held my gun and I look forward to it. I look sideways at Caleb who has a little smirk on his lips.

"First thing in the morning," he promises.

"Alright, we've milked about as much out of this as we can for now, let's grab Emma and hit the diner for some grub." Gus pushes back from the long conference table and goes in search of his better half.

"It's growing on me."

Beth, a long time waitress at the diner, just showed us to the table when Arlene, the owner and Emma's best friend, comes walking up from the kitchen. She waves her hand at my hair.

"The short hair; strikes me as more of a pixie than a dyke look now."

"Jesus, Arlene!" Emma slams her menu on the table. "You have the sensitivity of a warthog!"

"Whatever, Ems. Don't know why you're getting your knickers in a twist. At least I'm not terrorizing you today," she fires back, rubbing her hand through Emma's fiery curls. "Besides, Katie knows I'm yanking her chain, right girl?" The last was directed at me.

"You bet, Arlene," I chuckle. Those two are a constant source of entertainment with their bickering. Caleb and Gus hide smiles, pretending to study their menus.

"For the special, Seb has a huge pot of roasted red pepper soup and some fresh baked pesto bread. Can I start you off with some drinks?"

We all put our order in.

"I'll give you a minute to decide and be back with your drinks," she says as she heads toward the kitchen. Halfway there, she turns and calls out, "Hey Ems; hakuna matata!" Chuckling to herself, she disappears through the doorway.

Dinner is a lively event with frequent visits from the various locals who know either Gus, Emma or Caleb, and in some cases all. Seb, Arlene's man and the diner's cook, stops by for a chat as well. Caleb often slips his hand under the table to rub or squeeze my leg, or looks to see if I'm doing ok. I'm soaking it all up. When I was here before, I didn't take the time to get to know these people and I'm realizing I missed out. No one looks at me funny, and I figure it's because they all probably know my story. Not much stays hidden in a place like Cedar Tree. But it feels comfortable, not restrictive or cloying like it imagined it would.

I'm finally allowing myself to think of a future that might not look the way I planned it, but one that could be full of promise and possibility nonetheless, when a large burly man walks up to the table.

"Evenin' folks. Good to see you, Caleb. Just the man I wanted to talk to. Is this your woman?"

Emma snorts across from me and from the corner of my eye, I can see Caleb closing his eyes as if in pain, but I'm focused on the big ape that just called me Caleb's 'woman'. I open my mouth to give him a piece of my mind, when Caleb grabs a hold of my knee, hard, and intervenes.

"Clint, good to see you. This is Katie, yes. Katie, meet Clint Mason, my contractor. He also did the work on Gus and Emma's house. You'll be seeing a lot of him." The last he says looking at me from under his eyebrows, daring me to make nice. Very well, I'll try my best. I hold out my hand and find it wrapped in what is probably the largest hand I've ever seen, but that doesn't stop me from squeezing the crap out of it. By the time Clint pulls it back, he's shaking it out to restore blood flow. Good.

"Quite the grip you've got there, Katie," the moron points out.

"Must be all that knitting and crocheting, Clint," I tell him, a saccharine smile on my face.

The table bursts out laughing and Clint looks around a bit confused.

"I fucked up again, didn't I?"

Gus decides to come to his rescue and pats him on the arm, "It's ok. Better you find out now not to call Katie anyone's 'woman'. There are witnesses around, you're lucky. Katie's one of my top notch operatives and could probably sweep the floor with you, wheelchair or not."

That right there makes me feel ten feet tall, but then Clint does it again.

"I apologize. Don't mean anything by it, little la... Holy shit, there I go again. Sonofabitchin' southern upbringing kills me every time. No wonder I can't keep a woman around long enough to eat my breakfast!"

Now I'm laughing along with the rest of the table, especially when Emma regales the story of when Clint first came to quote on the diner after they'd had a fire. Apparently, Arlene tore him to bits. I would've loved to have seen that.

The next half hour or so is spent sharing stories over coffee and discussing plans for the upcoming construction on the barn. When Caleb moves his chair back and announces it's time to get home, I'm surprised to see it's pitch dark outside and the diner is virtually empty, except for our table which has an expanded circle of chairs now.

"Oh my God, that was so much fun," Katie stretches her arms over her head and yawns.

We're having a drink behind the guesthouse, on the patio off the small kitchen, enjoying a rather mild spring night. Mild, but with enough of a chill to warrant the quilt, which Katie has herself wrapped in.

"Can't remember the last time I laughed that much, but I'm fried. Going to turn in if you don't mind."

She gets busy folding the quilt and wheels herself around to go inside, doing her best to avoid my eyes. Thankful for my long arms, I manage to grab hold of both her armrests before she makes it past my chair and twist her to face me.

Cupping her chin in my hand so I can look her in the eye, I steal a hard predatory kiss, my tongue taking a deep sweep of her warm mouth.

"That's better. I had a good time too, little one. I'll be there shortly, just going to lock up."

The slightly shocked look on Katie's face is not going to stop me from getting a little more intimately acquainted with that luscious body that's been tempting me for days now, and I suppress a chuckle when she skirts out of sight as fast as she can move her chair. I make quick work of the few glasses we dirtied by hand and leave them to dry before locking the doors and turning off the lights. By the time I get to the bedroom, Katie's managed to get in bed and is rolled up in a ball, perched on the far side, her back to the door and her wheelchair abandoned by her side of the bed. After a quick clean up in the bedroom and the addition of my clothes to a fast growing pile of laundry in the basket, I slide under the covers behind her. A quick intake of breath and total lack of movement lets me know my little one is still wide-awake, however much she may try to convince me otherwise.

"Not fooling me, gorgeous," I breathe against her neck as I fold my body around her rigid one. My arms snakes around her waist and up to cup her breast unapologetically and my leg pushes between hers, pulling up snuggly to press against her warm pussy. Fuck yeah. On the release of a shuddering breath, she lets the tension out of her body and relaxes against me, allowing herself to lean into my hand and ride my thigh.

"That's it, baby, just feel me."

I work my hand under her tank so I can feel her skin and quickly find my way back to pluck at her tight little nipple. My own raging need to sink into her is almost impossible to control as I lick and kiss the skin of her neck and shoulder.

I growl my disapproval when Katie starts squirming in my arms.

"I need to touch you too," she says as she manages to twist around and loop her arms around my shoulders, fingers trailing down my arms and tracing the tattoos on my biceps while studying them closely.

"Hi."

When her eyes meet mine I see a slight hesitance and before it has a chance to grab hold, I slide my mouth over hers, plunging my tongue deep and letting her feel my need for her. One of her hands skims up my shoulders and scrapes over my scalp, shooting electric impulses straight to my balls.

"Too many clothes."

I start pulling up her tank and before she's even pulled it all the way off, I latch on to one of her soft plump breasts, sucking the pink tip deep in my mouth while my hand pinches the nipple on her other breast. Her back arches off the bed.

"Oh my God, Caleb. I won't last..."

"Yes you will. I need to taste you, little one. Scoot up."

In one tug, I have her shorts and underwear off and flung over the side of the bed. The sight of her softly rounded body sprawled on my bed gives me pause. Flushed cheeks, lips plump and slightly open, breasts moving in tandem with her rapid breaths. Her one leg open to the side to expose the deep red color of her aroused swollen lips, wet with her juices. I know I'm staring, but fuck she's beautiful. When she starts grabbing for the sheet to cover herself, I snap out of it.

"Oh no you don't," I yank the sheet out of her hand and pull it out of her reach, "You steal my words and take my breath, *Yázhí*. You're that beautiful."

Lowering myself on top of her, I kiss her softly before whispering against her lips, "perfect."

Slowly nipping and tasting my way down her body, I insert myself between her legs and raise my eyes to hers.

"Please, Caleb."

Using the tip of my nose to tease the hood of her clit, I push the soft dark curls aside before using the tip of my tongue to get my first taste of heaven. Christ she's delicious. With my thumbs I spread her open wide so the flat of my tongue can reach every part of her. Licking and sucking, I pay attention to her full pussy lips, lightly tugging and listen to every moaned encouragement from her mouth. When I finally enter her with my fingers and pull that little bundle of nerves in my mouth, her hands claw the back of my head and she bucks against my mouth.

"Fuck! I'm coming, Caleb."

"You'll wait for me," I say firmly when I pull back, drawing a whimper from her lips. It takes me two seconds to rip down my boxers and grab a condom from the nightstand before I'm back between her legs, pulling her knees up against my hips, my cock lined up at her soaking wet entrance. Fuck, I have to go slow or I'm done before I get started.

My mouth on hers, I slowly push my way inside her.

"Christ, little one. You're so tight. You ok?" I back up to look at her. Her fingers dig in my ass and pull me back inside her.

"Ahh, don't fucking stop now, Caleb. Don't you dare stop. I need you to fuck me, please..."

When I see nothing but need in her eyes, I let mine take over and without another thought, I pummel myself inside her, spreading her legs wide, grunting my effort as my release comes barrelling at me like a tidal wave.

"Fuck me, Katie, here I come. You with me?"

"God yes, Caleb, yes. Ahh."

The first ripples of her orgasm triggers my own. A surge down my spine, my asshole puckers and balls pull tight before the strings of semen jet from my cock, causing my body to buck and jerk.

"Jesus," I pant, still twitching, burying my face in Katie's neck, trying to catch my breath. "Long time coming, sweets. Long fucking time coming."

We lie there for a while slowly stroking each other's skin, breathing each other in. Finally I roll myself off Katie's body, earning a sigh from her.

"Wow," she mouths, making me smile.

"Yeah. My thoughts exactly."

CHAPTER ELEVEN

"She's nice. I like her. It's just odd she seems to know all about me and I'd never even met her."

Caleb shrugs his shoulders, "Not that surprising really, considering she was the attending physician at the ER at the time you got hurt, and you may have gone straight to Durango, but Emma ended up here. Besides, she's become pretty friendly with Emma and Arlene. Those two talk."

"No shit," I snicker.

So between Dr. Naomi Waters, who offered to monitor my progress and liaise with the neurologists in Durango, and Kendra Schmitt, who is going to be my physiotherapist starting Monday, it appears I'm all set. Hmm, haven't thought about 'recovering' in a few days now and it's been kinda nice, but I know I have to keep going.

"Ready for the shooting range?"

"Fuck yes! I can't wait to hold my baby again," I fist pump with a huge smile on my face.

Chuckling, Caleb reaches over the centre console and brushes his knuckles over my cheek. He brought over my beloved M&P Shield today, which had been stored in Gus' safe all this time. Damn it'll feel good to wrap my hand around it.

"You're lucky they have an official shooting range here in Macon where we can do some decent target practice. They even have a few courses set up we could try at some point, although to be honest, I wouldn't even know where to start on how to run those properly when you need two hands to manoeuvre the wheelchair."

I smile, and rest my head back against the seat letting the changes of the last few days play out in my head, and I've gotta say, I feel more alive than I have in a long time. Changes have come at me fast and furious, but truth be told, life had been nauseatingly boring and predictable since I landed in a wheelchair. I had started to think that's the way it was going to be. Apparently not. So far with Caleb it's been anything but boring. He doesn't seem to be affected too much by the wheelchair, and actually makes me forget it's there half the time as well. I sure as hell don't need a wheelchair in bed, and Caleb doesn't need help of any kind in that department. Fuck me, but that man has skills. When I woke up this morning, my body was still tingling and throbbing from the workout he put it through last night.

For someone usually on the cautious side, I sure am letting my hair down. It's fast, but it doesn't really feel like it. Maybe 'cause we've known each other for a few years, or maybe because he's been explicitly clear on where he stands and what he wants, which really minimizes risk for me. Not like I'm the one putting my heart on the line, or am I?

"What are you thinking so hard on?" Caleb gaze hits me before keeping an eye on the road ahead once more.

I snicker, "Oh, just everything. About a year's worth of excitement in two days and some life-altering events thrown in for good measure."

"Life-altering. That good, huh?" he says with a smile. That earns him a smack in the shoulder.

"Smartass."

"You like my ass."

"God help me, I do."

"Don't need any help there, sweets. It's all yours if you'll have it."

The smile on Caleb's face emphasizes the crinkles by his eyes. I love those crinkles. I've seen more of them in the last few days than I have in all the time I've known him. Instead of responding, I take my time studying his profile as he continues to watch the road, smile still plastered on his face. He really is a beautiful man; normally quite stern looking, but when he smiles, his eyes light up his entire face. An ageless face—one I could easily stare at for years to come. Holy crud, what am I thinking?

"Looking for warts?"

"What... Sorry?"

"Are you looking for warts? Trying to find flaws? I can feel your eyes scanning me, like you're trying to decide if I'm worth keeping around."

Turning into a parking lot of what I assume to be the shooting range, he pulls into a parking spot, turns off the engine and twists around in his seat so he's facing me. The question lingers in his eyes, laced with what might be some uncertainty. I quickly unclip my belt and turn to him, putting both my hands on his face.

"Not. Was simply contemplating how gorgeous you are, especially when you seem happy."

His eyes darken, his hand grab the back of my head and pulls me into a heart-stopping kiss. When his lips finally pull back and I can catch my breath, he whispers, "I don't just seem happy, I *am* happy, and I can't remember the last time I've felt this way."

I can't hold his intense eyes any longer and plant my face in his chest, struggling to swallow down the huge lump stuck in my throat. There is nothing to say to that, so I just let myself feel.

"Oh my God! Did you see that? Nailed that sucker right in the gonads."

Katie has been tirelessly shooting clip after clip for the past half hour, getting more hyped up by the minute.

"Yes, I see, and it would surely maim a man for life, but wouldn't necessarily stop him from shooting back at you. Come on, little one. You need to adjust your trajectory now that you're shooting from a sitting position. Different ballgame."

"Bahahaha... You're funny. I thought you wanted me to stay away from the genital area. I'll have to remember that."

The little tease. I lean down and grumble in her ear, "Just remember I can exercise great control, sweets."

From the way she squirms in her seat, I can tell she knows exactly what I'm referring to.

Just as I'm about to give her some pointers, my phone rings. I step outside so I can take the call, indicating to Katie where I'm going.

"Gus, what's up?"

"Change of plans. There were two meth-related deaths last night in Albuquerque and the Feds are cranking up the heat. They want this pipeline closed and closed fast. This was a deal gone bad, and one of the casualties was a member of the Klesh; it wasn't your brother," he adds quickly when he hears my sharp hiss, "but this might be a good time to get some decent intel. Tongues will be wagging after losing one of their own."

"Alright," I hesitate, looking through the glass in the door to where Katie is emptying yet another clip into the target's crotch. "When do you want me to go?"

"As soon as you can get on the road. Neil is on his way here already; I got hold of him before you. He'll stick around Katie. You sorted your shit with her?"

"Not that it's any of your goddamn business, but we're good for now, so yes." I answer reluctantly. What's between Katie and I is just that; between us.

"Don't need to know anything but that, jackass. Keep your panties on. Oh, and I'm fucking thrilled for you. Now get your ass in gear." Gus is chuckling when he hangs up. Dick.

"I'll be fine, really."

Katie is doing her best to convince me she's not disappointed, but her smile is strained and I'm not thrilled myself to lose out on another night with her in my arms.

"Sooner I can get this job done, the sooner I'll get back. Would you make sure Clint gets the keys to the padlock at the barn so he can get going on Monday? I'll hurry and program all the pertinent numbers in your phone when we get home, and I'd also wanted to talk to you about transportation. I have a small SUV lined up, a rental, with a swivel seat and a manual gearbox, so you can start getting yourself around. The chair will slide back once you're seated so you can easily pull in your folded wheelchair beside you in the passenger space. It's been specially adapted, but had to be ordered from Freewheel mobility and isn't going to be here until Monday. You can get Neil or Emma to take you to Cortez to pick it up. I'll leave the number for you."

When Katie doesn't respond, I check to find big tears rolling down her face. I reach over and wipe at them with the back of my hand.

"Hey, what's with the tears?"

"You got me a car," she sobs, tears coming in earnest now.

"*Yázhí*, I want you to be able to get around. I know Neil is going to be there to keep an eye on things, but you need your independence."

"See? How am I gonna keep myself from falling for you when you do shit like this, Caleb? It's impossible."

"First of all, I hate that we're needing to have this conversation on the road, and I can't have you in my lap where you should be when you're crying and we're talking about stuff like this. Second, why the fuck do you want to keep from falling for me? I'm already out for the count, Katie. Balls to the wall, remember?"

Frustrated out of my mind, I pull over on the side of the road, just outside of Cedar Tree and make quick work of getting her in my lap anyway.

"There. Now I feel slightly better. Talk to me," I urge her with one arm anchoring her to me and a hand in her short hair, pressing her head in my neck where she is getting my shirt soaked.

"I... I just don't know that I'm worth all this," she mutters.

"Worth to whom? To me? When all I could call you was my friend, you were invaluable. Now that you've let me become more, you're worth everything and anything. This is what friends do, what family does; what lovers do. I get as much of a kick out of giving you some of the tools you need to grab hold of your freedom as you probably do."

"Not used to kindness," her mumbled voice comes from somewhere in my neck.

"I get that, and I'm sorry you never had that, but you better work on a thicker skin if kindness is all it takes to pierce it, 'cause I have a feeling there's a lot more coming when you stick around Cedar Tree."

She sits up and wipes her face with her sleeves while I grab a box of tissues from the glove compartment and hand them to her.

"I'm done now."

"That's good, little one," I rumble, sweeping a few stray hair off her face.

"What color?"

"Excuse me?"

"The car you got me; what color is it?"

I throw my head back and laugh out loud. "You're such a girl."

"Am not."

"Oh, you are most definitely a girl," I chuckle as I lift her back in her seat, before getting back on the road, happy with the return of the light-hearted banter.

"He got you a car?"

Emma is helping me put away the groceries we just picked up at the tiny local grocery store. It doesn't have a big selection, for that you have to head into Cortez, but it's good for topping up the basic needs. Exactly what Emma decided was needed when she found me moping around a couple of hours after Caleb took off. We actually made quite a pair; between my wheels and her walker, we struggled to get ourselves in and out of her truck, but managed. With some support and a good handhold, I do okay moving myself around, and Emma had a bit of a struggle with the chair after that, but seeing as she doesn't know the meaning of giving up, managed to wrangle the chair in the back. Of course, guileless and without reservation as Emma is, she managed to get me to talk about these past few days with Caleb. For someone who isn't used to girl-talk, I was sure as hell learning fast, and the last person I'd have expected opening up to was Emma.

I just finished telling her about our trip to the shooting range, which I'm sure Gus won't be happy about since Emma now wants to go shoot at 'stuff' too.

"I can apparently pick it up in Cortez on Monday at this medical supply store. I have the number, I just have to call in the morning to set a time 'cause they want to give me some driving instructions. No foot pedals, so I need to know where everything is."

Emma is almost jumping with excitement, her curls bouncing.

"The man got you a freakin' car!"

Making me laugh, "I know. He wants me to have my independence and *'Grab my Freedom'*." I use my fingers to make air-quotes for emphasis.

"I know! Makes me happy he gets to do this for you." At the confused look on my face she adds, "that man's been sitting on his hands for far too long where you're concerned."

Before I get a chance to react, the front door opens.

"Honey, I'm home!"

With a big smile on his face, Neil James comes striding into the kitchen, sweeping first Emma off her feet in a big hug before lifting me clear out of my seat.

CHAPTER TWELVE

It's been exactly a week since Caleb left, and despite some pretty intense phone calls I miss him. Not that I've been bored. Hell no. Over the weekend, Neil filled me in on some of the information he has found on my adoptive mother. Apparently she hasn't had her license renewed in the past fifteen years, but was picked up in Denver eight years ago for soliciting. Eewww. I shudder to think how desperate you'd have to be to stand on a street corner when you qualify as a senior in some states. Oh, and double yuck to the type of clientele she might have drawn in. I don't have very good memories of her but I wouldn't wish that life on anyone. Anyway, Neil says he can't find a trace after that but he has a buddy with the Denver PD who will put some feelers out on the street, for whatever good that might do.

We also spent some time with Gus going over a few current trace cases, and he had Neil set up shop in the conference room. I think Neil must've emptied out the Grand Junction office, because every surface in that room is now covered with one computer or another, large screen, police-scanner or other electronic device. How he managed to pack all that shit up in his truck on such short notice is a mystery. Gus seems to be set on the idea of me doing some work again, because he had Neil hand over some of the computer tracking to me. I'm surprised I'm actually enjoying it.

As of Monday morning Clint came and got the key for the barn and Gus has been off on a job but left us with keys to the separate entrance for the office, so we don't have to bug Emma all the time, and I got my call in to check on the car. A navy blue

Toyota Rav4 and a sweet little ride. Caleb did well and I told him so that night when he called. He chuckled when I mentioned I approved of the car.

"Such a girl." To which I promptly issued a, "Shut up," making him only laugh harder.

It took me a while to get the hang of driving 'hands only', but the guy at the rental place had me do loops around the parking lot and then had me drive around Cortez before he felt secure enough to send me on my way. I had Emma in the back seat squealing the whole time. Crazy chick.

Tuesday was my first real day of physio and I was pumped to be able to drive myself, even though Neil was complaining from the passenger side the whole time. Caleb and Gus apparently have told him in no uncertain terms that he is to keep an eye on me at all times, a task he takes to heart, a little too seriously at times if you ask me. He was like a kid in a candy store when I had to ask him to drive the Rav back home because I was too sore, though. He had a blast speeding down country roads with his hands. A big kid.

I've had sessions every day since, and let me tell you, Kendra seemed nice, but now I almost hate her. Not really, but she's a tough taskmaster and will only entertain absolutes. No talk about adjusting to not walking again, only talk of when I do.

Yesterday Naomi came and checked in while I was walking between parallel bars, being held up by a harness.

"Hey! Good to see you up and about," she grins at me.

"Hilarious," I huff out at her, beet red and sweating from the exertion.

Not insulted at all, she takes a seat and spends the next twenty minutes watching me being put through my paces by the

ruthless Kendra, who finally lowers me back into my chair when
my knees won't stay straight anymore. She wheels me over to
where Naomi is sitting and pulls up a chair herself.

"So," Naomi starts, "how does it feel with the first week's
sessions done?"

"Fucking sore," is my response, making Kendra cackle.

"Good." She nods her head, apparently quite happy to have
made me miserable.

Naomi chuckles. "You're gonna hurt like hell, and I'd be
happy to give you something for the pain, but you seemed
adamant you didn't want anything. Just to be clear, pain will be a
huge part of what you need to do to get back on your feet, so if it
is a deterrent or gets to be too much, tell me. Although you strike
me as a tough broad." She inclines her head, waiting for my
reaction.

"Not taking drugs, I told you that. I don't like how they make
me feel loopy, but fuck if I don't wish I had a big ol' hot tub I
could sink into."

Suddenly Naomi jumps up and claps her hands, "Oh wait! I
know - we should go to Ouray; do the hot springs this weekend.
Let me call the girls." And with that she is out the door talking on
her phone.

That was yesterday and here I am, overnight bag packed and
waiting for 'the girls' to pick me up. The girls being Arlene,
Emma and obviously Naomi, who set this whole thing up.
Apparently it doesn't take much to persuade the other two into a
night away at the hot springs. I've never been, but I am looking
forward to it. Crud - Caleb is right, I am turning into a real girl. A
year ago the prospect of a night away with a bunch of chicks

would have sent me running in the opposite direction and now I find myself actually excited about it.

The two-and-a-half hour drive is gorgeous, especially once we get past Durango. Naomi is driving her fancy Denali, big enough to carry all four of us, wheels and bags. I'm riding shotgun and the Bobbsey Twins are in the backseat. Poor Neil, determined to stick to us like glue, is following behind in his truck. Arlene apparently had been the hardest sell and if it hadn't been for Seb virtually shoving her out the door, she would've waved the diner in our faces as an excuse. By the laughs coming from the back seat though, she wasn't regretting it one bit. Naomi and I have a chance to chat a little and I'm surprised to find out she is a single mom with a teenage son. I didn't even think she was my age, but it turns out she has a couple of years on me. The boy had been given her some trouble and wasn't liking the rules she tried to enforce, so when he turned sixteen, he decided to move in with his dad in Phoenix. Not happy with that decision, given that the ex was apparently a dick of massive proportions, there wasn't much Naomi was able to do about it without risking completely alienating her son. So she let him have that choice, preparing herself for what she believes will be inevitable fall out. Cripes. Kids sound like work.

"So Doc? Which one of us gets to room with the mini hunk?" Arlene pipes up from the back seat.

"Arlene. You dirty thing!" Emma admonishes. "You already have a gorgeous, tatted up hunk at home, who by the way, is younger than your ratty old ass."

"You're welcome to kiss that ass, Ems. And don't worry, I never leave Seb unhappy."

Rolling her eyes in mock disgust, Emma's only response is, "bite me."

"It never fails," Naomi giggles.

I've talked to Katie three times and each time just the sound of her voice has me harder than a fucking rock. Stuck in this shit room at the same Travelodge in Farmington as before, with only my hand as companion, but since having had a taste of her, for the first time in almost four years, my hand is not enough to ease the burn.

I've been back to my parents' house only once to find my mother alone and out of it as usual. The place was still in pretty decent shape and they hadn't made much of a dent in the groceries Mal bought them. No sign of him or my dad though. I've stopped in at some old hangouts in hopes of picking up on some of the local buzz and managed to put out some careful feelers. Also made contact with both the reservation authorities and the police department in Farmington, but so far very little has materialized. Malachi seems to have gone underground. I wonder if it has anything to do with the deaths in Albuquerque and the resulting increased heat from authorities.

I crumple my take out bag with the remnants of another lonely dinner when my phone rings. I don't recognize the number.

"Hello?"

"Señor Whitetail. You are a nosy man and as you know, curiosity killed the cat. We seem to be in search of the same man, but for quite different reasons. Should you find him first, tell him it would be in everyone's best interest for him to own up to his debts. I have very little patience for interference and less for traitors. Best you use extreme care." The heavily Spanish accented voice sounded pleasant enough, but the threat was undeniable and the hair on my arms stands on end immediately.

"Who is this?"

"That is of far less importance than the message of caution I suggest you consider. Perhaps a small incentive to convince you of my utmost sincerity is required."

Dead air indicates I have been hung up on. And warned off in no uncertain terms. Immediately clicking on my laptop, I check the software Neil has installed to automatically trace all incoming calls, but it only confirms what I already suspected; not nearly long enough for a result. Next I dial Katie's number, needing to assure myself she is ok. No fucking answer. I try Neil's number with the same result and leave him a message to call *immediately*. He should have his phone at hand at all fucking times. Furiously pounding at the numbers now, Gus is next on the list, and I feel slight relief when I hear his voice come on.

"Caleb, what's up?"

"Girls ok?"

"As far as I know. Why, what happened?"

"Just got a call. Likely cartel, a Mexican voice, poised but telling me an incentive would be given for me to not stick my nose into business it didn't belong in. Katie's not answering and Neil's not answering. Can you get a visual?"

"Negative, I'm on the road. The girls are at an overnight stay at the hot springs in Ouray. Emma told me about it last night when I called in. Neil was going with them. Calling her cell, I'll get back to you."

Fuck. I had skipped calling last night in favor of checking out some backwater hangouts I might find my brother at. For the second time in as many weeks I feel uncontrollable fear course through my body at the thought of any harm coming to Katie, and time crawls by as I wait for Gus to get back to me. What seemed like hours, but was likely only minutes, the phone rings.

"Not fucking answering. I'm gonna tan her hide when I get my hands on her. Sit tight, I'm getting Dana on the phone with the hotel they're staying at. Don't fucking panic yet."

Don't fucking panic. Right. I'm already half way done packing my shit and it doesn't take me long to throw the rest in my bags. Not waiting for a call back, I hoist my stuff on my shoulders, keep my phone at the ready and make for my truck. Like fuck I'm waiting around. I toss my bags in the back, hop behind the wheel and am about to turn the key when my phone rings.

"Yeah?"

I can hear a lot of commotion in the background and then Neil's tentative voice saying my name, "Caleb?"

CHAPTER THIRTEEN

"Oh my God, this is frickin' bliss," Emma exclaims as she sinks down in the hot springs pool beside me. The outside air is pretty chilly but once you hit that water you heat up quickly.

"Isn't it?" Naomi moans her contentment from my other side. "If I could set up practice here I would. Every night after work I'd hop in here. I bet ya I'd sleep like a baby all the time." She wiggles her toes above the waterline.

"I still say we should've put that wine in water bottles. Nothing wrong with having a little social drink in the hot tub. Stupid rules."

We all chuckle at Arlene's grumblings. Her bottle of wine and plastic glasses were confiscated at the gate to the pool and her attempts at sweet-talking the guard were to no avail. Although sweet-talking and Arlene in one sentence should be enough of an indicator of failure. She perks up noticeably when Emma reveals she has brought some of her special chocolates.

"You did not." I smile widely at Emma, having heard the story of their over-indulgence in Emma's medicinal pot-laced truffles from Caleb.

"What? What am I missing?" Naomi wants to know.

With Neil sitting at the edge of the pool, shaking his head at our antics and giggles, Arlene and Emma take turns filling Naomi in on that particular story, but it isn't long before they turn their attention to me.

"Soooo..." Arlene drags out teasingly. "What's up with you and Caleb?"

I knew it was coming, it was inevitable, but I don't know if I'm ready for this inquisition, so I try to brush it off.

"Just testing the waters."

"The waters huh?" Arlene turns to throw Emma, who is stifling a snicker, a significant look. "And how are those waters feeling?"

Unable to hold back, Emma laughs, "Arlene, leave her alone. It's none of our business." Then she turns to me with a mischievous grin, "not that we're not dying to know."

"Right. What she said; dying here," Arlene adds.

I shake my head knowing full well they won't let it go. "Fine. He seems to be hoping I'll settle in Cedar Tree."

I laugh at the three faces turned toward me, full of anticipation.

"Yes, that's not news. And?" Arlene waves her hand urging me to say more, "Geeze it's like pulling fucking teeth, here - Come on Pixie, spit it out already."

"I like it, and I'm willing to see how I do in Cedar Tree." I smile knowing I'm driving them nuts by being evasive.

"No one cares about Cedar Tree - we want to know how you feel about Caleb." This from Naomi, who's been quietly observing so far. Traitor.

"I'm still getting used to it… to us. Thinking of him differently, or maybe not so differently, but allowing myself to for once. Caleb is different. I'm used to him being so stoic, but he seems almost rattled to the point of distraction at times. It's new, all of it is. I'm still adjusting to the wheelchair thing."

"Don't get too comfy in that chair, you won't be there long enough," Naomi interrupts firmly.

"And adjusting to a whole different set of rules to live by. I'm just taking it all in and I guess Caleb is part of that."

"Rules? What rules?" Emma grabs my hand, "if there is anything I can teach you then let it be this; there are no rules. There is no can or cannot do, there is only a future with opportunities that can change by the day, and you need to grab hold of them before they're gone."

I soak up her words and hear the truth of what she says, but it's not easy to let go of a once rather regimented life and open yourself up like that.

"And please don't hurt Caleb. He may be an experiment to you, but you have been a lot more to him for a long time."

I turn to Arlene. "He is not an experiment," I bite out, "never was. I care for him. A lot. It's just new..."

"I get that, girl. Just needed to hear you say it." Arlene gives me a quick hug before flopping back in the water.

I allow myself to float on my back staring up at the night sky, amazed at the changes in me. Everything feels so vibrant, so crisp. For the first time in my life I feel like I fit in my skin and it surprises me. My situation is nothing I'd ever have expected or envisioned and yet here I am, completely content. A small pang of guilt hits me when I think of the mess and the question marks I've left behind in Grand Junction, but with it comes the realization that not everything is in my control. And for once I can let that be ok. Yes I want to know what happened to Juan, and I will do my best to help GFI and the GJPD find out as much as they can. And for sure I want resolution to Sue's murder, which I am convinced is connected, but I recognize I don't hold all the necessary pieces to make that happen, nor do I control the timeline. I'm learning just to be, and isn't that just the most amazing thing ever?

A tug on my foot almost has me going under.

"Falling asleep there, Pixie?" Of course it's Arlene. "We're just about to grill Naomi here about her interesting chemistry with our buddy the recently appointed Sheriff Joe Morris."

"Buzz off Arlene," Naomi balks, "nothing happening there."

"Oh I know nothing's happening now, but something did at some point. Sparks like those don't fly all by themselves. Come on, girl, you've been holding out on us long enough. You know every bit of dirt there is to know about us. Time to spill."

"Ugh, you're relentless, woman. Fine, but I warn you; it isn't as interesting as you might think it is." Naomi concedes. "I met Joe three years ago when I just started my rotation in the ER in Cortez. He came in with someone in custody who had gotten hurt driving drunk and needed stitches. I was relatively new in town and had come off a nasty drawn out divorce, he asked me out and I said yes. It was a big leap of faith for me, because I hadn't been with anyone but David. We'd been together since we were fifteen, so the prospect of even a date terrified me, but having just moved myself and my kid to a new place, I figured it would fit in with the whole 'new beginnings' thing. It was pretty much a disaster."

"I can't imagine," Emma sighs, "Joe is such a sweetie."

"Yeah, well, the physical chemistry was all there. No complaints on that front, but when his phone kept blowing up during dinner and souring his mood, and then some bimbo eventually stopped at the table demanding to know why he wasn't answering 'his wife's' calls, I figured it was time to call it a night."

I think we all gasped at that, but of course Arlene piped up.

"Joe is married? No shit! I've known him for years and I would know if he was. Are you sure she wasn't some disgruntled ex pissed at being passed over?"

"Pretty damn sure. In fact, he tried calling afterward for days, which I ignored. Until finally he cornered me in the ER, wanting to explain. I said there was only one thing I needed to know and that was whether he was married, and that that answer only required a yes or a no. His answer was yes, so I told him I had had enough of adulterers for a lifetime and left him in the hallway. That's the end of that." A shrug of her shoulders indicates she is done with it, but a shadow in her eyes tells me the experience still stings.

In an effort to steer the focus away from what seems to be an uncomfortable trip down memory lane for Naomi, I bring up a sure-fire topic, "So what's this about special chocolates?" And with a loud cheer of approval, the girls get out of the pool and make their way to the dressing room, leaving me to call after them, "Hey! Excuse me, some help here please?"

"Neil? The fuck is going on there... Neil?"

"Yeah. Sorry man, I got your message. Reception is for shit up here. Been checking my phone every couple of minutes while the women were in the pool."

I blow out the ball of tension that has been sitting on my chest like an anvil. The instant relief makes me almost light-headed and I bend over, leaning on the hood of the car.

"Everyone good? Haven't seen anything out of the ordinary?" I prompt him.

"Nah man. Just these crazy broads having a good time, why? Something happen?" The concern is evident in Neil's voice.

"Keep your eyes peeled. Make sure you have connecting doors in the hotel or sleep on the goddamn floor of their room if you must. I'm guessing they'll all be bunking like a bunch of schoolgirls, yeah?"

"Guess so," he says with a snort, "although I can't for the life of me figure out what's so fun about that."

"This time, just be glad they do weird shit, because I'm not sure we can get more coverage up there on short notice and we might be in a shitload of trouble. I got a call tonight, I pegged it as a Duarte family member or someone closely connected, telling me to back off and the promise I would be left with some incentive. I'm worried about Katie. If they've had eyes on me the whole time, they would've had them on her too. You hearing me?"

"Loud and clear. Want us to head back tonight?"

"No. Safer to bunk down for the night and travel in daylight but it might be a good idea to split the women over two cars. Did Katie bring her sidearm?"

"Didn't see it, but that doesn't mean it's not there. I'll have her in the car with the doc and Emma and Arlene can get in the truck with me, and I'll be behind the doc."

"If she has her gun, then yes that's a good option."

"Want me to talk to her?"

I'm pretty sure this is not something I can leave Katie out of, nor do I really want to. She has every right to know that she might have an even larger target on her head now.

"Hand the phone to her. I'll talk to her, but Neil? You give Gus a call and let him talk to Ems after. He's been trying to get through too."

"Sure."

I can hear him call out to Katie and a minute or so later I can hear her out of breath voice on the line.

"Hey you. How come you're calling on Neil's phone?"

Always sharp on details, she knows right away something is off.

"We may have some trouble heading your way, sweets. Nothing specific, but I was given the message that something might be coming down in connection with this cartel business. You'll see a few missed calls on your phone from me too. Couldn't get a hold you, apparently your reception sucks there."

"Fuck. You safe? Do you need back up?"

I chuckle at that, because I am likely better covered here, with the Farmington PD as well as the Feds backing me up should I need it.

"I'm good, little one. You, however, are a bit exposed. Are you carrying?"

"Brought my baby with me. In my bag, but she'll be on my hip from here on in."

I want to say much more but I have another call coming in so I have to cut it short.

"I've got a call, gotta go. Discuss course of action with Neil, okay?"

"Gotcha. And Caleb?" Her voice dips down to almost a whisper, "please try hard to come home to me."

I love you is in my heart and on my lips, but no way in hell am I going to tell her over the phone. She knows anyway.

"Always."

With a quick glance at my phone to see who's calling, I answer the other line.

"Gus. They're fine. Just talked to Neil, they have dick all in reception up there." I quickly fill him in.

"Thank fuck for that. Tell 'em to stay the night?"

"Yeah I did. Neil's gonna be calling you soon. I'm heading back inside. It's getting fucking cold here in the parking lot."

I can hear his chuckle coming over the line, "Bags packed and ready to roll, right?"

"Absolutely," I admit.

"Figured you weren't gonna listen when I told ya to wait. What else is new? Stay safe; I'll see to it we get some more eyes on the girls for tonight. I'll be in touch."

I slide my phone in my back pocket, open the back door to my Tahoe and am about to haul out my bags again, when I hear a car pull up beside me. Cops.

"Caleb Whitetail?"

"That's me." I notice the young officer who addressed me is doing his best to avoid my eyes.

"Sir, we need you to come with us."

Just then I notice the second officer standing by the patrol car.

"What's going on?"

"Detective Jonas asked us to pick you up. There's been a problem at your family home."

Fuck.

"I'll follow you." I move to get into the truck when the other officer's voice stops me.

"We were instructed to drive you."

I throw him a scathing look. "I'm not getting in the fucking patrol car with you unless you're willing to give me better information than you just did. My guess is you won't. So you either lead the fucking way or shoot me as I drive over to my parents' house where, as you point out, there is *'trouble'*. I'm sure your Detective Jonas as well as the FBI, with whom I am working closely together, would be thrilled about that." Fucking son of a bitch little punk ass cop thinks he's gonna sit me in the back of his patrol car.

I tear out of the parking lot in the direction of Shiprock with the cops on my tail trying to keep up. They wanna lead, they're gonna have to go faster.

CHAPTER FOURTEEN

I can see the thick plume of smoke from a distance. Fear and anger course through me as I pull the truck in behind a collection of emergency vehicles and jump out. There is fucking nothing left of my parents' house. Not a damn thing but a pile of burned out and smoking rubble.

Walking up to the remnants of my childhood home I barely notice my name being called until a hand is slapped on my shoulder.

"Hold up, son." A familiar deep rumble comes from behind me.

Detective Manuel Jordan is probably only ten or so years older than I am, but has a fatherly way about him.

"Where are they?"

My eyes closely scan the small crowd that has gathered, but the slight pressure of the hand on my shoulder warns me that I won't find my parents' faces among them.

"Your father was found just outside the door and has been taken to Farmington. No sign of your mother outside. Waiting for word from the Fire Marshall to go in and look for possible remains. I'm so sorry."

I haven't left the safety of my Tahoe since filling Manny Jordan in on the threatening phone call and suggest he call Gus to inform him of the latest. I just don't have it in me to talk to anyone right now. I'm not sure how long it's been; likely hours.

Silently I watch as a group of three men starts sifting through the rubble in what I know to be a search for my mother's body. All the while I try to honour her with memories of who and how she was before my sister's death broke her. I don't really need the confirmation; I can feel she's gone.

My eyes shoot up when I hear a yell and I see one of the men standing in the still smoking remains of our house, his arm in the air, marking the location where my mother died. It's her; don't need the confirmation, I know. Rubbing my hands over my face, I'm surprised to find them coming away wet with tears, and that makes me pissed. Why the fuck was my father out the door, but my mother still inside?

"Caleb?" Manny is standing in the open passenger side door, a look of concern on his face. "Can't confirm until the coroner has done his thing, but it looks like it might be her."

I simply nod at him and get out. "I want to see her." I start walking toward the group of men now huddled around their find, but Manny holds me back.

"I hear there isn't much left. Not a good idea, Caleb."

Shrugging his hand off my arm I walk on. "Not negotiable," is all I say.

"So glad you guys convinced me to come," Arlene is laying with her head on Emma's lap, a goofy smile on her face. I'm pretty sure she's three sheets to the wind with the white wine and truffle combo she's been hitting.

Neil and I managed to get our rooms changed to a suite with two bedrooms and a pull out couch, which put us all within the same walls and that makes protection a shit load easier. Only one door to watch. I feel bad about leaving the others in the dark, but Neil was right when he pointed out there was no use in spoiling everyone's night. Wasn't like we weren't gonna say anything tomorrow. They're likely to find out when they get wind of the driving arrangements that something is up.

Not wanting to dull my rusty reflexes even further, I made up the excuse that I couldn't drink because of medication, something that was quickly accepted in this group.

We're lounging on the big king-sized bed in one of the bedrooms and just finished watching some sappy movie on the big flat screen when Arlene sighs, "I used to be like that you know? All lonely and frustrated... Sad, really. Having to go without two or three good orgasms a day should be a crime."

Naomi and I burst out laughing, but Emma just smiles dreamily, "I used to get so fucking horny, I'd wonder with every guy that passed me on the street or stopped next to me at a light, how he'd be in the sack. Some of those fantasies would be so hot; I'd live off them for weeks. Nowadays, who has time for fantasies?"

Ahh. Slightly uncomfortable for me, knowing exactly what she has... or maybe that's not fair. I don't really. There is no comparing what I thought I had with Gus and what he and Emma have. No comparison whatsoever.

"I have an admission to make," Naomi slurs next to me, "I'm on a dry spell that's going on–" She starts counting the fingers of both hands before she says, "four years now, and I get turned on in the produce section of the grocery store, imagining random shoppers doing me in the potato bin."

I'm laughing so hard, tears are running down my face and I'm pretty sure I peed my pants a little. Arlene just manages to catch Emma before she rolls off the bed in hysterics and with a loud snort and a shake of his head, Neil finally has enough and pulls the bedroom door shut on our raucous laughter. Of course this is only 'cause for more hilarity. To think I didn't even have one sip to drink.

Not five minutes later I am grateful for that fact when Neil sticks his head back in the door.

"Need you in here for a minute, Katie. Business call," he says, giving me a pointed look that takes all the giddiness right out of me. I scramble to get off the bed and in my chair, and with the others barely noticing I'm leaving, I head into the other room.

"What's up," I question Neil when I notice his cell phone laying on the table.

"Gus just called. There was trouble in Shiprock."

At my panicked gasp Neil throws up his hands and adds quickly, "Caleb's fine, but his parent's house was burned down. Nothing's been confirmed but arson is suspected and his father was found unconscious just outside the door. He's in the hospital in Farmington."

I know there is more when he keeps looking at me with his solemn eyes.

"His mother?" I have to know.

"Remains were found inside the home and are en route to the coroner's office for positive identification, but the general consensus is that it's her."

My heart breaks for Caleb. I know his relationship with his parents has been non-existent for most of his adult life but there was a time when they were a happy family. I know he loves his family regardless. This must be killing him. I wheel myself into the other room to start packing my bag when Neil stops me.

"What are you doing?"

"Have to get to Farmington," I say without looking up from my task.

"We can't. Katie, think. I get it, I do, but things just got really serious and you and I are all that's between these three women in there and potential trouble."

He's right, I know he's right but I'm so fired up, I need to do something, I need to be with Caleb right now. Fuck, why is this so complicated! Any action impeded by circumstances, I have nothing left but to give in to my emotions. Big tears of sadness and frustration start rolling down my face and Neil looks on in shock, but soon is kneeling next to me, awkwardly wrapping his arms around me in comfort.

"I'll have you know I hate this feeling, shit. I just started and it's not working out so good right now," I mumble in his shirt, making him laugh quietly.

"You were always too much of a hard ass for a girl. Gotta say I like you better like this."

"What? Weepy and weak?"

"No. Beauty, balls and heart. You know; the whole package?"

He gets up to get a box of tissues from the bathroom and I observe him as he hands them over.

"You know you're gonna make some woman extremely lucky one day, don't you?"

"Whatever," he says with a smirk, "come on, wipe the slobber and let's wait for Gus's call. He was going to make some arrangements while I talked to you."

When we drive on to the parking lot of the San Juan Regional Medical Centre, it's near noon on Saturday.

Gus met us in Durango where we had a quick late breakfast before I transferred my stuff to his truck. Gus had his hands full trying to calm down a pissed off Emma and Arlene, who had wanted to come for support. Explaining to them they'd be walking into a potential dispute between a notorious Mexican cartel and a well-known gang, went a long way to calming them down. Finally tucked into Naomi's fancy car with Neil ready to follow them back home, Gus and I finally get on our way.

"So you never got through to him?" I ask again. I asked him last night too and tried calling myself a few times, but Caleb never answered.

"No, Manny Jordan, the lead detective, who was working with Caleb already, mentioned Caleb had very determinedly turned his phone off. I've been in touch with Manny a couple of times though and know Caleb's here waiting for his father to regain consciousness. He's been out this whole time."

"Is he gonna make it?"

"It would appear so, although with some serious third degree burns and they haven't been able to assess the damage from smoke inhalation. He was drunk out of his brain, which is the only reason they figure he hasn't woken up yet."

Gus walks up to a portly middle-aged Latino man who comes toward us in the lobby.

"Detective Jordan?"

"Manny. You must be Gus Flemming." They shake hands and Gus introduces me as his associate, immediately making me feel less awkward about being here.

I'd been having second thoughts about coming, the closer we got to Farmington. Starting to doubt whether he'd even want me here, thinking he would've called or at least answered my calls if he needs me. I hate the uncertainty eating at me.

"He's up on the third floor. Mr. Whitetail has still not woken up and they're keeping him in the ICU, but in a private room because of the police investigation. Let's go up." Manny indicates the elevators on the far side of the lobby.

"Actually," Gus suggests, "why don't we let Katie head up while we go over some things here. Okay with you, Katie?"

I'm eager to see Caleb, but nervous as hell about how he's going to react to having me here. I simply nod and make my way to the elevators.

There is no one stopping me on the third floor so I peek in the doors along the hallway until I see Caleb sitting beside a bed, his head in his hands. He must've heard something because his head shoots up and he looks straight at me.

I stumble over my words, "Hi. Sorry to barge in, but I... I needed to see you."

Without a word, Caleb gets up, walks over and grabs my chair, only to turn me out into the hallway again. That did not go well.

Been sitting in this damn hospital room for hours listening to the beep of the various machines my father is hooked up to, thinking about how detached I'm feeling compared to another time in recent memory when I was sitting by the side of a hospital bed, waiting for a sign of life. I felt like my heart was being ripped out then, but this time, I feel nothing but a deep anger and sadness.

The soft groan from the bed startles me. He blinks a few times before his eyes finally settle on me and without needing to hear the question, he answers it for me with the guilt that clouds his eyes and the hastily whispered, "Sorry."

Nothing left now. I only stayed because I needed to know for sure. Needed to hear from him how he could save himself and leave my mother, his wife, to burn.

I saw her body, or what was left of it. If there was any doubt, the horseshoe shaped picture frame clutched in her charred fingers confirmed it. She never went anywhere without that picture of my sister. Never. I hope it gave her some comfort in the end.

A small sound from the doorway alerts me and I can feel my hard resolve crumbling when I see Katie there.

"Hi," she says in a small voice, "Sorry to barge in but I... I needed to see you."

Unable to speak for the flood of emotions coming at me, I turn her chair around, away from my bastard of a father and roll her into the adjoining small waiting room, which luckily is empty. I don't think, just lift her out of her chair and on to my lap as I sit down on the single couch in the room. Wrapping my arms tightly around her I bury my face in her neck and feel a shudder go through my body. I'm holding my family in my arms.

Tentative hands slide over my shoulders and into my hair, holding my head close and I can't hold back the sob that's been trying to escape me. Fucking hell. How is it possible that a normal, happy family like ours got so destroyed? Wasn't it enough we lost Nascha? Times like these I really have trouble believing there is a God, or any other benign higher power for that matter.

I don't exactly know how long we are sitting like that. At some point I could hear movement but I never bothered looking up. All I care about now is in my arms.

"Thank you," I manage to croak out my head still in her neck, breathing in her scent.

"I want to be here, no need for thanks," she whispers so softly I can barely feel the air moving.

She sits up and reaches over to grab a box of tissues of the side table. I notice her tearstained face and red eyes, and imagine I probably look about the same. She makes quick work of her own tears and the smudges of make up under her eyes, before she gently wipes my face. I let her. I'm raw, fully exposed and completely at her mercy. When she's done she takes my face in her hands and kisses me softly on the lips, sliding a hand over my head.

"I tried calling, to see if you even wanted me here," I open my mouth to interrupt, but she places two fingers on my lips to shut me down, "And I wasn't sure I was doing the right thing all the way up to the moment you took me on your lap. I'm so glad I followed my gut and came."

I take her hand away from my mouth after kissing her fingers, "I turned my phone off. My instincts were to run home to you as fast as I could get there and I knew that I would, if just heard your voice. I had to see this through—I needed to know why my father breathes when my mother was burning to death just a few feet away. And I needed to hear it from him."

"Shhhh, I get it."

CHAPTER FIFTEEN

"I smell like a pot roast."

I almost choke on a sip of coffee when I hear Katie's comparison.

We just got back to the hotel room from my mother's combined Navajo and Christian funeral and Katie had been fascinated with the smudging ceremony. The side effects of the smoky sage are apparently less appealing to her.

Turning toward the choking sounds I was making, her eyes suddenly turn big as saucers.

"Oh no. That slipped out, that was terrible. I'm so sorry. I wasn't trying to be disrespectful."

A deep rumbling chuckle escapes me as I lean in and quickly kiss the worry off her lips.

"It's fine, little one."

Relief slides over her face as she says a bit sheepishly, "Phew, seriously. The more time I spend with you, the less control I seem to have over my filters."

"For your information, I'm considering that a compliment. Don't want any filters, just you is perfect."

A light blush creeps up from the V-neck of her long-sleeved t-shirt and slowly spreads over her cheeks under my scrutiny. I'm looking my fill, having kept myself a little distant the last few days leading up the funeral. With so much to sort through and organize, my father still in the hospital and my brother in the wind, there was only me. Gus stayed on to focus on the investigation while I have been dealing with the arrangements for my mother, and despite Katie's offers for help, I needed to do this myself. Honour my mother in a way I know would've pleased her.

No hiding my hunger for Katie now, and from the look on her face, she knows it.

"I... I've been wanting to show you something," she says almost shyly, immediately peaking my interest with visions of sexy underwear and soft naked skin. Instead she rolls her chair back from where I'm sitting on the edge of the bed and locks her wheels. Gripping the edge of her armrests, she pushes herself up to stand in front of me. Automatically my arms shoot out to grab hold of her but I pull back when she shakes her head.

"Yeah, I've been working pretty hard with Kendra while you were gone. It's not much, but progress for me," she says as she's about to sit back down in her chair, looking defeated because I haven't been able to say a damn thing.

Fuck me.

"Katie," I manage to get out before I grab her around the waist and twist her onto the bed, throwing myself over her with my elbows by her shoulders and my hands holding her face in place. I rub my nose along hers and kiss her lightly. "So fucking proud of you. You're incredible, and you can do whatever you put your mind to, my *Yázhí*. So fucking fierce."

"I missed you."

"I know. Me too. I'm sorry for not showing you how much it's meant to have you with me these past few days," I tell her, peppering her face and neck with kisses. "Sorry I haven't paid attention to this amazing body except to take comfort holding it at night. Sorry I..."

"Shut it and kiss me properly," she interrupts with heat in her eyes.

"Yes ma'am." I have no problem complying. I'm so hard for her, I don't care Gus is waiting to meet us at Manny's office in an hour. I don't care how we spent our morning. All I care about is getting inside this woman, right fucking now.

Our mouths clash, so hungry for each other. My tongue licks inside her mouth and I'm immediately immersed in her rich coffee-laced flavor. So fucking delicious. Hands are everywhere; hers are trying to get into the back of my jeans and the feel of her blunt nails on the skin of my ass almost has me blowing my load. Mine are pulling and jerking on her shirt, trying to get it off her but unwilling to break the voracious feeding of our mouths. I'm grinding my cock against the wet heat between her legs, growling in frustration at the layers of fabric between us.

"I need to feel you," Katie hums against my mouth.

I have to force myself to pull away and within seconds my clothes have been yanked off and I'm back on the bed, working on Katie's jeans. She has already flung her shirt aside and is sliding off her bra, exposing those full luscious breasts to my view.

"Hurry..." she urges me on.

In one move I have her flipped over, two pillows under her hips and with one cock tease through her soaking wet cunt, I surge balls' deep into heaven with a loud roar.

"Fuck, baby. I'll never get enough of you. Never." I mumble into her neck as I fold my body around hers and fuck her hard.

No words from Katie but deep moans each time my hips lift hers a little when I am seated deep. One of her hands is clenched around the back of my head, trying to grab on to my hair, the other is slipping between her own legs. Fucking hot. She's bucking underneath me with a finger furiously working her clit when I feel her finger push alongside me into her opening, stretching herself and putting incredible pressure on my cock.

"Christ, yes. Just like that. Fuck that's incredible. I'm gonna come..."

I'm Not gonna leave her behind and slide my hand over top hers, putting added pressure on her clit and her inserted finger.

"Caleb!" She screams out her release right before I hurl over.

"God, Caleb. So, so good," she mumbles with her face pressed down in the pillows. I roll my upper body off her while still connected. My heart is pumping so hard I can't trust myself to speak right now, so I soothe myself and her by stroking her shoulders and her back, bringing us both down from an intense ride.

When she rolls her head to face me with a smile I can't hold back any longer.

"I love you, Katie. Have for a long time. I get that it may be soon for you, but it's been years for me. I loved you with long hair, hard-edged and athletic just as I love you now; rounder, softer and with pixie hair. I loved you battered, bruised and in a coma. Loved you cranky and ready to give up. I even loved you when you were loving another. It never went away; it only got stronger."

An emotional roller coaster. This whole day has been an emotional roller coaster, and we're not even halfway through yet.

After a very moving and sad funeral this morning for Caleb's mother, we're supposed to head back to the hotel to pack up and meet with Gus at Detective Jordan's office, but we got slightly distracted.

I've been on pins and needles for days, 'cause even though I know intellectually that Caleb wants me here; he's told me so, I feel unsure of my place. At night he's been in bed with me, even wrapped around me, but he's made no attempts to touch me sexually. Mind you, neither have I. The whole atmosphere is loaded and heavy and I have to fight my instincts to run off the whole time. The next thing I know I say the most god-awful thing you could ever say having just buried someone who died in a fire. If my gun wasn't tucked away in the glove compartment of Caleb's Tahoe, I'd've shot myself. *Pot roast*? I'm floored when Caleb actually laughs.

Somehow we end up here, face to face, Caleb half on me half off me and still partially inside me. And saying possibly the most beautiful words ever spoken. I can feel the tears rolling down my face, again with the crying, and I don't know what to say... or to do, for that matter. I'm overwhelmed and terrified to give into this feeling of happiness at perhaps having found something lasting. So I hold on to all the emotions that are struggling for the surface, determined to work through them first. Instead, I lean in and pour as much of what I feel into the kiss I give him. Caleb pulls back, wipes my face with the back of his hand and smiles.

"Gonna get something to clean you up. Sit tight."

It isn't until he finally slides all the way out of me, that I feel his come running down. Crud. Up on my elbows, looking down at the wet spot between my legs I'm trying to get my head around the fact that on top of everything else, I've just had unprotected sex. No condom.

Caleb sits on the bed beside me and calmly starts wiping himself off me.

"We didn't use a condom."

I can hear the panic in my own voice.

"I know," Caleb says calmly.

"How can you be so calm? Did you know?" I admit, that last question does come out a bit accusatory and he notices, giving me a lift of his eyebrow.

"I just noticed now when I got up."

Again with the calm, when I can feel a mild hysteria nibbling at my sanity. Mind going in twenty different directions at once, not the least of which that I'm in no shape to take care of a baby. Hell, I'm still trying to figure out how to take care of myself. Two warm big hands grab my face and tilt it up so I have no choice but to look in his mesmerizing eyes.

"Don't panic. Deep breathing, sweets, you're starting to hyperventilate." A few deep slow breaths help slow down my racing heart—a little.

"I'm sorry I was too caught up in the moment to protect you. I swear that has never happened to me before. And Katie, I'm clean; I've been tested just last year."

"I'm at much at fault as you are, Caleb, but tested last year? Surely you've been active in the meantime?" Not that I had, but I've kinda been out of commission. When he shakes his head no, my mouth drops open.

"Seriously? It's been a year?" I immediately slap my hand over my mouth, "Sorry, it's really none of my business."

"Stop that," he growls, a dark look in his eyes. "It is very much your business, especially now, and yes, it's been longer than a year and I know you've been checked out top to bottom more than I'm sure you'd care to remember recently. I'd say we're pretty safe on the transmittable diseases. That leaves a big one, because I'm guessing you haven't been too preoccupied with birth control the last few months?" he teases with a slight tilt to his mouth.

"Pffff, not particularly. No."

"Then we'll deal with whatever happens if and when it happens."

"We could get the morning-after pill?" I suggest carefully, even though it feels completely wrong. I have to try and stay rational, but it's hard when Caleb's eyes are glaring at me.

"Is that what you want?" An edge has crept into his voice, one I haven't heard before and it gives me a chill.

"It's not just about what I want, Caleb. I happen to think you should have a say in this too," I try to explain.

"If by chance I got you pregnant, however rotten the timing might be, I don't think I could be happier."

"Wow. Okay no. I don't like the idea of messing with nature."

Before the last syllables were out of my mouth, Caleb's tongue was invading, leaving me absolutely breathless.

"Good, good answer," he mumbles against my mouth when he finally lets me up for air.

"Just be prepared for an occasional massive freak-out, okay?" I warn him, "I'm not really getting a chance to wrap my head around one thing before another blindsides me. And Caleb?" I want to give him something, "You know I have all this stuff in here," I take his hand and put it on my chest, "all these feelings, most of them for you that I'm just not used to."

"I know, and there's no rush, although the simple solution would be to stop trying to wrap your head around things, and start free falling." He presses his lips to my forehead before he gets up off the bed. Then he bends to bring his mouth to my ear and whispers;

"Life won't wait, *Yázhí*."

CHAPTER SIXTEEN

"Makes no sense to keep you here, Caleb. That is, unless you changed your mind about your father?"

I shake my head. Not a chance in hell am I changing my mind about that one. When my father decided to save himself and leave my mother to the smoke and the flames, he became lost to me. I'll never understand how it was even possible for him to walk out that house, leaving his wife of almost forty-five years to die. I'm not sticking around to sit by his hospital bed, holding his hand. Not gonna happen.

We're almost an hour late getting here and although Manny seems in a forgiving mood since I'd just buried my mother. Gus is obviously irritated with the delay and lets us know it. The blush on Katie's face doesn't help when he takes a long and pointed look at the clock on the wall above the door in Manny's office. I'm sure he can guess the reason we're late.

"I guess I don't get where you're coming from," I tell him, trying to keep my own irritation at bay. "It's possible my brother will still come out of the woodwork. I'll just start beating the bushes again. Perhaps..."

"This is what I mean! You're not thinking straight, Caleb. This is not like you. Where is your focus?" Gus suddenly blows up, startling everyone.

"What the fuck? Gus, you and I need a word," I say walking to the door and holding it open. I'm not about to get into a pissing match in front of everyone.

"Be right back, guys. Excuse us for a minute," I tell Manny and Katie who are watching Gus stalk out the door in front of me.

He keeps walking until we hit the far side of the parking lot and stands there, head down and hands in his pockets.

"You have an issue with me, you come to me. You don't blurt it out in the middle of a meeting with the local PD."

Gus blows out a big breath and runs both his hands through his hair.

"I'm sorry. My bad. This case—the threat, worrying about Emma and the girls last night. I can feel control slipping away and frankly; I'm scared. Fuck, Caleb. Your mother is dead. That may not have been the intent but whoever set that fire had to know that possibility was there with people in the house. It's frustration that we can't find a hard lead. Nothing to get our teeth into. And before you get up in arms," he cautions, hand up, as if he knows I'm a second away from jumping in, "I'm not questioning your efforts or your abilities. I'm saying that with the obvious attack on your family, your brother's involvement in dangerous illegal activity. I'm not so sure anymore that people would want to talk to you. The mere fact that you are related will have them going another block just to avoid you. Can't you see?"

I see the sincerity in his face, and fuck; he's got a point.

"Yeah. Put that way, you make sense, but Christ, Gus. Do you have to fucking act like an absolute dick?"

The smirk on his face shows he's well aware.

"Point taken, but there's one more thing I want you to consider: Katie's safety."

"Nothing will happen to her," I bite off, bristling at the suggestion that would be something I wouldn't be constantly

154

aware of. Now with the added awareness she could be pregnant. Hell, *we* could be pregnant, I was even more driven to protect her.

"No it won't," he agrees, "because I want you to stick close to her. Fuck Caleb, go home, check on the progress of your house and for God's sake, keep her close at all times. I'm so not having a good feeling about this one. These guys have resources we can't even begin to imagine and having you up front in this investigation would be a constant burr up their ass. You are the closest connection they have to your brother and if burning down your parents' place, killing your mother, doesn't bring him to the surface, they'll be stepping it up a notch to get what they want. I know you don't want to think it, but you're vulnerable, more so because you have a woman who is vulnerable."

When he sees my raised eyebrow, he chuckles. "Both you and I know she's not half as vulnerable as she looks, even in that damn wheelchair, but they don't."

Once again I have to agree with him.

"They could kill two birds with one stone by targeting her. She's had eyes on the oldest, Ernesto, and can place him at Larchwood at or around the time that nurse was killed. You think the Feds aren't digging into that investigation to try and get him on murder? Katie's been too visible, from both sides." Rubbing his hands over his face and through his hair again, it's starting to look like he just rolled out of bed.

It feels fucking uncomfortable discussing Katie with Gus. She's my concern, my responsibility, but I've gotta admit I'm so in awe of that woman, I've had my head up my ass and underestimated how vulnerable she is.

"Could've done without a dressing down from my woman's ex-lover, but I hear you."

"Can't erase the past, my friend. Trust me, had I known then how you felt, I'd have pulled out right away," he says both hands up defensively.

"Fucking bad choice of words, man," I growl in response and the bastard starts laughing. It's all I could do not to put my fist through his face. I'm having a fucking hard day here, but he only laughs harder when I glare at him.

"I guess; 'I'm sorry, slip of the tongue' wouldn't be an appropriate apology then either, would it?"

Can't hold back the involuntary chuckle at his attempts to loosen me up. With a slap on my shoulder and a push in the direction of the door, Gus leads us back inside.

"Left them waiting long enough. Surprised they didn't send out a search party yet."

With Gus staying behind in Farmington for a few days, Caleb is coming home with me.

Funny, how fast saying 'home' when referring to Cedar Tree or even the small guesthouse has taken over my vocabulary. Not a word I ever remember using without a lot of hurt and anxiety attached to it. Not now though; now it just is a place I want to be; a place I'm starting to belong. Somewhere I am wanted.

On the verge of tears, again, I force my mind in a different direction.

"So what happened with you and Gus? For a minute I thought you guys were going to come to blows."

Caleb shakes his head and chuckles, "He was being a dick and he knows it, but he was also trying to make a point, and he made it. A few reasons he needs me away from the investigation, which makes sense. At least they do now, after he forcefully removed my head from my ass."

"You're the most even-keeled and responsible person I know, what the hell do you mean you had your head up your ass?" I want to know, ready to turn back and tear a strip off Gus again. Almost did that when these guys came back into Manny's office, but Gus was quick to apologize for his words.

"Thanks for jumping to my defence, little one, but the boss pegged it. Things were too close for me to see the forest for the trees; one of the reasons I've always been good at what I do is because I've been able to detach myself emotionally. Can't do that here, when everyone I've ever cared for is affected. I needed to step back and he made me see it. Wasn't pleasant, but it did the trick."

Picking up my hand from my lap, he twines his fingers with mine and rests our joint hands on the centre console.

"Still," I sputter; not as ready to forgive, but a squeeze of his hand and a quick stern look my way tells me in no uncertain terms that this subject is closed. Fine. I'll just wait to have my own showdown with Gus.

"Tell me about the house. What has Clint been up to?"

And just like that I am distracted when I enthusiastically tell him of all the progress that has been made since he's been gone. In fact, he hasn't even seen it since Clint started. He'll be blown away when he sees most of the downstairs done. At least it was when I left last Friday? Christ, I've been gone almost a week already.

"All of the downstairs had floors poured and was framed in already and they were starting drywall on the weekend. Clint had some guys come down from Durango for the job and rather than sending them back and forth, he's wanting this part done at once. He'll get them back when the time comes to finish the upstairs. Kitchen was next on the list, although I think he said something about putting the heating in before the flooring? I didn't quite get all he was talking about but he said they were on top of things. Of course I haven't been to see it, it's not really my place."

It's true, I've been itching to go have a look, but it just doesn't seem right to go and drool over a place that isn't mine. I was hoping to see that dog again too, though.

"What the hell, Katie? Of course it's your place, as much yours as it is mine. We'll go right away as soon as we get our stuff tucked away. I want to see the progress myself and find out how much longer before we can move in downstairs."

Warmed at his reassurance, I'm also fighting down the panicked thoughts that this is moving fast. Way fast. Another quick squeeze on my hand has me look up to find Caleb's eyes fixed on me.

"Thoughts, baby. What is going through your mind?"

"Just scrambling to keep up, that's all," I admit.

He lifts our joined hands to his mouth and kisses the back of mine.

"Don't overthink it, just feel."

Right. I do more than my share of 'feeling' these days, and old habits die-hard, so I still find myself trying to control every emotion, but it's almost impossible.

158

It's late when we finally hit Cedar Tree. Dark already when I open my eyes from a much needed nap after the eventful day and find myself lifted in Caleb's arms and straight into the front door of the guesthouse.

"I need to practice my muscles, you know," I tell him, secretly loving the way he totes me around like I weigh nothing, especially knowing I weigh more than my share these days. I forcefully silence the other part of me that has always been determined to be independent. The old Katie would've bristled at the thought of being hauled around like a piece of luggage. The new Katie is trying to see it as the loving and protective gesture it's meant to be.

"I like having you in my arms," Caleb's voice rumbles from where my hand is pressed to his chest as he walks me over to the couch. With a gentle kiss on my lips, he's back out the door to grab our bags and my chair from the Tahoe.

"Guess it's too late to head over to the barn now, but you okay going first thing in the morning? We'll have a quick breakfast, check in with Emma and Neil and head out."

"Sounds good, babe," I say, the endearment slipping from my still sleep muddled mouth. It doesn't escape Caleb, though. He's beside me on the couch, hauling me in his lap right away.

"Did you just call me 'Babe'?"

A smug smile on his face, this obviously pleases him.

"I'm sleepy, can't be held responsible for the stuff that comes out of my mouth," I try to evade, not that I have any illusion he will let me. The low growl deep in his chest only confirms that.

"I like it."

"Yeah?" I tease him shifting slightly on his lap when I feel the evidence of his appreciation lengthening under me. "Quite a bit, it seems."

"Playing with fire, little one," he growls in my ear, making my nipples pucker up and pay attention. His hand slides under my shirt and skims over the skin on my lower back before dipping down in my waistband to palm my ass, and just like that I'm lit up like a flame. I kiss him hungrily while grinding myself down on his lap, the hand on my ass not doing anything to stop my wriggling. His fingers slide down my crack and I involuntarily stiffen. Something that doesn't go unnoticed.

"Easy," he mumbles, his lips still attached to mine, "going nowhere you don't want me to go, but I suggest we take this to the bedroom. I want to be able to take my time with you."

"My chair... I'd like my chair," I tell him, before he starts carrying me around again.

"Later," he mumbles, licking my jaw before settling his open mouth on my neck. My entire body is tingling, but I'm desperate to regain some control.

"Please..." I'm just about to give in to him when there is a sharp knock on the door.

"Fuck!" Caleb is just able to pull his hand out of my pants and his mouth off my neck when the door opens and Neil comes walking in.

Taking in my ass on Caleb's lap and I'm sure my flushed face, his mouth twists into a cocky smirk. Brat.

"Am I interrupting something? I can come back later."

"Wipe the stupid grin off your face, kid. Damage is already done. What's up?" Caleb asks as he slides me off his lap and on the couch.

"Right. Emma sent me over to see if you wanted something to eat, she says she has kept some dinner warm if you're hungry and to come right over." He's about to head back out the door when he turns around. "No pressure, but knowing Emma, she'll be packing it up and bringing it over here herself. Either way, you'll have the company." Chuckling he pulls the door closed behind him.

"I'm thinking we probably should show our faces," I suggest to Caleb, who doesn't look pleased at all. "She's been stuck here all week without Gus and with only an occasional phone call and besides, she was really upset when Gus sent her home instead of bringing her to see you. Both her and Arlene actually. They seem to have a soft spot for you."

"Half an hour tops," is his response, "I want back here, with you under me in half an hour tops."

CHAPTER SEVENTEEN

"Want some more coffee?" Emma asks puttering around in the kitchen after feeding us some fucking amazing shepherd's pie.

"No thanks, we should head out."

We've been here almost two hours now and when I look over at Katie, she is nodding off in her chair. Time to get her home and in bed. I filled Neil and Emma in on most of what I know so far; which isn't saying much. The fire has been confirmed as arson and was started in the mudroom off the kitchen and it looks like they approached the house on foot through the fields in the back. The only evidence found where some size twelve-foot prints at the edge of the property leading to the house. Generic brand of runners so not particularly helpful at this time, until they get something to compare it to. Frustrating as all hell, since I know damn well who was behind it.

Neil has little to report, other than that things have been quiet in Cedar Tree. Time to take Katie home. She isn't happy when I push her chair along the path to the guesthouse, but only grumbles half-heartedly. She looks exhausted and so I leave her to do her thing in the bathroom and bedroom while I tidy up and lock up. By the time I get to the bedroom she is already asleep in bed. Not gonna wake her up just because I am still walking around with a hard-on. Instead I opt for a shower before I slide in beside her. The warm water and my hand can take the edge off tonight.

A slight shift in the mattress wakes me up the next morning and I can just see Katie slipping into the bathroom. Lying there contemplating how I can get her back in bed, I hear the shower turn on, which immediately creates a new possibility. I'm out of bed in a flash and with a quick grab from the bedside table, I slip into the bathroom, just in time to stop her from sliding the shower door closed on me. Startled she tries to cover her body and looks up from the specially installed seat that folds out from the wall.

"What are you doing?"

It takes me less than a second to step out of my boxer briefs and slide into the extra large shower stall.

"I woke up alone. That messed with my plans this morning, so I am adjusting to the new situation."

From her position, Katie is eye level with my cock and damn if that is not a huge turn on. Already hard with morning wood, her close perusal of my crotch only makes me harder.

"Mmm, last time I found myself in this position you didn't know how fast to get away from me," she says with a teasing smile on her face, "I just don't know if I can take the risk."

"Maybe I can convince you?" I sink to my knees in front of her, letting the hot water run down my back. Holding on to the back of her knees I pull her forward to the edge of the seat, I spread her legs and move in between while pulling them up on my shoulders and pushing the front of the seat up, so her pussy is lined up with my mouth—just where I want it. With one hand holding on to the grab bar on the side and the other the seat under her butt, Katie's head falls back against the wall while she bites her bottom lip. When I blow on her distended clit, just visible as I spread her open with my thumbs, I can see the goose bumps rise on her skin and a sharp hiss escapes her. So fucking beautiful and responsive. Her heavy-lidded eyes never leave mine as I put my mouth over her and slide my tongue into her entrance.

"Ahh," she breathes out with a slight shiver running down her limbs.

"I could live off you, you know that?" I mumble, lapping at her arousal that is now thickly coating her swollen lips. With one hand I reach and twist one of the showerheads so it is pulsing a steady stream just above the hood over her clit and her mouth falls open as her body is starting to ready for relief. By raising and lowering the seat I control the angle of the pulsating water and tease her mercilessly, keeping her teetering on the cusp of an orgasm.

"I need to come, please, Caleb,"

Both her hands are clawing at my hair in desperation, so I plunge and twist two fingers inside her while sucking hard on the little nerve cluster. With a high-pitched scream, she finally finds her release and I can't take my eyes off her. Her mouth wide open, panting and with a high flush on her cheeks she is the most beautiful thing I've seen. Lowering her legs and the seat, I put my cheek on her thigh, looking my fill while lightly stroking my fingers over her softly curved stomach. So soft. Her fingers drift through my hair as she comes down from her high and smiles.

"I can't reach you when you're down there."

No need to tell me twice. I've imagined her mouth around my cock for years. I'm on my feet in an instant, making her chuckle.

"Eager much?"

"Baby, have mercy," I smile down at her, her short hair slicked down like a helmet on her head, her eyelashes clumped together under the downpour of the water. Eyes bright and challenging as she leans forward and holds my eyes as that little pink tongue peeks out and licks the bead of pre-cum off the crown of my dick. When her hand folds around me with a firm grip and she slides me into the warm heat of her mouth, a low groan escapes me.

"Won't take much, little one. Your mouth feels amazing on me," I grunt out. Unable to hold back my hips start surging forward, fucking her mouth, and when she swallows on the tip of my cock all control slips away. I struggle not to pound out my release and her hand wrapped around the base of my shaft is the only thing protecting her from my cock being buried balls deep down her throat. Her other hand anchors on my hip, both encouraging my movements and holding me back from going to deep.

"Fuuuck, Katie!" I bellow as I try pulling out. I feel my balls drawing up tight and my orgasm surging through me, but she sucks me deep without spilling one drop.

"Morning!" Beth greets us as we enter the diner. "Early lunch or late breakfast?"

Katie snorts when I say, "Had a late start."

We had moved our activities from the shower to the bed after Katie gave me that earth shattering blow job, and I was surprised to find myself ready to go almost immediately again. Maybe it's the years of drought, or maybe it's just Katie, but I'm insatiable around her.

"How's the house coming along?" Beth inquires. "That Neanderthal of a contractor, Clint, comes in regularly, but he rarely does more than grunt at me. What an ass. Good thing he does good work, at least he did on the diner."

Beth hands us menus as soon as we take our seats.

"We haven't actually been to see it. Plan is to go after breakfast."

"I had no idea you felt so strongly about Clint, Beth?" Katie teases, "Not that I haven't had my run-in with him, but after our initial clash, I've actually found him to be not too bad."

"For all his looks, he has the personality of a primate," Beth returns through tight lips. "Anywho, coffee?"

After she pours us a cup and we put in our orders, she goes to check on her other tables.

"Interesting," Katie observes, looking after her, and I agree. Methinks the lady doth protests too much.

When she comes back with our breakfast, I ask how things have been at the diner.

"Actually, pretty busy. We're getting a lot of 'new' regulars from the Cortez area coming in since the re-opening. This past week we've had another few new faces, although only one less friendly. On Tuesday he was downright rude. He just wanted a coffee and must've sat at that window table for about two hours straight. Every time Julie or I would check to see if he wanted something else, he'd just glare until we walked away. The next time was over the dinner rush on Thursday and at that time at least he ordered a burger, although he hardly ate a thing. Sat at the same damn table though."

Katie throws me a look, obviously having similar thoughts.

"Other than that he was rude, did anything stand out about him?" I ask Beth calmly. She puts her hand on her hip and tilts her head when she looks at me.

"Something going on? I can't help noticing the gathering of the GFI team. First Katie here moves down, then you take off and

Neil comes down, following Katie around like a puppy. Now you're back, but I haven't seen Gus in a while and Arlene mentioned something in passing about a fire at your parents?"

Should've known nothing much would go unnoticed or stay quiet here for long. So I give her as much as I'm comfortable with. "Yes, we're working a case that may draw some unwanted interest to Cedar Tree, which is why I'm kinda interested in any new faces."

"Oh, wow. Well, I can tell you the first time he was well dressed, shoes polished, creased slacks and an earring in his right ear. Brown eyes and clean-shaven, I'd say about thirty-five years to forty years old and likely Hispanic from his coloring and his initial order for coffee. Not married that I can recall, at least he wasn't wearing a ring and it didn't look like he'd worn one for any length of time. The second time he was more casually dressed, jeans, work boots and had I not seem him dressed up before, I would've pegged him for a working man because he appeared to have some kind of injury on his hand. It was bandaged up. Curiously, this time I couldn't detect an accent but I'm sure it was the same guy. You think that is significant?"

My mouth is literally hanging open. This woman is amazing. She had pretty complete descriptions for both times the man was in. I see Katie with the same stunned look on her face I must be wearing.

"Wow, that is quite the party trick, Beth," Katie manages, "why the hell aren't you working for GFI yet?"

Beth lets out a bark of laughter, "You kidding me? Arlene can barely handle me, what makes you think Gus can?"

"Got a point there," I agree, surprised and impressed by Beth's observation skills. "If I leave you my phone number, you think you can shoot me a text or give me a call if you see anyone else who seems out of place?"

Big grin on her face, she answers, "Abso-fucking-lutely! This is so cool. Wait 'til I tell my son."

"Yeah, perhaps keep the whole investigation bit to yourself for now, okay? I don't want to alert everyone."

The barn is not the quiet place it was before; trucks and piles of building materials are littering the front drive and it's clear activity is at a high level when we drive up. Both barn doors in the front are open and a crew is busy installing massive curved windows in the openings. It looks fantastic. When we get out of the truck Clint, who must've seen us coming up the drive, comes out to greet us.

"You came at a perfect time. Big glass doors in the back went in this morning and we're just doing these ones now. Floors were finished yesterday and we can finish cabinetry in the kitchen as soon as the window is placed. Top cabinets are in, and we were waiting for the flooring to go down for the bottom ones. Give us another day or two and the downstairs will be habitable."

"That's great, man," I tell Clint. I've been eager to be able to do some of the detailing and renovations myself, but with this case blowing up, plus Katie in Cedar Tree a little sooner than anticipated and no chance in hell I'd leave her alone anywhere, I'm glad Clint has gotten this far and made it liveable.

"Can we see?" Katie wants to know eagerly looking around.

"Yeah sure, just keep an eye on the crap on the floor. Don't want you to spring a leak," he says with a wink for Katie.

Entering through what is now the front door, beside the big new window that the guys now have shimmed into place, I get my first glimpse of the dream I've been carrying in my mind for years. A huge open space with light streaming in from both sides, exposed beams now all cleaned and stained high above and a rustic large tiled new floor that is hiding a coiled heating system on the ground. I am pleased to see the large stone fireplace built centred on the long wall on the left with it's chimney exposed mostly on the inside going straight up, the height of the barn.

"I can't believe you got that in already," I tell Clint. "Wouldn't have thought that could be done so fast."

"We were lucky, I wanted the base laid so the floor could go in, but when the sub came here with his crew and saw he had no additional floors to break through but could go straight up to the roof on this side, he decided to finish right away. Works better for us, one less contractor under foot while we finish up the kitchen.

Katie is moving around the space taking everything in trying to avoid the odd stack of building materials left out. I walk up to her just as she opens one of the few doors this house will have and goes into the space beyond.

"What's this?" She eyes the medium sized empty space with one large window and a connecting door to an ensuite bathroom.

"A spare bedroom or eventually a den, once the upstairs is done and the elevator is in."

"Is that what the space in the wall at the base of the stairs is for?"

"Yup," Clint says from behind me having followed us into the room. "Come see the kitchen."

The space is bright with light coming in from the new sliding doors on the back of the barn and a corner of windows in the kitchen itself. The top cabinets are hanging, giving a rough idea of what the layout will be once finished. All the doors have been stained to match the dark beams in the ceiling but are still missing hardware. Something I wanted to save until last to order, hoping Katie might want to weigh in on that. I look at her and a deep satisfaction fills me. She seems excited and is beaming from ear to ear when she turns to me.

"This is fantastic! I mean, I've looked at the plans and all, and I have a pretty decent imagination but to see it all come together like this. It's so much better than I thought."

We chat with Clint about a few more things before getting out of their way. At the door, Clint stops us. "Do you know who a big ratty dog belongs to? Damn thing keeps showing up early in the morning when I drive up, but every time I try to approach him he takes off."

Katie's face lights up her face at the mention of the ugly mutt.

"I'm thinking he's waiting for Katie. She's suckered him in," I tell Clint with a smile.

CHAPTER EIGHTEEN

The next few days were spent picking up bits and pieces of hardware for the kitchen and downstairs bathroom in Cortez, usually coupled with my visits to see Kendra for my therapy, and one trip into Durango to look for some furniture. Most of the shopping was done online though, and I was secretly tickled that Caleb asked me to take the lead on this. Initially I resisted, telling him it wasn't my place to furnish his house, but there was no way Caleb could be swayed from this. What finally persuaded me was the argument that he had no idea when it came to furnishing or decorating since he had mostly rented furnished before. As much as I dislike shopping for clothes and such, given the blank canvass of such a great space to fill was too much fun to resist.

This morning I'm scheduled for another session with Kendra in Cortez. Things are really starting to progress, I can tell. Each time she's done with me, I can feel more strength in my legs and she seems sure it won't be long before my brain kicks in and remembers the necessary impulses to put one foot in front of the other automatically. I'm driving myself, which I still get excited about. It's such a feeling of independence to be able to get yourself from A to B without needing help and for a change, Caleb is my passenger, although grudgingly so. With him home I'd hardly had a chance to use my car so this morning I put my foot down. He still wouldn't let me go alone.

"I've gotta be in Cortez anyway, I can drop you off at the clinic, go meet up with Joe and be back to pick you up," he tries to convince me but I'm not that easy.

"Or *I* can drive, drop *you* off at the sheriff's office, and pick you up when you're done. Likelihood is I'll be done before you are, and I'd rather not sit around the clinic waiting for you. Gus is going to be there as well, right? So if you're done earlier, you can always hitch a ride with him."

"I don't want you on the road alone, Katie."

"Oh please - I'll be driving in broad daylight in a busy town and I'm carrying. Seriously?"

That draws an unhappy growl from Caleb, who seems torn between not wanting to insult my abilities and his need to protect me. Kinda sweet.

"Fine, but if you do leave early, make sure to call or text me before you head back home, and I'll let you know if I'm gonna be longer."

I try really hard not to gloat when I get behind the wheel, showing him how I'm able to manage by myself, when he tries to do the usual; picking me up and dropping me where he wants me. Still grumbling he folds himself in the much smaller cab of the Rav.

"Should've gotten you a decent sized truck." That made me laugh out loud.

"That would kinda defeat the purpose, don't you think? I'd never be able to hoist myself up into anything higher than this. Besides, I love this little SUV, and you're not touching it."

A smile twitches at the corner of his mouth when he leans over, grabs me by the back of my head and pulls me to his mouth for a panty-melting kiss.

"Love you. Love the feisty you," he mumbles against my lips, but when I open my mouth to say something in response he swallows my words with another kiss. When he finally pulls back he taps a finger to my nose and jokes, "You're making me late, woman. Let's go."

When I drop Caleb off at the sheriff's office, he comes around the car and motions for me to roll the window down.

"Careful?"

"I promise," I tell him, seeing it is a bit of a struggle for him to let me go on this two-block drive by myself. With a hard kiss on my lips and a knock on the frame, he turns and disappears through the doors, leaving me truly on my own, and mobile. A grin spreads over my face when I think of all the possibilities, but although I'm sure driving to Vegas by myself at the spur of the moment is not the greatest of ideas, I can't say it didn't enter my mind. Instead I turn toward the clinic.

"I want to try you without a harness today," are Kendra's first words when I come in and they stop me in my tracks. A feeling of panic hits me at the thought of not being secured in that contraption should I not be able to hold myself up, and I guess it shows on my face, because Kendra chuckles, "You'll do fine."

Yeah well, I'm not so sure about that.

"Right now your biggest issue with moving forward is your brain."

I roll my eyes, because she really isn't telling me anything new. "Ya think?" slips out before I can get my lips pressed together hard enough, but it only makes her laugh harder.

"What I mean is that aside from the obvious, at this point your mind is boycotting your progress because it no longer has faith in your body's abilities—*you* no longer have faith in your body's abilities. We're gonna change that today."

Setting me up at one end of the parallel bars where usually she would hook me up, she now simply says, "roll as close in between the bars as you can get and lock your wheels. Then stand up and place your hands on the bars, and keep reminding yourself that no matter what happens, your upper body strength is enough to hold you up. Because it is, Katie," She smiles at me.

I do as she says and feel a brief moment of panic when I feel her moving the chair away from behind me, but then her arm slides around my waist loosely and she says, "ok, now we walk." And one foot at a time, with a little nudge from Kendra behind me, I manage to shuffle my first independent steps. It feels fucking phenomenal.

"I'm sorry, little one, things are running a bit long here - do you want to come and sit in?" Caleb calls just as I'm getting ready to head over and pick him up.

I'm exhausted and elated from the best ever physio session I've had and the last thing I want right now is sit in on a case meeting with the guys.

"I think I'll pass, I'm really tired. Can you get a ride with Gus and I'll meet you at home?"

The brief silence on the other side lets me know it wouldn't have been Caleb's preference, but he comes back with, "Sure, go on and be careful please."

"I will. See you at home."

Making my way out of Cortez, I am trying to keep close track of my surroundings, but my mind drifts to this morning's session. I catch myself daydreaming about things I'd been afraid to think about. A future that would have Caleb and I living at the barn when it's finished. My chair doesn't feature in my fantasies. I'm able to walk without issue and that silly dog seems to be around everywhere. Another thing I seem to be stuck on is the way my hand keeps lingering on my stomach and the realization I am envisioning myself pregnant snaps me out of my daydream. That, and the jolt of an impact that has my head snapping back and my hands almost coming off the steering wheel.

What the fuck?

A quick look in the rear-view mirror reveals a large silver pick up – a Dodge Ram or something – gaining on me for another hit and my hand goes to hit the hand's free unit Caleb's made sure the SUV was outfitted with. Scanning the road ahead for room to evade, I can hear the phone ring and pray Caleb hasn't turned it on silent. Just as I hear his "Hey sweets," another impact almost has me knocked sideways. This time they tried to fishtail my little Rav, and each time my hands slide off the controls and I lose speed. Fuck.

"Caleb–"

"What the fuck is going on!"

"Silver Dodge Ram trying to get me off the road. Just turned onto County Road G and they popped up behind me. Gonna find a turn."

"No!" Caleb bellows, "don't turn off the main road, whatever you do. Gus has Neil on the other line, hang in. Keep heading to town, and drive full width of the road, alternate your speed to keep them off track. Do it!"

I see the Dodge coming in for another hit and brace myself for the next impact, but it doesn't come. Instead the truck starts inching up beside me and I kick up on the gas trying frantically to stay ahead.

"Coming alongside me now," I report, short of breath with all the adrenaline coursing through my blood.

"Don't you let them, dammit! Whatever you do, stay ahead. Veer into them if you have to."

I vaguely register Caleb's heavy breathing, as if he is on the move, when the rear window implodes, showering me in glass. Fuck, game change.

"Shooting, Caleb. They've shot out my rear window. I can't fucking shoot back and drive at the same damn time!" I yell frustrated beyond reason.

"Jesus, Katie. Move that car all over the goddamn road. Neil is coming toward you and we're hauling ass in behind you, but girl, you better fucking keep yourself standing until we get there."

Another shot is fired; this one hits the dash on the passenger side. Holy hell I'm in deep shit.

"Tell me you're ok, little one. I hear the shot, I don't hear you, and I don't fucking like it! Talk to me."

"Sorry, dashboard beside me. Other than glass, no holes yet. Two in the cab of the truck, one driving the other shooting. Fucker is half out of the cab taking aim. Hang on—" I can see him take aim and swerve the Rav the width of the road, but apparently he counted on that manoeuvre because I can feel the burn of the bullet before I even hear the sound.

The moment I get the call from Katie I'm running, Gus and Joe close behind without asking. Gus points to his Yukon once we get to the parking lot and I realize I'm without wheels. He is on the phone with Neil, having picked up enough from my conversation, which I threw to speakerphone as soon as I figured she was in trouble. I am hitting myself over the head for not getting the fuck out of here when she was done her physio. Not that nothing would've happened, but at least one of us would've had our hands free.

"They're fucking shooting at her," I tell Gus when I hear the unmistakable sounds over the phone.

"Flooring it, buddy. Joe is clearing the road."

Joe is ahead in his official truck with lights and sirens going and is literally blasting through intersections and in no time has us out of Cortez and turning onto County Road G. Then I hear another shot, a muffled noise that could be Katie and the next thing I know the connection is dead.

"Fuck! Fuck, fuck, fuck! I've lost her."

Panic grabs at my chest and hampers my breathing and I let out my frustrations in a loud roar.

"Neil's got a visual," Gus says, touching the Bluetooth in his ear, "Rav's on the side of the road, no sign of the truck."

"Katie?"

"Hold on. We're coming up on them now."

"No truck... we didn't pass any truck. Where the fuck did they go?" I'm looking over my shoulder to see if we've missed anything but the road is clear.

"There's Neil's truck and the Toyota," Gus points ahead of us where I can see Neil stalking around Katie's ride and Joe stopping on the other side of her car. No sign of Katie. Fuck. I get a sinking feeling in my stomach. No sooner has Gus pulled up on the other side of the vehicles or I'm out the door and running. Neil is yelling something at me but I'm not registering a word he says, I need to see for myself. Yanking open the driver side door I let out the breath I've been holding on a hiss when I see Katie slumped in the seat with blood running down the side of her head, her eyes closed. Like the impact of a truck, images of a scene in the hallway of Emma's house almost a year ago slam my memory and all I can think is; *too late.* My knees buckle and I drop to the asphalt, a foreign sound ripping from my chest and rolling out my mouth unchecked. I'm busy emptying my stomach beside me, deaf and blind to my surroundings until I feel a hand clamp on my shoulder and hear Gus's voice in my ear.

CHAPTER NINETEEN

"Fuck. Hey buddy. Snap out of it. She's ok. Caleb, man, it's a scrape. She'll be ok."

Slowly registering his words I look up to see Gus nodding in Katie's direction, and when my eyes follow I see her sitting with a shirt pressed against her head, looking at me with concerned eyes. Next thing I notice is Neil, shirtless, in the passenger seat beside her with his hand on her shoulder and a feeling of a different kind starts rolling in my gut.

"Out." I bark at him, up and at Katie's side in a flash. When he looks at me confused, I hear Gus snickering behind me.

"Better move your ass, Neil. Let's give them some space."

Katie makes room when I get in the front seat with her and then proceed to pull her on my lap. Her arms snake around my neck, her hands rifling through my hair.

"You're crushing me, honey."

I can't speak; I just hold her and breathe her in. Not sure why I lost it out there. The only thing I am aware of is that I am holding my entire world in my arms, so I tell her, "Something were to happen to you – to the life we may have made together – *Yázhí,* I don't think I'd be able to survive. I've had to stand by helpless when cancer took my sister before my eyes. I was too late to protect my mother. But losing you would end me."

My emotions are raw. Seeing this strong and contained man come completely undone before me, hearing him exposed and vulnerable is ripping me open. All the reservations I've been hanging on to fly out the window. The harrowing experience I've just escaped and Caleb's reminders when he talks about his sister and mother, hammer home how fleeting life is. You'd think I would've learned that lesson already, but this man clinging to me like he needs me to breathe deserves all of me.

Placing my hands on either side of his face I force him to look at me, and the pure emotion I see there encourages me.

"I've fought it, but it's so much stronger than I am. I've wanted it but been so afraid of giving in to it—to give myself so completely. I've never had these deep feelings and they scare me to death, 'cause they're so intense; so all consuming. I've been afraid to get lost in them, lost in you. But I'm done. Done being afraid to give you what you deserve. Hell, what I deserve. I love you, Caleb, so fucking much it hurts sometimes."

If eyes are the mirrors of the soul then Caleb is showing me everything in his right now. No words, but the deep pools of hazel and dark gold speak volumes. The arms around me tighten and his head disappears in my neck where he mumbles quietly, "Means everything. You've just given me everything."

"Hate to break this up, guys, but we have a situation here?" Joe stands in the open passenger side door, trying not to look at us but eying the blown out back window and the holes in my dashboard. With that reminder, Caleb snaps into action and carefully pulls away Neil's shirt that is half-stuck to the gash in my head from the bullet that grazed it.

"Shit baby, I'm sorry. You'll probably need some medical attention for that. Where else are you hurt?" He gently probes my head and my upper back, which is a bit sore.

"Turn around. Here, let me move out so I can have a good look." Sliding out of the cab, Caleb turns me so I'm sitting with my back to him and I hear him swear behind me.

"What?"

"Jesus, I'm so fucking sorry. You have glass in your back, little one. Some of it on the surface but some looks to be a bit deeper. Not gonna touch that. Some bleeding."

"Ambulance is already on the way, Neil called first thing," Gus informs us. "Before they get here, Katie, what went down?"

"It was weird. At first they seemed dead set on getting me off the road, I assumed to get me out of the car, and I was actually surprised when they started shooting. Back window was first, that's when I noticed there were two guys in the truck. Dark tinted windows, silver Dodge Ram, I didn't get the license plate - I tried but couldn't keep my focus on it long enough and it looked like they had it dirtied up or something. Never got a look at the driver, although I can safely say both guys were short from the way they fit the cab of a big truck like that. Think Arlene would be taller, easy. Maybe 5'9"? Shooter was Hispanic looking, thirties or early forties, wearing a leather jacket from what I could see and more significantly, he had a bandage on his left hand." That little bit of information had all the guys look at me and at each other.

"You thinking the guy from the diner Beth mentioned?" Gus asks.

"It was my first thought," I tell him. "Anyway, the last shot grazed me and I momentarily lost control of the wheel and the controls, next thing I know I ended up on this side of the road almost in the ditch and the truck was gone. All I can figure is that turnoff we had just passed a few hundred yards back but Caleb had said to keep heading to Cedar Tree, so I ignored it. I don't think it leads anywhere."

"Actually," Joe suggests, "it's County Road 21 and leads to a back road into the Cortez airport. Not only that, but there is a Budget rental office on that side too."

Just then the sounds of the approaching ambulance can be heard and another patrol car is just coming into view.

"Now are you two going to be ok here while we go check out that route?" Gus wants to know, while Joe walks over to the sheriff's unit to fill them in.

"Go." Caleb says, his eyes never leaving me. Even when an EMT comes over to check me out, I can feel the heat of his eyes on my skin.

"Ma'am, we're gonna have to take you in to the hospital, I'm gonna get you on a backboard and then on the gurney."

Before I even have a chance to protest being strapped down to a backboard, Caleb has me out of the SUV and in his arms, moving toward the open ambulance not even entertaining a discussion. Once the EMT catches on that I come with an entourage he makes quick work of securing me on my side on the gurney and has Caleb sitting close to my head. Last time I was in an ambulance he was with me too, I guess, but I had no clue that time. Looking at him now I can see how much it costs him.

None other than Naomi waits at the emergency entrance of Southwest Memorial Hospital in Cortez. It shouldn't surprise me since she works as an ER physician there, but apparently I surprise her.

"What the hell? You crash that sweet little Rav already?" She mutters on as she rides me to the first treatment room on the right, Caleb close behind us.

When one of the nurses tries to tell him to wait outside, he says nothing but simply looks at her and doesn't move an inch from the spot he has taken up against the wall beside the door. My sentry.

First thing Naomi does is look a bit closer at the gouge on my scalp. "That's a bullet graze," she holds my chin and turns my head back to give me a stern look. "Why is someone shooting at you?"

"Not quite sure what to tell you," I chuckle a little, "the boys are out there trying to figure it out."

"Boys?"

"Yeah, Neil, Gus and Joe. I'm sure they'll pop in here eventually," I say, noticing the slight tightening of Naomi's mouth at the mention of Joe's name.

It takes a few stitches and a bit of glue to fix the graze on my head, but digging the glass out of my back takes a lot longer and is much more unpleasant. Some larger pieces left significant holes that need thorough cleaning and stitching and some smaller ones have embedded so deep, Naomi has to use a scalpel to dig them out. Just lovely. I feel like a slab of raw meat.

While she is working on me, the ER nurse is going over a checklist with me.

"Any chance you could be pregnant?"

I freeze and my eyes slowly find Caleb's before saying, "Yes, it's possible."

I can feel Naomi's hands still on my back and in that moment everything seems temporarily suspended, but then Caleb winks and for some reason that tickles my funny bone and I burst out laughing.

From behind me I hear Naomi's voice say, "Girl, you have *got* to be the weirdest chick," as her hands start moving on my back again.

I just laugh, until I discover I'm crying and Caleb is right there. Of course he is. A big hand holding the back of my head while my face is buried in his midsection, the other stroking my shoulder and arm. A click of the door indicates we've been left alone, I think.

"We'll move tomorrow," Caleb says as he puts a bowl of Chili on my lap.

No sooner had Gus walked into the ER with my chair, or Naomi had shown up with my discharge papers and wound care instructions that Caleb snatched from her hand. To my question where Joe and Neil were, Gus answered vaguely something about following through on a few leads, but he wasn't particularly forthcoming. I had a sense it was more about the surroundings than the company, so I let it go… for now.

Arriving at the guesthouse it was almost five in the afternoon and Emma is ready with a big pot of Chili to feed the troops. Gus must've called her from the road and filled her in, because she hauls me in for a bone crushing hug that makes the stitches on my back pull something fierce, but there is no way in hell I'll let her know. This woman who stands so awkwardly bent over my chair, just to give me her seemingly unending supply of care, never ceases to amaze me. She pushes back and wipes a few strands away from the bandage on my head, tears pooling in her eyes.

"Holy crap, Katie. I would've totally lost it, and you totally handled yourself. Look at you; all banged up and still as strong and beautiful as ever. You floor me, girl."

Wait, what? If only she knew what a simpering mess I've just been all over Caleb. I open my mouth to burst her bubble, when Gus slips his arm around her waist and pulls her away.

"These guys probably figured they'd pick on the weakest link when they tried to tackle Katie," he chuckles, "little did they know they chose one of the grittiest fighters. Come on, Peach. Let's let them get settled in next door."

Emma isn't letting us go without a pan of her Chili and some freshly baked cornbread.

"Okay, but why the rush?" I want to know. Hell, I'm eager to get to the barn, but I'd thought Caleb might want to stick closer to Cedar Tree for a while after today's events.

"The barn is off the beaten track on the other side of town, and it is still a construction site which will distract from the fact someone is already living there. Besides, I have Neil talking to Clint right now to move the installation of the alarm system ahead to first thing in the morning. Since most of it was hardwired in when they worked on the downstairs, it's only a matter of hooking everything up."

"Okay," I say again, because it sounds reasonable, "but I just want you to know if that dog shows up, I'm keeping him."

"The big rangy mutt? I'll get you a nice puppy when this case is settled."

"Nope. I want him," I'm half teasing, knowing Caleb has his doubts about the stray, but I had already promised myself that if the dog is really looking for me—if he wants me, he can have me. Gladly. I know only too well what it feels like not to belong. Caleb is changing that for me, and I'll change it for the dog. If he'll let me.

CHAPTER TWENTY

I just left Katie in bed asleep. She was exhausted and couldn't keep her eyes open, but as much as I'd like to crawl under the covers and take in her smell, hold her warm body to me, I need to get a handle on how the guys made out this afternoon. So I carefully close the door on the guesthouse and head over to the office door where I can see lights on.

Gus lifts his head when I walk in, but Neil's stays focused on the screen of the computer he is furiously working on.

"She out for the count?"

"Yeah. Exhausted, but she'll be pissed missing any updates, so I will fill her in on anything you tell me. Just so you know." I look Gus straight in the eye, needing him to realize that I will not be keeping any secrets from Katie come morning. He acknowledges with a curt nod.

"We don't have much, but we're getting there. Followed the turn off all the way to the airport, which is no more than a strip, a few hangars and a tower. A silver truck was coming out from behind a hanger just as we were driving on to the field, and Joe managed to cut him off. Some poor teenage kid was behind the wheel, told us he worked for Budget and was told by his boss to go pick up one of their trucks at the airport, so his buddy just dropped him off. Keys had been left on top of the sun visor. That's all he knew. The grill had some scrapes, but they were smart in picking that truck, 'cause it was minimal compared to the damage it did to Katie's SUV. Joe called in some back up to take in the truck for processing. Neil spotted a guy working on an old plane in a hangar, and he had seen two men of a similar general description get into a small Cessna, which had been sitting on the tarmac all morning with a pilot at the ready. He had noticed because that seemed odd. When he saw them leave he figured they were businessmen. Apparently, chartered planes tend to be delegated to this end of the airfield. Neil and I headed over to Budget and Joe went to talk to the tower to find out more."

"Let me guess. All matching descriptions but fake names and payments in cash." I observe.

"Pretty much," Gus admits, "but the mechanic did mention an odd logo on the tail of the Cessna that could be significant and he had memorized its registration numbers. It's what Neil is working on now. Trying to figure out who the plane belongs to."

"And the truck?"

"Was rented a week ago. Rental place got a call requesting a pick up at the airport and the need for a large truck. Same kid we found with the truck had gone to pick them up, drove them to the Budget office and they paid cash, although they did leave a credit card number. Neil ran that and it's a stolen identity. Guy's been dead three years now."

None of this should surprise me and still I'm frustrated. Fucking slippery assholes. I'd much prefer there was some legal way to pin something on them, but knowing we're probably dealing with a cross-border issue only complicates that.

"Got something!" Neil's head pops up from behind his current choice of computers. "Alto is a tiny charter company out of Monterrey, Mexico. The logo the guy described sounded like a griffon and although the tags on the plane were US, they didn't belong on that particular plane. The griffon is not a familiar logo for any local charter companies so I checked south of the border.

We'll have to do a visual confirmation with him, but this looks like it could be it." He looks up with a big grin on his face, "Especially since the owner of the company is listed as Ernesto Duarte."

"Shoot it through to Joe and the Feds right away," Gus says, "I have a feeling this may become a multi-departmental case soon, if it isn't already without our knowledge."

"Malachi," I change direction, "do we have anything? Did Manny come up with any leads?"

Gus shakes his head. "A vague description from a farmer working nearby on the day of the fire. One man running into the fields from the direction of your parent's house. No good physical other than that he wasn't too tall, was average build and not too old. Guy wasn't a great deal of help, but one thing he said keeps coming back to me; he was grabbing one arm with the other."

The guy with the bandage immediately springs to the front of my mind and my eyes snap to Gus who simply looks at me.

"I see you coming to the same conclusion. Guy who set fire to their house could well be the same guy who showed up here, shooting at our Katie."

Instantly my blood boils, I shoot up out of my chair and bite out, "My Katie."

The surprise is evident on Gus and Neil's faces, but I don't back down. Slowly realization dawns on Gus and he raises his hands. "Absolutely and without a doubt she is yours."

Neil's head swings back and forth between us in confusion until he finally rolls his eyes and focuses back on his computer screens.

The raw feelings of possessiveness and sudden jealousy surprise me and I can't help wonder if my friendship with Gus will withstand the changes.

"Go get some rest, Caleb," he says with a hint of sadness in his eyes, "tomorrow is moving day."

After a quick shower I slide in behind Katie, who hasn't moved a muscle since I put her to bed. Pulling her body carefully to mine she lets out a little sigh from between her pouted lips and one of her hands searches around blindly until it finds mine, and she pulls it up and rests it clenched in hers between her breasts. That's how I fall asleep, wrapped around her soft, warm body with my nose buried in her neck, breathing in her unique citrus scent.

Sometime in the early morning hours I wake up to find myself on my back with Katie draped over me and my hands holding on to her juicy ass. How or when that happened during the night I have no idea, but having her front plastered to my chest sure has peaked the interest of certain parts of my anatomy. The only offensive thing is the nightshirt she is wearing which I can't wait to get off her. I start sliding my hand over the soft globe of her butt to the curve of her spine and under her shirt. She moans softly as I trace my fingers lightly over the skin of her back, taking the hem of her shirt higher. I stop my track suddenly when I encounter the first of the bandages I now remember dot the upper half of her back, and Katie emits a soft grunt of protest.

"Don't stop," her sleepy voice cracks as she mumbles against my chest. "Please."

"You're hurt, *Yázhí*," I whisper in her hair, "we can wait."

With my dick throbbing from the close contact with the source of all my erotic fantasies for the past few years, on top of my morning wood, I gingerly slide myself from under her body. On my way to the bathroom I give her half exposed butt-cheek a nibble, leaving her grumbling in the sheets. After relieving myself and pulling on some track pants I head to the kitchen for some much needed coffee.

It may be early yet with the sun just starting to rise, but we have to pack. I'm determined to get us settled into the barn by sundown and yesterday was a total loss in terms of prep so we need an early start. I'm just sipping on my first cup when Katie rolls in, her short hair sticking every which way and a scowl on her face, pointedly ignoring me while she makes a beeline for the coffeepot.

"Come kiss me, little one," I coax only resulting in a loud snort.

Minx.

"Katie. Need a kiss, babe."

"Well crud. That's just too damn bad, Caleb. You got me all worked up in bed just to leave me hot and bothered, so I don't particularly feel in a giving mood right now."

I have to bite my cheek not to chuckle at her sour mood. I've observed Katie long enough to have seen just about every side of her, but this pouty mood is new, and fucking cute. The moment she puts the coffee pot down I grab the back of her chair and swing her around, caging her in with my hands on her armrests.

"Kiss," I demand, but when she rolls her eyes at me I pick her up under her arms and lift her on the counter, moving between her legs. One hand on her butt, sliding her toward me and the other on the back of her head so she can't turn away.

"Kiss," I repeat.

"Manhandling me is not gonna make me feel more amorous, Caleb. You had your chance."

Stubborn woman. If we weren't on a time constraint I'd continue playing with her, but with a full day ahead I need my fix, so I take it. I lick her tightly closed lips with the tip of my tongue, but it isn't until I lightly pinch her butt that she opens her mouth in protest and I can slip in. The moment I taste her, the world settles around me and it's the damnedest thing. I would do anything for this woman, anything to make her life complete, because she already has done so for me.

Small hands that were propped against my shoulders to ward me off, slowly relax and slide up and around my neck, winding their way into my hair and Katie's tongue begins a languid and erotic tangle with mine.

"Can't anybody find a bed here? Jesus. What's in the water here in Cedar Tree? Maybe I should move here to get some action, everyone else seems to."

I am instantly aware of my half-naked ass sitting on the kitchen counter as Neil barges into the guesthouse. Caleb just chuckles. He would, *ass*.

"Troops have arrived. Go get some clothes on, babe." He orders as he lifts me back in my chair. Bossy much?

Christ, I'm in a mood today. Don't know whether it is the after effects of yesterday's events or whether I'm really that ticked off at being worked up and then left cold. I just feel out of sorts. I really don't feel like hanging around with the guys in my shirt and barely there panties, so I go and get dressed. Not because Caleb said to, but because I want to.

Cleaned up and in my now familiar get up of comfy yoga pants and for today a man's flannel shirt, I head into the kitchen only to find Gus has joined.

"Morning, Gus," I smile at him, but other than a rather curt "Katie", I'm not getting much. What the fuck is up with that? Tension seems a bit thick, especially between him and Caleb. When I catch Neil's eyes, he just rolls his. Guess I'm not the only one noticing.

"Ok, tell me the plan," I ask, as I finally take a sip of coffee from the mug Caleb just hands me.

"Neil and Gus are going over now to meet up with Clint to finish installation of security. In the meantime you and I pack up our belongings here and head over to Emma who is apparently waiting with breakfast for us. These guys have already been fed."

"Cripes, you guys are early."

"No rest for the wicked," Neil quips," and besides, you guys are all like bunnies anyway, everywhere I turn. Doesn't matter what time of day or night; someone's going at it. I'm starting to feel seriously deprived. And what the heck is with the kitchen counter?" The baffled look on his face is hilarious and instantly has the rest of us laughing hard, immediately breaking the tension that lingered in the room.

"If you have to ask, you're not ready to go there yet, grasshopper," Gus chuckles, slapping him on the back, "let's get going and let these folks get ready before my Emma gets impatient. She feels the need to feed."

There isn't much to pack. Most of what I own is still in a storage unit in Grand Junction and although I've gotta figure out eventually what to do with that, for now I won't have to worry about it. Other than clothes, toiletries and my laptop, there really isn't anything else. It's much the same for Caleb, although he still has a furnished rental place somewhere. I never paid much attention to be honest.

Just half an hour after the boys left, we are sitting in the kitchen with Emma, having another coffee and eating a massive breakfast of pancakes, scrambled eggs, fresh muffins and orange juice. The woman is nuts. I swear she must've been up at four AM to be able to get this spread on the table. It's only nine-thirty now.

"Emma, this is delicious," I say around a mouthful of blueberry pancake, "but I have to admit, part of me is glad we won't be this close anymore 'cause I'd grow to massive proportions under your watch, I'm afraid."

A growl and a tap to the back of my head lets me know Caleb is not pleased with my observation.

"Really? You wouldn't be able to do your caveman thing and haul me off everywhere if I were twice the size now, would you?"

"Katie..." The low vibration in his tone should be warning that his patience with my irritable self is coming to an end, but I don't care and Emma only seems amused with our back and forth.

"I'll be big as a house before you know it, Caleb," I can hear a whine in my voice and shocked I snap my mouth shut before more slips out. My fork clatters to my plate when I suddenly realize the source of my unusual crankiness with utter clarity. My eyes slowly creeping up to where Caleb's black t-shirt ends and that delicious hollow right under his prominent Adam's apple where I like to nuzzle begins. With a finger crooked under my chin, he lifts my face so I'm now finding myself looking in his deep hazel ones. The gentle warmth I see there tells me he is

196

aware of my little revelation; maybe even experienced it at the same time I did. When those last words tumbled out of my mouth.

Without taking his eyes off me Caleb says to Emma, "Thanks for breakfast, Ems. Beautiful, as usual. I think we'll wait for the boys in the guest-house."

"Absolutely," I hear her say, before Caleb wheels me out of the kitchen, out the door and down the path.

"I don't get it," I mumble with my face pressed to that delicious spot on his neck I was ogling moments before. Caleb has me out of my chair and on his lap on the couch seconds after we walk in the door, apparently his preferred position for conversation, and if I have to admit, it's fast becoming mine too. "How is it possible to suppress something that momentous from my mind? Pregnant, Caleb? Me. It's just hitting me now. Actually no, that's not true. It hit me yesterday in the hospital when they asked if there was a possibility and I answered yes, but somehow I managed to push it away. What kind of person does that?"

"Someone who's been uprooted, almost run off the road and shot at perhaps? Someone who has always had a tight reign on her life and her surroundings, who suddenly finds herself at the mercy of circumstance and needs to compartmentalize a few things to get through yet another trauma? Honestly, little one. Give yourself a break."

Still disappointed in myself, but hearing what he says and feeling a little better I slip my arms around his waist and give a little squeeze.

"When do you think we'll know for sure?"

"Not really my area of expertise, but when is your period due? If it doesn't show, that should tell us something, right? Or we could get an over the counter test?" he says with an eyebrow raised.

"Anyone ever tell you, you can be a bit of a smartass, Mr. Whitetail? Not due my period until sometime next week, but they've been a bit wonky since my injury. Don't ask me why."

"Picking up a test then. And wonky? Is that a scientific term, Ms. Acker?" he counters with a smile on his face.

"Whatever. You're a pain in my ass," I grumble.

"I like your ass. Plan to tap that ass."

I turn to him with my mouth open in mock disbelief. "Oh Em Gee! For your information, I like your ass too, but if you don't watch it, you'll end up with my footprint all over it."

The world suddenly rights itself again when Caleb throws his head back and belts out his beautiful laugh.

CHAPTER TWENTY-ONE

Bliss.

Breathing in the fresh air, while sitting out here in the early morning sun that is slowly warming the day ahead is simply bliss. A quiet little void for me to collect my thoughts and reflect on the last few days that have whipped by since we moved into 'the barn', as everyone now calls Caleb's new home.

I know Clint's crew will be arriving in an hour or so, they've been putting finishing touches on the laundry room down here and the elevator shaft, and are ready to move it upstairs and start roughing in the plumbing and electrical. After that Caleb wants to take over and get his hands dirty.

So far we've been preoccupied with furniture arriving. The huge natural leather sectional sits proudly in the great room across from the fireplace. It's still rather pristine looking, but is supposed to weather and age with time, giving it an interesting rugged and natural patina. The kitchen island boasts four dark metal stools with seats and backs in the same leather as the couch and a rustic looking long knotted kitchen table and chairs sits in front of the sliding doors.

The last thing to arrive yesterday had Caleb almost as giddy as a kid at Christmas. We've spent our nights here on a couple of mattresses borrowed from Arlene, since Neil moved into the guesthouse right after we came here, but they were about five inches short for Caleb's long frame. With me sharing the bed, he hasn't had the luxury of lying across the bed diagonally so his feet ended up dangling off the end every night. Apparently that is not conducive to a good night's sleep. When the bed arrived yesterday afternoon, he literally dropped everything he was doing to put his baby together.

I sip my coffee with a smile on my face, recalling the enthusiastic and creative ways he found to 'christen' the new bed last night. I left him sleeping like a baby this morning. He has a few hours to catch up on.

A faint sound has me turn my head to the grove of trees to the side of the barn and my breath hitches. Standing right on the edge, still as a statue and looking right at me is that glorious pooch. Alright, he's a bit ratty, but all I can see is potential when I look at his eyes.

"Morning my friend," I say softly, not wanting to startle him, "finally you come for a visit."

His ears twitch when I start talking, as if trying to pick up the vibrations of my voice.

"Did we move in on your territory? Hope you don't mind. I'd like to be friends. Do you remember me?" I ramble on in the same soft voice, trying to let him get used to my sound, and slowly his tail starts moving from side to side. I carefully put my cup down on the ground beside me.

Just like before, I turn my hands palms up and put them on my knees, never stopping the cooing nonsense that falls from my mouth, and just like before, the dog starts inching his way closer, his tail wagging more enthusiastically with every step he takes.

I have no idea what I'm doing, it's not like I grew up with pets or know anything about them, but there is something about this dog that draws me. For all I know, he could be dangerous, but somehow I don't think I have anything to fear.

His head within reach of my hands, I resist reaching for him, and patiently wait for him to come to me.

"You're gonna need a name, boy, if you're gonna stick around. Or even if you just come to visit from time to time. I don't want to keep calling you 'Dog'."

His wet nose is sniffing over my hands and I gently curl my fingers under his chin to scratch. The steady wag of his tail and the weight of his large head now on my lap, tells me he desperately wants a friend too, and when he lifts his eyes to look at me I suddenly know what I'm gonna call him.

"I'm gonna call you Blue, baby. You like that?" I smile when ears perk up at the name. His eyes are an incredible shade of icy blue.

We sit together for a while, Blue and I, one of my hands scratching him, the other holding my coffee cup again. Blue has shifted and is sitting next to me, staring out into the distance, seemingly content just to hang out. I'm good with that too.

Suddenly I hear a low growl come from him as he jumps up, turns around and moves behind me.

"Whoa, boy," I hear Caleb's low voice from the doorway.

When I turn around, he is leaning against the doorpost, a coffee in hand calmly eyeing the dog, whose neck hair is standing on end.

"Morning, little one. Your friend is a little protective of you. You seem to bring that out in us guys. Now, I want nothing more than to taste you, but I'm thinking we should handle this situation with care."

I should've guessed Katie and that dog would find a way to connect again. It was only a matter of time, but what surprises me is the instant possessive and protective instinct the dog has over her. As long as he doesn't get in my way, I'm happy to add an extra guard to her.

"Babe, talk to him and then slowly move to me so he knows you belong with me, or rather, I belong with you," I chuckle.

"S'ok Blue, that's Caleb. He lives here. You'll see a lot of him, especially when I'm around since he can't seem to stay away for very long, but I don't mind, I'm kinda hooked on him too."

With an impish grin and an occasional peek my way, Katie slowly rolls her chair over to me, trying to calm the dog down at the same time. He stops growling and moves his head back and forth between Katie and me, trying to get a handle on the situation. Funny that he isn't moving off the deck though. He is staying right there.

I'm careful not to move too much when Katie reaches me and starts touching me, coaxing the dog to come closer. Reluctantly, he starts sniffing; first the air in my general direction, and then slowly moving closer until I have Katie on one side, holding my hand, and the dog on the other, sniffing.

"His name is Blue," Katie says softly, a smile on her face when she lifts it up to me.

"Blue," I repeat and notice the dog's eyes on me too.

Carefully I nudge his fur with my finger where I can reach it, and before you know it, he's sitting down beside us, just outside the sliding door on the deck, looking out in the distance. Katie's hand squeezes mine.

When I finally bend down to taste her, the dog looks but doesn't move or make a sound. Good, 'cause that would've been a problem.

With the sound of the first of the work trucks rolling onto the drive, Blue's head turns and with one last look in our direction, he lopes of into the trees.

"Who the fuck is Blue?" Gus walks into the kitchen with Joe in tow.

It's early afternoon and the morning has slipped by since Clint's crew showed up, turning our peaceful oasis into a cacophony of construction noise. Katie escaped out the front to sit at the picnic table put out there for the workmen, and is working on her laptop.

"Katie's dog," I explain, putting the finishing touches on the dough for the flatbreads I want to fry for tonight's dinner.

"Katie has a dog? Since when? Didn't know what she was jabbering on about out there."

"A stray who has taken a shine to her, and the feeling is mutual. Big sucker too. Must have some wolf in him somewhere. He doesn't want to stick around when there are others here though. Barely seems to tolerate me, but loves Katie," I shrug.

"Huh. Never figured her for a pet owner," Gus contemplates.

"By the way, hello Gus and Joe," I say pointedly, "what brings you here?"

Joe just chuckles.

"Caleb. Starting to look great. Never thought a barn could turn into something like this," he says looking around appreciatively.

"We've got a few developments we want to go over. Joe just got a call from Manny in Farmington this morning and thought we should stick our heads together."

"Sure. Let me finish this and put on some coffee, unless you guys want a beer?"

Both Gus and Joe opt for coffee so I make short work of wrapping up the dough and leaving it to rise and fixing us a pot.

Armed with coffee, I lead the guys outside to where Katie is still sitting by the picnic table but with her laptop now closed. Putting the two mugs I'm carrying down on the table in front of her, I bend down and kiss her head before taking a seat on the bench.

"So what did Manny have?" I ask Joe who takes a seat across from me.

"One of his men is dating a nurse from Shiprock, who works at the medical clinic there. Apparently she let it slip that her brother had texted her a week or so prior, asking her to stay after hours with an excuse. He needed her help. She was worried about him and after the on-call doctor left, she locked up and waited by the back door. He showed up with a Mexican guy, she said, whose hand was blistering. When she told him he needed to go to the hospital in Farmington, he pulled a gun on her, so she cleaned him up and bandaged him the best she could."

"Why didn't she come forward right away?" Katie questions.

"He threatened her and told her he'd first take care of every member of her family before he would put her out of her misery. Manny says you might know the brother though," Joe says, turning to me.

"Yeah? Who is it?"

"Benjamin Chee, apparently he's your brother's second hand man?"

A heavy feeling settles on my shoulders.

"Malachi's best friend since they were little. Those two would get into shit all the time, started calling me El Jefe when I would try to wrangle them. Dammit. Now I get why I couldn't get a straight answer from him. He not only is more involved with the Klesh than I knew, he also has a foot in with the cartel. Something smells."

"Something smells alright," Gus agrees, "Why would the Klesh' second in command be involved in any way in the torching of his leader's family home? A life-long friend to boot. Doesn't sit right."

"You think your brother might have been set up?" Katie grabs my hand as she voices the thought that had just formed a persistent seed in my mind. "I mean, think about it. It makes sense, doesn't it? He must've suspected something was off with his right hand man or else he would have taken him into confidence. He wouldn't have walked out on his gang like he did."

I squeeze her hand. What she is saying is more plausible than the idea that my brother, however fucked up, would care enough check up on and look after his parents just to ignore an attack on them. That never sat well with me.

"Okay," Joe offers, "let's follow that train of thought through. So, if Chee and his Mexican pal are in cahoots and intercepted a load of drugs from the cartel intended to be distributed by the Klesh on the street—a scam they managed to pin on Malachi. They've effectively gotten everyone; Klesh, cartel, and law enforcement barking up the wrong tree. No wonder they want to find Malachi themselves first. They need to take him out. Can't run the risk of him talking to anyone."

"He has proof," Gus slams his hand on the picnic table, "he has to have something that's got them running scared. We've gotta find him."

"Why me though?" Katie wants to know. "Why come after me? I'm nothing to your brother."

"You're everything to Caleb though," Gus responds for me with a nod in my direction, "and he would do anything, and everything, to keep you safe. Even give up his brother. That's what they're hoping for. Hell, counting on probably."

I head inside to get the pot of coffee for refills, needing a minute alone to process. It's like the tumblers of a lock slowly clicking into place; the way this whole tangled web of a case is starting to become clear. Not that it helps much. Malachi is still on the lam with a price on his head and the cartel is still a danger to anyone associated with me, it seems, until he's found. Unless...

CHAPTER TWENTY-TWO

Caleb leaves the table quite abruptly, but I get it. It's a shatload to absorb, and I'm not so sure how that last remark by Gus comes across, but it's gotta create some sort of internal conflict.

A sudden shiver runs down my spine, like someone just walked over my grave, and I look around the barnyard to the edge of the trees, but there is nothing to see. Weird. I've learned to trust my instincts and they rarely steer me wrong. I could've sworn I could feel eyes on me.

"You ok?" Joe asks, having picked up on my jumpy behavior as well. Gus is already wordlessly scanning the tree line.

"Yeah. Just a weird vibe, is all."

When Caleb walks out with the coffeepot, it doesn't take him long to cotton on and without looking at me, he puts a hand on my shoulder and squeezes. "Where?" is all he says.

"Not sure if it was anything."

"You guys are freaky 'in-tune'." Joe looks between the three of us, shaking his head.

"Years of working together," Gus grumbles, still facing the trees.

"It's a bit creepy."

A vaguely familiar rustling sound comes from the trees and all three men have their guns drawn and aimed before I can stop them.

"No! It's Blue," I yell, almost certain it's him I hear when I wheel my chair between the guys and the sounds, right in the line of fire, to their great displeasure. At least by the sounds of their swearing.

"Fuck Katie. Would you use your head?"

"Shut it, Gus. Don't stop trusting my instincts now."

With his neck hair up, but tail wagging hesitantly, Blue comes forward from the shrubs at the edge of the trees.

"What the fuck is that?"

"Katie's dog," Caleb chuckles at Gus, "that's the Blue she was telling you about."

"I need another coffee." Joe sits down and fills up. "Guess that's what you heard?"

"Possibly," I say, not quite so sure as I watch Blue's apprehensive approach, not taking my eyes off his. Amazing how much trust this animal puts in me to walk up to a yard filled with strange trucks, strange people and enough of Alpha testosterone to drive a rocket ship. Trust, or loyalty?

At least Blue has broken a bit of the tension. Having found his way to my side, he seems to keep himself between me and the trees at all times. I would've thought he'd be aggressive toward Gus and Joe, but he barely gives them a look and seems to have accepted Caleb completely. No, his focus is solely on me. Don't I feel special.

I scratch his ears, which he seems to like, since he'll occasionally groan loudly, making Caleb chuckle.

"You molesting that dog, little one? Should I be jealous?"

"Perv, that almost brought my coffee back up. Knock it off." I elbow him in the ribs for emphasis.

"Enjoying the display of domestic bliss – dog and all – but let's get this wrapped up so I can get back to the office?" Joe says with a hint of bite to his voice, raising the eyebrows of both Gus and Caleb.

Alrighty then. I just smile, thinking little horrible thoughts to myself, about a certain someone who might want to get his own shit in order so he can enjoy his own version of 'domestic bliss', or maybe not. After all, he did fuck over my new friend. Great, now all three are looking at me strangely. Must be the smile that took on a hint of evil I guess.

"I may know where to find him," Caleb says from beside me, causing all eyes at the table to snap his way. "Malachi. I think I know where he is, and it would make perfect sense now."

"Where?" Gus wants to know, but Caleb shakes his head.

"Sorry, boss, not gonna share, but I'll find him and bring him in."

"What the fuck, Caleb?" Gus pushes up off the table, ready to go a round. The tension that's been swirling around these two almost to a boiling point.

"Whoa, easy there, Gus. Give the man a chance to explain," Joe tries to settle the waters.

I stay out of it, sensing I might be the source of a lot of this new friction between them. Besides, the low growl coming from

Blue is enough to have me focus all my energy on keeping him calm in the face of all this negative energy.

Caleb takes a deep breath, obviously trying to settle himself before he responds. "It's obvious as you pointed out, that they're trying to use those closest to me to get to Malachi. I tell you where he is, it only makes you and yours more vulnerable."

His eyes are on Gus while he talks and I can see the anger slide out of Gus's glare with every word spoken.

"Right. See your point; don't like it, though. You go off on your own, no back up. What if we're wrong about Malachi? Things can go to hell in a hand basket. Then what?"

"If I can suggest something," Joe interjects, "there are some safety measures that can be put in place. It isn't that complicated and will allow us to find him if he doesn't check in with one of us within a certain time frame. Your Neil can work his magic with a tracker and a burner phone."

Gus nods, thinking over the possibilities while Caleb sits stoically his hand clasped over mine in my lap. I know we'll talk later and I can fire off all the questions I'm saving up for his ass 'cause I'm just a little bit fired up myself, but not about to throw down in front of the guys. He better give me that.

"So you'll never be further then two hours away from here?"

"That's as much as you're gonna get out of me, babe."

I grumble my displeasure at not getting a more specific answer and turn away, but a strong arms wraps around me and pulls me into a much bigger, harder body.

We're lying in bed after a frickin' amazing dinner of Navajo fry bread tacos Caleb put on. Gus and Joe had left after hammering out some details that gave Gus relative peace of mind over the plans to 'extract' Malachi. Neil was to plant a tracker on Caleb's body or clothes in a few places and provide him with a burner phone, so there would be no chance of a trace on his own cell. He'd come here tomorrow morning, park his truck right up by the front door so he could get in and out without anyone having a good visual from outside.

After Caleb was hooked up, he would leave in Neil's truck, leaving Neil here with me. It's not likely they'd be tracking Neil. At least that's the gamble. Caleb says it's not too far, but he has some hiking to do so it'll take him a good five hours total at best. That is gonna kill me. The wait will be brutal, but he promised to try and check in every couple of hours, and not to panic unless I hadn't hear from him for seven hours. *Seven fucking hours.* Brutal. Which is exactly why I'm trying to get him to be a bit more specific. Not budging though... *Ass.* So I pout, and his response is to throw me over his shoulder and dump me on the bed. Guess he hopes he can sex the sass out of me. Good luck.

"Stop pouting."

"Not pouting."

"You're sticking out that bottom lip so far, it's throwing shadows on the wall, babe."

"Fuck off, Caleb," I slap his arm, but have a hard time containing my chuckle.

Snuggling a little further back, I let the comfort of his arms lull me, until Caleb's low voice rumbles in my neck.

"Want to keep you safe, little one. You gotta let me try to keep you safe."

I'm instantly sobered by the serious tone I detect in his voice, and completely alert to what he says. He's not just talking about me. Turning around to face him, I find his troubled eyes and stroke my hand over his bristly jaw.

"Honey, I'm sorry. I..." His mouth covering mine cuts off the rest of what I want to say and my mind turn blank. When he lets me up for air, all he says is, "nothing to be sorry about."

"Well, actually. If I could've finished my thought there, I probably would've had something really sensible to add to that, but I'm afraid you kissed all the words right out of me. Except maybe I love you."

"Second time you tell me that and in case you're afraid you'll wear it out? Not a fucking chance. I'll never tire of hearing those words out of that mouth."

That mouth is receiving quite the workout right this minute and again all coherent thought disappears.

She drives me to distraction and soothes me emotionally, can challenge and match me intellectually, and fuck if there is another in existence who sets me on fire like she does.

"Love you too, *Yázhí*."

I kiss her nose, when she suddenly pulls back and says enthusiastically, "Perfect! This is actually the perfect moment I've been waiting for."

Not a clue what she's referring to I'm surprised when she pulls her wheelchair over and lifts herself in, only to come around the bed to my side.

"You've gotta sit up or stand up, Caleb. I can't do it with you laying back."

Confused, I do as she asks, and stand up as she wheels her chair back along the wall—a good 5 feet away from where I'm standing. She puts the breaks on and braces herself on the armrests, pushing herself up. I'm as excited as I am terrified and battle the urge to run and swipe her off her feet before something happens, but the determined grimace on her face has me rooted in my spot; hands clenched at my sides. She wants to show me this. It's important to her.

Slowly she straightens up on her legs, moving one arm from the chair behind her to the wall beside her and her eyes come up to meet mine. A slow grin stretches over her face as she tentatively moves one foot forward, letting go of the chair with her other hand and sticking it out to her side for balance. My heart almost stops when her knees seem to want to buckle, but she raises her chin, pushes her shoulders down and simply keeps moving forward, tiny little steps at a time.

I can't help myself, when she is just a step or two away from me I take one big one forward with my arms out and catch her around her waist, lift her up and land with her on the bed.

"Fucking hell, Katie. That's un-fucking-believable! How? When?"

Laughing through her obvious exertion, Katie hugs me tight.

"Saturday, at my session with Kendra... something clicked," she pants, "she took off the harness and had me practice without. Been doing it since. Twice this week already. I can do better with the parallel bars. I didn't think it was gonna be this hard without them," she laughs at herself. "But I did it. I wanted to be able to show you myself. Alone."

"So fucking proud of you, little one. Never doubted you, I honestly didn't, and it wouldn't have made even a hint of a difference in how I feel about you, but I am so fucking happy to see you battle so hard for something and win. You win, sweets."

The smile she throws me is brighter than the sun at noon and just like that I need inside her.

"Need you, Katie," I tell her right before I take her smiling mouth hungrily. I can fucking taste the positive energy on her tongue. I need it—need her to fill me with it so I have the balls to leave her tomorrow. I touch the connection of our lips with my fingers before tracing them down her jaw and neck. Shifting myself slightly off her without ever losing contact with her mouth, my hand follows the contours of her body, finally coming to rest on the soft swell of her stomach where I let the heat penetrate my palm. Glorious. Fucking glorious.

I treasure every inch of her as I slowly kiss and nip my way down to that warm spot on her stomach. She looks down at me, smile still on her face, but her eyes now darker; deeper. Her hand slides through my short hair.

"Where are you going?" she asks huskily.

"Shhh. I have one stop to make before I reach my destination," I mumble with my lips against her skin and my eyes fixed on hers. Her belly button is a brief distraction that almost has her giggling. A tad ticklish I find out. My lips finally replace where my hand has been resting, and just for a moment I put my cheek to that gentle rise and close my eyes, hoping.

But the scraping of Katie's fingers against my scalp and the hot, sweet smell of her arousal draw me in. One move and I'm down on my knees beside the bed, have Katie pulled to the edge with her legs held over my shoulders. Fuck. She's a smorgasbord.

As self-conscious as she was at first about her body, now she is spread eagled, pulling pillows under her head for a better view, and is licking that damn pouty bottom lip in anticipation. Short dark hair going every which way, full soft breasts falling slightly to the side as she props herself up a little and that sweet soft belly I can't fucking get enough of.

"Gonna make you come hard on my tongue, baby. You ready? Eyes on me. I need to see you."

Katie's eyes darken with lust, and she just nods.

I slowly lower my head and with our eyes connected I proceed to make true on my promise. Teasing her clit with my tongue and playing my fingers through her juices and into her pussy has her on edge and pleading.

"Make me come, honey... I need to come."

"Eyes on me, little one. Always."

Snapping her eyes open, her frustration is clear. I run the flat of my tongue in a few long teasing strokes over her clit, then finally at the same time I slide a soaking wet finger in her small puckered hole, I suck that bundle of nerves deep into my mouth. I can feel her orgasm take over in the pulsing muscles around my finger and Katie's body almost comes off the bed as she screams her release, "Caleb... Ahh!"

Holy crud. I think I blew a few blood vessels with that orgasm.

Gasping for breath I squint down to see Caleb's face, shiny with my juices and grinning wide, peeking up from between my legs.

"Holy crud," I repeat out loud, making him smile only wider as he drops my legs down and climbs up on my body, which is in no shape to move. Nose to nose now, he whispers against my lips, "Taste yourself," before sliding his tongue inside and infusing me with a heady combination of flavors; my own and Caleb's.

His hands slide up under my arms and he rolls over and pulls me on top of him.

"I want you to ride me."

But when he moves my slightly unwilling leg over his hips to straddle him, a frown creases his brow.

"This may not work. Hang on."

Sliding out from under me, he leaves me in bed to watch his tight ass flex on his way out the door. Okay then. Not two minutes later he's back with one of the end chairs of the new dining set, his erect cock bouncing with every step. *Hmmm.* A nice big chair with high armrests, which he proudly puts at the end of the bed.

"Come here, little one," he pats the mattress.

When I raise my eyebrow, he just chuckles, reaches over and hauls me off the bed as if I'm no more than a throw pillow.

"Hey!"

As usual, my protests fall to deaf ears and by the time he has us situated, him seated with his bare ass on our new dining chair; me straddling him with my legs through the armrests. I can suddenly see the purpose of his maneuvering. He wants something, he's gonna make it happen.

"Put your hands on the armrests and ride me, baby. Your arms are strong as fuck. I want you to take me."

How I can be primed and ready so soon after an orgasm that surely left me with a few more dead brain cells than my daily quota. I don't know, but I can feel the wetness seeping out of my pussy. Grabbing the armrests firmly, I push myself up while Caleb positions the crown of his straining cock at my entrance. Slippery and still soft from my orgasm, I don't hesitate; I drop myself onto his red-hot length, eliciting a strangled groan from his lips.

"Fuuuck, woman. Killing me here."

The almost pained expression on his face as he fights to gain control gives me a wicked sense of power. I slightly swivel my hips and feel the slight burn of him stretching me. His eyes squint slightly, knowing I'm teasing him.

"Careful, little one," he growls, grabbing my hips firmly.

With the strength of my arms and the help of his hands on my hips guiding me, I slowly but thoroughly fuck my man. Every time my body slides down his cock, I feel filled to capacity and spread so wide; I can feel every fucking inch of him inside me. When Caleb changes his grip to clasp my ass cheeks in his big hands, spreading them even wider and using the tips of his fingers to tease our slippery connection, I start to lose control. Panting hard from exertion and so turned on, my mouth is hanging open and I begin to mutter nonsense. Caleb breathes in short grunts as he starts to raise his hips, pounding in me from below, his intense glittering dark hazel eyes never leaving mine.

"Never had the urge before, but soon I want to take you here," he croaks as he begins fucking my ass with his finger. "I need to have all of you."

The simultaneous filling of my ass and my pussy is overwhelming and I am teetering on the brink.

"Oh. God. Don't stop... Fuck. Please—I'm coming."

"Come for me, *Yázhí*," he growls.

"Trying to. Harder! Please..."

"Grab my neck."

I do as he says and cock still embedded in me, he stands up with his hands under my ass, and puts me down on the bed. I whimper at the loss of that wicked finger in my backside.

"Hold your legs open, sweets."

My ass is almost hanging off the bed, and with one hand firmly gripping my hips, the other pushing my knee open, Caleb starts slamming inside me with such force it knocks the breath out of me.

"I. Need. You. To. Come." He bites out, releasing my knee and sliding his hand to where we are connected where he squeezes my clit between his fingers. *Hard.*

And I burst into a million little pieces.

CHAPTER TWENTY-THREE

I hate it.

Watching Caleb drive off in Neil's truck from the small window in the front door sucks. As in, big hairy donkey balls, especially since I have to stay behind instead of making sure his back is covered. He goes off alone, and I'm safely tucked in a well-secured house with my personal bodyguard.

Neil showed up this morning and as agreed parked his truck so close; you could almost leap from the door into the cab. Caleb had just come out of the shower and hadn't bothered to get fully dressed since he had no idea where Neil was planning to stick trackers.

"Please don't tell me I'm interrupting some kind of sex marathon again?" Neil complains, his free hand shielding his eyes. His other hand toting a bag, which he dumps unceremoniously on the couch.

"Keep your shorts on, kid. Just trying to be helpful, since I don't know where you're gonna put those gadgets of yours."

I sit back with my cup of coffee and watch while under their constant back and forth barbs and bickering, Neil pulls out a selection of tiny electronic gadgets no bigger than grains of rice. He picks two of them, and sticks them with a dot of glue in Caleb's hairline and armpit. A third tracker is shoved in a hole he pokes in the heel of his boot, which Caleb is none too happy about.

With Caleb rigged up he motions me into the bedroom.

"Kid, grab a coffee. I'll be right there," he directs at Neil, who rolls his eyes when he sees where we're headed.

"Better not fucking dislodge those trackers, man," he calls out as Caleb shuts the door behind us.

He doesn't say anything to me while he gets dressed, but his eyes never leave me. They speak volumes to me, especially since I can still smell the evidence of our almost frantic activities of last night lingering in the room. We're both remembering the near desperation in our lovemaking. Fucking is probably more apropos. Intense, raw, exposing and absolutely earth shattering. Caleb's roar when he climaxed closely after I lost my mind had my ears still ringing this morning, and my 'nether regions' were definitely a touch tender this morning.

Slowly stalking towards me, he tilts his head to one side. "What's on your mind, little one?"

"You need to ask?"

He shakes his head. "Nah. It's like a movie on a loop in my head; I'm feeling it too."

"Don't want to, but I've gotta go," he says, sitting on the end of the bed pulling me up by my hands. He wedges my legs between his knees, and wraps his arms around my waist. Tilting his head back, his beautiful smile breaks through, "Love you, Katie-girl. Keep yourself busy and I'll be back before you know it."

I want to snort at that, but then he puts his cheek against my stomach and I don't want to kill the moment, so instead, I run my fingers through his thick shiny hair and curl myself around him. Just grabbing on to this one moment more.

"Why didn't you tell me before?"

This does not make me happy. Not that I was in a good mood to begin with, but hearing from Neil that all inquiries into the woman who adopted me have netted nothing really bites.

"You guys had all kinds of stuff going on, I had a few sticks in the fire yet and didn't want to give you bad news if there was still a slight chance. Besides, Caleb has some feelers of his own out."

"What? What do you mean Caleb has feelers out?"

We're sitting at the big kitchen table with our laptops open, working on tracing as many of the known members Agave cartel as we can, until we find the man who took a shot at me—the man with the burned hand. So far, he's been elusive.

My attention now far from the man who might hold a key to this case, I turn my entire body to Neil.

"Feelers on what?"

"Ah shit. He didn't say anything? Dammit." Scratching his head, Neil looks at me guiltily. "I swear I didn't tell him about your adoptive mother, Katie. He knew when he called me."

"I know you didn't tell him. I did. What I don't get is why he called you?"

I'm not sure if I'm angry or confused; a bit of both, I guess.

"He seemed to know I was looking into it, because he called me shortly after you guys came back from Farmington. Asked what I'd been able to dig up and I gave him what I had. He said he had some ideas of his own, took her particulars and that was it."

Standing up from the table he grabs our cups, and refills them from the coffeepot in the kitchen.

"You realize he's really gonna hate me now right?" Neil grumbles as he slides my coffee in front of me.

"He doesn't hate you. Why do you say that?"

"Are you kidding me? The man calls me every diminutive name in the book. I even heard him call me a 'guard puppy' to Gus."

The disgruntled look on his face is so comical; I can't help but burst out laughing. My own irritation with Caleb for going behind my back instantly forgotten.

"You're a goof, Neil."

"Whatever," he says; shaking his head and turning his attention back to the computer screen.

Left to my own thoughts, I'm about to turn back to my own computer when the phone rings.

"Everything go ok this morning?" Gus jumps right in without the customary hello.

"Off without a hitch. He's been gone for three hours and I got a text about an hour ago saying he was going to be out of reach for a while. You want to talk to Neil?"

"No. Why don't you guys head over to the diner and I'll meet you there for lunch. On the off chance anyone was paying attention, seeing Neil instead of Caleb with you at this point is not gonna make a difference. Caleb's safely gone."

"Yesss. Can't wait to get out for a bit. I've gotten too used to the construction noise around us and it is too quiet today without the crew here."

I don't know why I hadn't thought of it before. With the possibility Mal may not be hiding from me necessarily, but rather from the cartel and his own gang, it seemed obvious he would pick a place only I would know how to find.

For years our parents had taken us for weeklong camping trips into Arches National Park near Moab. On one of our first trips there, Mal had only been about six years old, I had been instructed to keep an eye on him when he disappeared. Just up the trail from the campground, we had found an area riddled with sagebrush and large boulders where we'd play hide and seek. Except when it was my turn to look for Mal, he was completely gone. I checked every rock and brush in that damn clearing and couldn't find him. About to go running for my parents, I heard a muffled voice call my name. It seemed to come from an area where three large rocks were grouped against the side of a cliff rising up. Afraid he'd hurt himself I ran over but still couldn't see a thing, until his little head peeked up from ground level from right underneath where the three rocks touched. He was stuck in a hole, well, not actually a hole; it turned out to be a mostly intact kiva. An underground chamber. Of course we didn't learn that until later, but for that camping trip and all of the ones that followed, we had found a perfect spot to hide out from our parents and Nascha, our sister, and arch-enemy number one in those days. Even as teens we loved hanging out in there, having cleaned and widened the opening to allow for easier access. When the sun hit at a certain time of day, it could fill the underground room with so much light, you'd never know you were basically in a hole.

God, I don't think I've thought of that place since Nascha died, but for some reason it seems like that would be the perfect spot for Mal to hide out. With a campground nearby, he could make use of the amenities there and Moab's not far away for necessities. On top of that, as far as I know the only other person who knows about that place is me. I certainly never told anyone about its existence. Yes, my gut tells me I'll find my brother there, but I'm not dumb enough to drive my car into the park.

It's not that difficult to figure out if you have a tail on the open roads between Cortez and Monticello, and by the time I get close to my destination, I'm fairly well convinced that I have no one behind me. When I get to the park gate, I follow the road a ways in, until I find a trail entrance that already has quite a few cars in the parking lot. I slide Neil's old truck between a minivan and a Ford-150 and send one last text to Katie, knowing that I won't likely have reception for long. A check of my watch and the small backpack with water and some trail mix and fruit on my back, and I'm setting off on the trail. But not for long.

Making sure there is no one directly in front or visible behind me, about a quarter mile into the trail, I head north, away from the path and in the general direction of the campground a few miles up the road. I check my surroundings constantly, but other the occasional small animal scurrying out of sight before I even have a chance to identify it, there is hardly a sound or sign of life. Yet I have no doubt of what I'll find when I get where I'm going.

I almost slap Neil when he tries to lift me into the Tahoe.

"Would you knock it off? I'm not an invalid."

"Could've fooled me," the ass grumbles as he takes my chair and folds it in the backseat while I pull myself up into my seat.

"Heard that." Guess he's still smarting 'cause I laughed at him, so I punch him in the arm as soon as he sits his butt down beside me. "Knock it off, you sourpuss. You've gotta lighten up a little. You're too young to be so damn grumpy half the time."

"Ouch," he grumbles, rubbing his arm furiously. "For a chick you have a surprisingly solid punch."

Just for that he gets another one.

"Ouch! Have some mercy will you? That'll leave a mark."

"Serves you right. Who the fuck are you calling a chick anyway? Besides, I was just confirming something for you, that way next time you won't need to be so surprised."

A small smile plays at the edge of his mouth. "Not surprised as much as impressed, I guess."

"Oh now you're just blowing smoke up my ass," I chuckle, finding myself enjoying spending time with Neil a lot. He is super sharp with all things electronic and can work the computer like you wouldn't believe, but even more I enjoy the casual familiar banter. Almost like a younger brother I never had. Yeah. I really like the kid.

Listen to me. Calling him kid like Caleb does—he's maybe ten years younger, if that. And he sure doesn't look like a kid, maybe his face, but the rest of him is ripped and toned like a man's body. There's a lucky girl out there somewhere, although he could use some help smoothing his game out.

In the diner the lunch crowd is thick, even for a Friday. Beth has us sitting at the counter, which meant I had to leave my chair and hoist myself up on a stool. Something that was closely observed by Arlene.

"You're doing pretty decent there, missy," she point out.

"Yeah. Getting there," I tell her with a wink, not ready yet to reveal my newfound ability to walk a few steps. Let them see me stand and manoeuvre myself around for a bit. I don't need gawkers anyway. Awkward enough as it is.

Seb comes out of the kitchen and gives me a hug. Cripes, he is a *nice* man, and Arlene is one lucky woman.

"I have home made elk burgers on special today guys, with sweet potato fries. You game?"

"Hell yes," belts Neil, whose three eggs fried over hard in my kitchen at 10:30 weren't enough to tide him over I guess.

"Yes to what?" Emma asks, just walking up in front of Gus.

"Seb has elk burgers and Neil is a bottomless pit," I announce, "he's already emptied our fridge and now he pretends to be starved again. Don't fall for it."

"Hey, I'm a growing boy," Neil protests, a big grin on his face.

"Sign me up too, Seb." Gus throws in his order and with Emma's and mine to match it's unanimous.

"No table?" Gus wants to know.

"Hang on, I think the corner booth is about to leave, I'll go wipe the table to help them along." Beth grabs a rag and heads over to the booth where Clint and some woman are finishing up lunch. Furiously wiping the table and slamming plates and cutlery together, she succeeds in chasing them out of the booth in no time. Clint with a confused look on his face and the woman by his side more than mildly irritated. With a wave in our direction he guides her out the door.

Heading our way is Beth with a giant smile on her face. "There," she says triumphantly, "your booth is ready and waiting." With a toss of her ponytail, she flicks the rag over her shoulder and heads into the kitchen.

"Oh boy." Emma looks at Arlene who is looking at the doorway where Beth disappeared.

Gus starts chuckling behind her. "Leave it alone, Ems. Whatever it is, leave it alone."

"But..." she starts, but she's cut short when he grabs her around the waist and moves her along to the now vacant booth.

"Come on guys," he says over his should to us, "we've got some business to discuss."

Four elk burgers, a mountain of sweet potato fries and some damn good diner coffee later, Gus finally is ready to go over the details of a call he mentioned earlier he received from Manny Jordan, the detective from Shiprock. Emma stopped him from discussing business while eating, which earned her a scowl, but he did eat first. Never thought I'd see the day.

"Manny says it was a routine traffic stop for speeding, the idiot. They took him in and are holding him for questioning."

"Who is this Benjamin Chee?" Emma wants to know.

"He was, or still is we're not quite sure, Caleb's brother Malachi's best friend and also his number two man in this gang he runs. He may be involved. At the very least, he knows a lot more than he should."

"So we're gonna sit and wait for news?" I ask, hoping I might finally be able to do something instead of waiting around twiddling my thumbs, but no.

"We should know more by the end of the afternoon. Anything else from Caleb?"

"Nothing since the text that he would be out of range."

"How long ago was that?"

"He's been gone for five hours now."

I approach the three rocks along the side of the cliff wall. It's taken me much longer to get here than I had anticipated. An hour's hike is what I counted on, but it turned out to be at least double that. And no reception to give the guys back home a head's up.

A slight rustle above me, has me snap my head up, but all I see is a bird taking off from some brush on the cliff above. Pausing a moment to make sure that is all it was, I rest my head against the sun warmed red and yellow sandstone rock of the cliff. Minutes pass without any further sound and I slowly push away from the wall to make my way over to the hidden kiva.

With a sudden change of light and a rush of air, a large form knocks me forward and flat on my face. The unmistakable cold steel of a gun is pressed to the base of my skull.

"Don't. Move." A voice hisses close to my ear.

CHAPTER TWENTY-FOUR

"Seb's already prepped tonight's dinner special; Jambalaya. I packed up a tub for you to take along."

Arlene is waiting at the cash register when we're ready to leave. Of course Gus wrangles Neil and I for the bill and wins. *Asshat.*

The bag is shoved in my direction and when I hesitate to accept it right away, Arlene scoffs and adds, "Don't make a big fuss, okay? I'm having a nice day - don't spoil it. Beth's made these ridiculous little pouches with some kind of wood eating tools for our new take-out menu, and I popped some in so you won't even have to do dishes."

I have a shit eating grin on my face at Arlene's obvious discomfort with having been caught doing something nice—in front of witnesses, no less! For all her abrasive bristle, the woman is a gem and I'm really starting to love her.

With a loud 'humpf', Arlene throws one last dirty look in our general direction, as if daring any of us to say anything, before turning and virtually stomping off into the kitchen.

"Better go," Emma chuckles, "all these kindly vibes are bound to pop her a blood vessel."

Outside I stop Gus by grabbing his arm, not able to forget my anxiety over Caleb despite our little chuckle at Arlene's expense.

"How long till we activate the trackers?"

"I promised him seven hours to get back in touch, Katie. Go home. Trust him to know what he's doing. If we haven't heard by three this afternoon, I'll be at the barn and we move."

Mildly placated with a timeline and a gentle reminder that Caleb is a highly trained professional who would take no unnecessary risks, I join Neil waiting at the Tahoe.

The drive to the barn is a quiet one, both of us alone with our thoughts, but pulling onto the yard the sight of Blue sitting by the picnic table instantly lifts my spirits.

"Whoa, what the fuck is that thing?" Neil exclaims when he gets his first glimpse of all that is Blue.

"Thing? That's not a thing, that's my puppy."

From the incredulous look he throws me, I gather he's not convinced and almost yanks me back in the truck, when I try to slide out.

"Hang the fuck on, woman. What if it mauls you?"

"Get over yourself," I call him on the drama, "he's just a dog. Let me get out and prepare him for you."

"Oh *that* makes me feel a lot better. Thanks." Rolling his eyes and with his arms crossed defiantly over his chest, he cautiously keeps an eye on Blue as I slide out of the truck and hold on to the door for balance.

"Come here, Blue!"

With a twitch of his ears, the dog gets up and gingerly moves closer. Always aware of any movement around him. There is no hesitation in his approach of me though. Nuzzling my hand, he flops back on his haunches and leans his body into my legs as I scratch him under the chin.

"Hey buddy. Did you come to see me? I need you to be nice to my friend. He's gonna help me inside, okay?"

When Neil opens his door to get out, I can hear the low growl vibrating through Blue's fur.

"I'll be damned," Neil chuckles, "that mutt loves you."

"Don't come barging up right away, he's very protective of me. Let me introduce you first."

"Every man around you is protective of you, Katie. Although it beats me as to why. You may look the part, but you're no damsel in distress. You're actually kinda scary."

I smile at Neil, who lingers at the hood of the car, careful not to come too close.

"Awww, you just gave me a compliment. That's so sweet."

"Me calling you scary is sweet? Fuck I have a lot to learn about women."

A few minutes later Blue is sniffing Neil's hand and is cleared to get my wheelchair out of the back. None too soon either; my legs are starting to buckle from exertion.

I wheel up to the house with Blue in tow, while Neil dives back in the Tahoe to get the food out. To my surprise, Blue actually leads the way once I have the front door open. It's the first time he's been inside. Curiously sniffing around he makes his way around the entry and the doors to the side leading to the laundry and bedroom, stopping only to look back at me as if for approval to move ahead.

"Go on. Have a look around." I urge him on. Neil walks in behind me with the bag of food and puts it in my lap.

"Here, you can put this away, I'm going back to work." He moves over to the table and boots up his laptop, ignoring the dog that does a 'sniff-by' as he passes Neil on the way to the kitchen. I follow behind, curious to see where he'll go.

Blue stops in the middle of the kitchen and sits down, looking expectantly at the fridge.

"You're not such a wild dog, are ya, buddy?" I chuckle; amused he knows exactly where the goodies are kept. Opening the fridge I plop the bag from the diner in and pull out a length of kielbasa Caleb bought last week when we were stocking up. I hate the stuff, but he loves it. Maybe Blue will too. Slicing off a piece I look at Blue whose ears are perched to attention and I swear the dog is licking the drool off his lips. Slightly dipping his head down, he gently lifts one paw and puts it on my lap.

"Well, you little bugger! Somebody trained you at some point didn't they?"

I hold out the meat and with his head tilted sideways he very carefully takes it from between my fingers, barely touching them.

"I'll be damned."

Neil is leaning over the counter looking on with a grin on his face.

"Don't know who's got who suckered in, but it looks like love to me."

Before I have a chance to come back with a response, the large window over the sink shatters and Neil dives over the counter and knocks me out of my chair on the ground, covering my body. Blue stands in front of us facing the window, growls coming from deep in his chest and shards of glass glistening through his fur that is standing on end.

"Phone?" I ask Neil, since mine is on the counter where I put it earlier. He hands me his cell from his back pocket, never letting go of the gun he has clutched in his right hand. I dial Gus' number as Neil shoves both of us up against the cabinet under the broken window.

"Gus, shots fired at the barn. Kitchen window, were hunkered down and ok."

"Fuck! On my way. Leave the line open."

Putting the phone on speaker I put it down on the ground and slide out my own side arm, which is strapped, under my arm. Neil is trying to have a look through the window, but dives down when this time a volley of shots comes flying in hitting surfaces around us. Blue's had enough and starts barking furiously. Fuck. That's all we need.

We're not visible from the big sliding doors, which are still locked, but we didn't lock or arm the front door behind us and whoever walks in has us in their direct line of vision. Stuck between the counter and the island is not the worst place to be.

"I'm checking the doors in the back," Neil starts making his way to the back wall, staying low to the ground with his gun at ready. My eyes flick back and forth between the front door and Neil's receding back. Poor Blue is not happy with the situation; he paces back and forth between the disappearing Neil and where I'm leaning against the cabinets in the kitchen, opting finally to stick by my side. I mumble soothing words to him to try and calm him down a little, but the truth is, I'm all but calm myself.

I hear a huge crash and a "Fuck" from Neil, which momentarily draws my attention to the back. At the same time I can feel a draft coming from the other side and before I can even turn around, Blue whips past me and charges the front door. I can't even see to shoot. The dog is in my way, but another shot rings and this time it's followed by a loud yelp as Blue crumples on the ground, halfway to the front door.

At least two hours have passed. Fuck. Katie must be getting frantic by now and there is nothing I can say to change that idiot's mind.

As soon as I hear his voice, I knew I was bested by my little brother, but the fucker wouldn't listen and just put handcuffs on me and tossed me down the hole into the kiva. He sat at the edge up top, just staring down.

"Mal, you can't stay here. People are getting killed over you." I try again.

"So what do you want, Jefe? Want me to give myself up? You think it's gonna stop there? I don't have the drugs they think I took. Don't have 'em… Fuck. You think I'm that stupid, going up against the cartel? I've had my suspicions. Benji had more money than was reasonable, had a cocky attitude that was new. Mouthing off about his Mexican 'buddies'. He's stupid as fuck, is what he is. At first I couldn't believe he'd do me like that, but when people started dying over this missing load and then eyes started turning my way, I knew I was in deep shit. I had to haul ass out of there. Can't go back. I'll just bring more danger to everyone. Been trying to figure out a way out of this mess."

With a shock I realize he doesn't know. He's been holed up so deep, he hasn't been in touch with anyone, so there's no way he knows what happened to our parents. Carefully I test him, "Mal, you talk to anyone back home? Anyone know you're even alive?"

"Nah. You're the first person since I left, other than the chick at the gas station check out."

Shit.

"Brother. You missed some pretty bad news back home," I start carefully, and proceed to tell him about the fire, our mother and our waste of space of a father.

"A few days ago, my girlfriend was run off the road and shot at. Gus and I, we want to go directly to the Duarte's and tell them our suspicions, but we need a name for the guy—the fucktard who burned down our house and almost took out my woman."

When I look up to where he is sitting, all the badass is gone from his posture. His gun laying harmless beside him, his knees are drawn up to his chest and his arms around folded around him. The ink-black hair he never cut off is draped around his shoulders.

"Gonna kill that son of a bitch."

"Get in line little brother."

"What do you want me to do?"

The defeat is now evident in his voice and even though this is what I was waiting for, it kills me to see him like this.

"Come with me. Let me keep you safe and away from law enforcement for now – at least federal law enforcement – until we can come up with a way to stop this endless clusterfuck."

Finally, he stretches his long legs, jumps down in the kiva with me and unlocks the cuffs.

"You think she suffered?" he looks at me and I don't want to give him an answer, but he sees it in my eyes anyway. Although he is almost taller than I am, I pull him into a firm embrace and feel the full weight of his guilt leaning against me. Fuck.

Making our way back to Neil's truck, Mal starts questioning me about Katie.

"So... girlfriend?"

I chuckle, "Whatever they call it. She's mine, I'm hers. End of story."

"That serious huh? Fuck man, at forty-two? Now you're gonna change your ways?" Mal shoves my shoulder like he used to do to get a rise out of me when we were younger.

"Not changing any ways, little brother. I was never a man-whore like you. Anyway, with a bit of luck you'll meet her soon. We're gonna try and find a way to get you into town without anyone knowing you're around, but at least you'll be close by."

By the time we get to Neil's old truck Mal has already agreed the better option is to leave his truck where it is; hidden from view behind an old shed on a service road not to far from the parking lot. The sun is getting low in the sky and I know Katie is going to be frantic with worry by now. Fuck I hate this. I pull the phone from my pocket and see I have two bars. I immediately dial and wait for a connection. Nothing. The damn thing goes to message. An uneasy feeling crawls over my skin.

"No answer?" Mal asks, waiting by the truck. I just shake my head as I immediately dial Neil's number with the same damn result. *Fuck!* This doesn't make sense. I'm starting to sweat now and climb behind the wheel, motioning Mal to get the hell in as well, while I dial Gus. Finally, Emma picks up.

"Emma? Where's Gus?"

"Caleb? Are you ok? Oh my God, Caleb..."

CHAPTER TWENTY-FIVE

The moment Blue is down, I see the outline of a man in the doorway. I don't think, I aim and shoot. I must've hit him, because he goes down, but not quietly. He's fucking howling like a pig. Keeping my gun trained on the front door, I yell out at Neil.

"Yo Neil! Status!"

"Down... Leg..." He sounds in pain, but pissed. Good. Pissed is good.

"Stay put, shoot anyone coming through that door."

"Fucking A."

I'm not even gonna try to get up. We have at least one other shooter out there, 'cause there's no way in hell one person could've come from the back to the front door that fast, so I'm staying close to the ground. One hand, my ass, my heels, I use everything at my disposal to crawl toward Blue, while keeping my gun pointed to the front. Not fucking easy, but I'm not gonna take chances. From behind I'll hear; Neil will make sure of that, from the front will be to fast for me to react. No one is gonna fucking take me out today.

By the time I reach Blue the son of a bitch's yowling in my doorway has reduced to whimpering. I place my hand on Blue's side and am relieved beyond belief to feel a fairly strong rise and fall of his chest. Alive. Quickly wiping a tear trickling down my cheek that I don't have the time for now, I lean over and mumble in his ear, "You hang in there, beautiful boy. I'm gonna get you help."

I'm almost to the front door, at level with the elevator door when I hear the crunch of footsteps on the gravel out front. Crud. I have no time to get myself into the bedroom so I reach behind me and with my fingers wedge open the door to the elevator. I reluctantly slip my gun in my waistband, curl my hands around the frame behind me and with all the strength left in me, pull my body into the dark space.

I hit the bottom of the elevator shaft with a big smack and it takes a minute for my head to stop ringing. Fuck me. Forgot about that. They'd had to dig down the shaft to make room for the elevator car and had just finished pouring the floor. Dayum. I think that was five or six feet down and I'm lucky I didn't break anything. At least I don't think so. My hand automatically checks the small of my back to see if my gun survived the fall and it is still safely tucked in my waistband. Thank God for that. I wouldn't be able to find a damn thing in here; it's pitch black. Ears tuned in to see if I could pick up any movement outside, I slide over until I find a wall and sit with my back against it. The remaining daylight outside is creeping through the crack left in the door opening and my eyes are able to pick up a bit more of my surroundings, such as they are. I can still hear the whimpering of the dickwad who shot my dog, but other than that there is no sound whatsoever. Not happy with my rather passive situation, I manage to work myself to my feet. Not an easy task, and with my ass and back to the wall, I shuffle my way along the wall to where I can see the light filter in. I'm hoping I can reach up enough to see along the floor to the front door.

The sudden ringing of a phone startles me so hard; I almost drop my gun, which has been back in my hand the moment I was on my feet. A loud cursing from inside tells me I'm not the only one taken by surprise.

"Katie?" A voice comes from outside this time. And again, "Katie? Neil? Stay down, fuckface. Move and you're done." The last I'm sure was directed at my friend by the door. Apparently the cavalry has arrived.

"Gus, head's up! There's a second shooter out there," I call out as I hear him moving through the house.

"Where the hell are you Katie? Jesus Christ, Neil."

"Is he ok? In the elevator shaft. I'm here!" I'm about to pound the bottom of the door with the butt of my gun when the door swings open and Gus looks down.

"This is fucked up. You're all bleeding. Let me get you up. We've gotta tend to Neil. Jesus Katie, and your dog... Joe is on his way. No sign of a second shooter and the fucker at the door has a hole where his dick used to be. Your work?" he asks as he grabs my arms and pulls me right up and out of the hole. With one arm around my waist and one under my knees he scoops me up and deposits me in my chair, which is still sitting in the kitchen. I hurry around the island to find Neil half sitting against the wall beside the shattered sliding glass door with his belt tied around his thigh, close to his groin, head rolled to one side. He's lost a massive amount of blood.

"Normally I'd say elevate that leg, but the way he's sitting with that tourniquet around his leg, it seems to have stopped the blood flow. You're probably better off leaving him," I suggest to Gus.

"Gonna check in with Joe, see where they're at. And you better see if you still have an open line on yours, I hung up when I got here."

240

I find Neil's phone on the floor in the kitchen and press end, putting it on the counter beside mine. Just then, Joe and two sheriff's deputies come through the front door.

Not ten minutes later, Neil is loaded in the ambulance on his way to Cortez Memorial where and we're following in Gus's Yukon where I'm holding a barely breathing Blue on my lap on our way to the emergency veterinarian clinic, holding a towel against a hole in his shoulder. Already his breathing is much shallower than it was the first time I checked and I'm terrified we'll lose him.

The EMT wanted me to come to the hospital to get checked out. Some of the stitches in my head have come loose and he's concerned I may have hurt myself when I fell. No shit, Sherlock, but those stitches were gonna come out anyway and unless I was missing a limb, this dog needs attention first.

"Emma? They'll be ok, darlin'" Gus answers his phone when it rings just once.

"Why'd he call there? ... Fuck, of course, I had an open line. It must've forwarded to the home phone. Come to think of it, one of theirs was busy as well; the other rang just as I approached the barn. Lemme call him right now." When Gus looks at me in the rear-view mirror I already know what he's gonna tell me and tears of relief start running down my face. Caleb was okay.

Un-fucking-believable.

I'm already almost out of Moab, tearing down the road in Neil's shit bucket. Malachi tries to ask questions but I can't fucking handle questions right now, so all I say is, "Bad fucking trouble at home," to shut him up. I don't wanna hear it.

"Hello?"

"They're all accounted for. Neil's shot, Katie's scraped up, the dog saved her life but he's barely hanging on. Everyone is en route to emergency care in Cortez. I know what you want, my friend, and I get it. But for all of our sakes stick with the plan so we can end this shit."

"Gotta see my girl, Gus."

"Asking you to trust me, Caleb. I've got her for you. You get Mal sorted and stay in touch. Wanna talk to her?"

Some rustling as Gus hands the phone over and the next I know my girl is sniffling on the other side.

"Ah, little one–"

"He ran out in front of me, Caleb," she sobs in the phone, "caught a bullet that was meant for me. Not even a hesitation."

"He's a good dog, babe. The best," I try to soothe her, grateful as hell for that rangy mutt.

"Shot the fucker, though. Fucker may not be an appropriate name for him an longer though," she chuckles through her tears.

"Why's that?"

"Remember that issue I had with my aim at the range? Well, I still have it."

After an extremely tense and stressful day, followed by ten minutes of my life I'd rather never repeat, the burst of laughter that explodes from the pit of my stomach feels fantastic.

"Ya hit his groin?" I ask when I can manage to get a word out.

"Annihilated his jewels, more like it," she deadpans, with a little snicker.

I can see Mal shaking his head beside me, a smile on his face.

"Atta girl, *Yázhí*. Atta girl. Gonna be there as soon as I can. We've just gotten on the road and I'll be another two hours at least."

"Do what you do, Caleb Whitetail. I'll be here when you're done. Love you."

"Back at you, sweets. Love you too."

When I hang up, I can feel Mal's scrutiny. *Wow*, he mouths. Smartass.

"She killed his dick? And this is your girlfriend? Fuck man, can't wait to meet this one," he chuckles.

"Better watch yourself too. Even from her chair, she could whip your ass." I tell him with a grin.

"Chair?"

Right. He wouldn't know, in fact, neither of us knows much about the other's life these days. Only what we think we do. We may as well spend the next two hours stuck in this rattling shit box getting reacquainted.

By the time I have Malachi safely settled in with the burner phone and one of the trackers Neil stuck on me, now wedged between the heel and sole of *his* boot, I finally head back in the direction of Cortez. Gus already called to say they had taken Blue into surgery and he'd had to virtually drag Katie out of there to get her looked over at the hospital.

He's waiting for me in the lobby when I drive up, eager to get going.

"Quick briefing and I'm off, but I'm relieved as fuck to see you in one piece. Things got hairy for a while there with you out of reach." Gus motions for me to sit, but I'm too wired.

"Malachi needed a bit of convincing," is all I share for now, not wanting a lengthy discussion.

"Fair enough, we'll get details later."

Like hell. Not sure I'm gonna volunteer how my little brother took me down and have it held over my head at every opportunity.

"The guy Katie castrated is alive and been flown to Durango with Lifeline and in surgery. Irks me that taxpayers are spending money on a douche like that, but whatever. Not a coherent word from him and no ID yet, but he's not our Mexican friend. He's Caucasian. Second shooter who was gone before I got there, apparently was picked up by one of the patrol vehicles coming in after Joe when he shot out of a back road into the Ute reservation. Looks like he'd been waiting there for all emergency vehicles to pass before making his escape and missed one. Some scared as shit punk kid off the street with a large scope rifle beside him. I'm off to the sheriff's office, where Joe has him waiting for questioning. I want in on that."

"What about Neil?"

"Jesus, he's lost a lot of blood, but that kid is tough. He's in surgery here and Emma is on her way in. I've called the office in Grand Junction as well. Dana's like a mother to him. She was gonna leave right away. Doc says he'll be ok. Nicked his femoral artery but the little fucker managed to tie himself off so good he didn't bleed out. Katie is livid with him; he made her believe it was 'just' a leg shot. She never saw."

This has taken way too long already and I'm fucking antsy as shit to get to my girl.

"Thanks man, but I gotta go see her now. Where?"

With a smile and a finger pointed in the right direction Gus slaps me on the back and without another word I take off to find her.

The room has three bays, all with the curtains drawn and I don't know which one she is behind.

"You're late..." I hear the smile in her voice and following it to the curtain on the far left.

"How did you know it was me?" I want to know as I pull back the curtain and take her in; covered in dirt and scrapes, with a fresh trickle of blood down the side of her head and her eyes red rimmed. But beautiful and bright smiling and so very fucking alive.

"I feel you," she says simply, and I kick off my boots, climb into the stupid little bed and wrap myself around her. I feel her too—everywhere.

After a few minutes of just breathing her in, I ask her about the events at the barn and I tell her about my day with Malachi. We don't let go, staying wrapped up together and whispering quietly as if we were just catching up on our days.

The clearing of a throat has me look up—straight into the smiling face of Naomi.

"Well, well, well," she says to Katie, "I see you picked up an extra blanket."

Katie sticks her tongue out, only making Naomi laugh out loud.

"Get your own hot guy, girlfriend."

"You guys are keeping me too busy here. And besides, every time I turn around, another one is off the market. So unfair."

Stretching, I reluctantly let go of Katie, but if they're gonna be talking about guys, I'm gonna find a coffee.

"Don't leave yet, Romeo," Doc holds me up, "I'm actually glad you're here. With Katie coming in banged up, *again*," she says with a pointed look at the patient, "And with her taking a six foot tumble down an elevator shaft, I decided it was probably a good time to get some confirmation on a question we had floating around last time you were in here already."

Katie knows just as well what Naomi is talking about as I do, guessing from the death grip of her hand around mine.

"Go on, we're ready," I urge her on.

With a little bit of trepidation showing on her face, unsure how we're going to take the news, she says, "It's positive. You're pregnant."

CHAPTER TWENTY-SIX

"That was Sergeant Teva from the Grand Junction PD," Joe says after hanging up the phone. "The little creep in our cell as well as the eunuch – courtesy of Katie here – are well known thugs to her. Never thought we'd come full circle, but apparently Brian Crowe's name and picture raised a flag when it popped up on her feed this morning, combined with the description of our injured perp, she is convinced that's his buddy Rolf Baird. Brian has a sheet with mostly small time stuff, nothing too disturbing, which may have been why he got cold feet, but Rolf is a different story. He's been in for two counts of assault and is suspected in the death of a prostitute last year. Lack of evidence has ground that investigation to a halt. These are local boys to Grand Junction though. She's confused as to what they would be doing all the way in Cedar Tree, unless they were sent out there. She'll beat the bushes today and get back to me if she finds anything out. Says to say hi."

Joe came in this morning, just as Clint and his crew were leaving. They had been here at the ass-crack of dawn with replacement glass for the kitchen window and a giant board to close up the hole left by the broken sliding door. The replacement for that would take a few days. If I'd had any reservations left about Clint, they flew out the window this morning when he came in, lifted me clear out of the chair and hugged me against his big bear body.

248

"Did good, little lady. Hear you blew his nuts to kingdom come - you're a legend in these here parts now," he put me back down with a chuckle.

Yeah. Big Neanderthal Clint was definitely growing on me.

After the shock/surprise/elation/raw terror of last night's news from Naomi, Caleb and I didn't talk much. I guess we both needed time to process what we had known was a possibility, but were shocked to find out that the hormone levels indicated a pregnancy that was at least a few weeks further along. That would mean it happened our first time together when we thought we were protected. When Caleb admitted that the condom we used was one he had carried around for at least three years, waiting for the right opportunity, I could see Naomi had a hard time keeping a straight face. At times I would find myself smiling at him and he'd smile back. It was like having a delicious little secret that wasn't ready to see the light of day yet. Let the knowledge settle in for each of us first. We aren't that young anymore and would be middle aged by the time the kid turns ten. Crud. Scary thought, that, but I have to admit there is no paralyzing fear and the shock is starting turn into an almost giddy excitement. Not even worrying about logistics that much anymore. Not after the events of yesterday. If I can handle a shoot-out, I can certainly handle a couple of dirty diapers.

Naomi made me an appointment to come see her for a prenatal visit and to see about an ultrasound in a month, and told me I was cleared to leave after she took out my remaining stitches.

We checked in on Neil before we left the hospital and I begged Caleb to take me to the veterinarian clinic to see Blue before heading home. Blue had just come out of surgery and was groggy, but lifted one eyelid when he heard my voice. I couldn't hold back my tears when I saw the shaved patch of skin where they'd managed to dig out the slug he took for me. After being assured he'd be well taken care of and could probably come home tomorrow to continue recuperating, Caleb had to drag me out the door.

With a patrol car stationed outside, we rolled into bed, with a pile of extra blankets to ward off the night cold that snuck in from the broken windows and wrapped around each other tumbled into a deep sleep.

"Huh," Caleb grunts, rubbing his hair, which is starting to grow a little longer. I like it. "Wouldn't be cartel. They wouldn't hire outside help unless high quality; not some thugs off the street. Odd."

"And it's not likely from Grand Junction either," I add, "this has to be connected to Sue's murder somehow. Unless there is something I am missing somewhere."

"Well I don't have a lot of details on that case, I'll defer to Sergeant Teva for that one, and I'm sure she's figured the same possibility. She's got a great rep with local law enforcement, so let's wait to see what she comes back with," Joe suggests.

"Any word from Manny on Benji? Is he talking?"

"Talked to him last night, actually; he's put the screws on Benjamin, told him right now he'd go down for aiding and abetting, but if he continued to protect the guy, they'd have no choice but to charge him with the arson and murder as well. Apparently, that had impact. Gorge Guzman. I called it in to Gus right away and he's been trying to get a hold of one of his FBI contacts. Still trying to work with their support, but they have about three years' worth of man hours invested in this case against the Agave cartel and aren't about to negotiate that away over a drug deal gone bad. I just don't see it happening."

I try to sort all the information, while I work on another pot of coffee in the kitchen.

"Better make that decaf. Right, little one?"

My hand halts mid-air with the scoop of full strength coffee grinds ready to drop in the filter. Right. Replacing it in the canister without being too obvious about it, I quickly pull out the decaf coffee and proceed, hearing Caleb's low chuckle behind me; which I pointedly ignore.

"Okay, so we have Malachi somewhere close by and safe. We now have a name for the rogue cartel guy who was working hand in hand with Mal's second in command of the Klesh, Benjamin. Those two were trying to pin the creaming of drug shipments for their own profit on Mal, putting the lovely Duarte brothers on his tail. Completely unaware of the rat in their own house, they're after Mal full force, ironically using this Guzman to flush him out by coming after me, with the added benefit of taking out the one person who can place creepy Ernesto at Larchwood the night of Sue's murder. How am I doing so far?" I pause to take a breath and am met with nods.

"Go on," Caleb encourages.

"To get them to back off us... off me, is to convince the Duarte brothers about Guzman's duplicity and Mal's innocence, at least as far as pilfering their drug shipments goes. But that still leaves the fact that I've seen one of them at Larchwood with their father the night of the murder; nothing can undo that. In fact, I'm surprised the feds haven't shown up on my doorstep yet. I would've thought they'd be thrilled to have another potential nail in Duarte's coffin."

I'm standing at the counter and take two cups in one hand, while reaching out to the island with my other. Without even thinking I shuffle the two steps it takes to get there and slide the cups in front of the guys; Caleb with an ear-splitting grin on his face and Joe with his mouth hanging open. Then I turn around, look at my chair and realize what I've just done. I swallow hard before looking at Caleb.

"I think I need crutches or something."

He smiles even bigger. "Done," he says.

After dealing with Joe's surprise at my progress and my own shock at my body's automatic movements, we spend some more time discussing the point I brought up. A valid one. Not to mention the oddballs from Grand Junction who showed up shooting out of the blue. Twenty minutes of talking in circles and Joe announces that he's heading back to Cortez and will be in touch with any news. Caleb and I are not far behind, hoping to get a few necessary supplies at Wal-Mart for when Blue comes home; my puppy needs food and a bed. And maybe we'll pop in at Walgreens to have a look at some crutches.

"What do you mean Blue can't come home?"

After spending an hour or so in a store I would rather not be found dead in, *Wal-Mart,* we finally make our way to the cash register with a cart piled high with what Katie deems to be 'necessary items' for the mutt's comfort. Of course I'm the sap pushing the damn cart, but the huge grin on Katie's face is well worth it. And it might be that it is me who wanders into the department with all the baby stuff... You know, just to look. So even though we haven't really talking about the baby, we both are pretty damn giddy picking out the tiniest fucking socks and shirts I've ever laid eyes on. Damn socks barely fit over my finger and the shirts are about as big as the palm of my hand. Now *that* scares me a bit. But Katie is happy and we had a fucked up day yesterday so it makes for a great way to kill time until we can get her dog.

Damn Wal-Mart even had crutches, so that saved us going into another store. Elbow crutches these things are called with a cuff to slide her arm in and handles for her hands to lean on. Seems to be a bit easier to manoeuvre than those things you stick in your armpits.

She's actually standing on them now, determined to use them right away, since the woman working in that department at Wal-Mart was kind enough to adjust them to size for her.

"Ms. Acker, I'm sorry, but Blue had a bit of a rough morning and although he is doing better now, I'd really prefer to have him get through twenty-four hours without complication before I send him home with you."

The vet gives Katie a sympathetic look.

"Of course," I answer for her, seeing her struggle to hold back tears, "can you tell us what happened?" I slide behind Katie and slide my arms around her stomach, to give her some support. Her body immediately leans in to me.

"He did fine through the night, but this early morning developed a fever. We understand he was a stray?" he asks, eyebrow raised. I simply nod yes, as does Katie.

"Not sure exactly what caused it... hard to tell when we don't have a medical history, but I can tell you that overall he's in pretty good shape or he would likely not have survived this. I put him on an antibiotic drip and fluids and almost immediately his fever went down, but he is still a bit lethargic. He is strong though, and will more than likely come through this little set back too."

With a smile to Katie and a hand on her arm he asks, "Would you like to see him?"

Almost. I almost grab the guy's hand and break his fingers. The urge is strong, and I don't care that he probably remembers the Beatles' first visit to the US as if it were yesterday. Katie must've felt the tension in my body 'cause she twists her head back and through the slight sheen of wetness in her eyes, the look she throws me sparkles with mischief.

"*Behave,*" she whispers. To the vet she says she'd love to see Blue, and we are lead back through a long hallway lined with wire kennels housing a variety of animals that, as the guy explains, are waiting for their surgery. Poor saps.

The smell hits me first; it smells like sickness in here. Now granted, I'm not digging the whole antiseptic smell of this place. It doesn't quite seem to hide all the underlying odors, but in here, it makes for a cloying combination.

He leads us to a kennel on the far side and opens the door on the middle one.

"We put him in here, so we could slide him in right off the gurney. He's a big boy and we didn't want to jar him too much by lifting him. You can lean right in."

Lying on his side, the poor mutt looks even worse than he did before. In fact, if it weren't for the fact that I can see his chest moving, I'd have passed him off as gone. Leaning into the kennel, Katie pushes one of her crutches at me to hold and sticks her hand in to pet his fur carefully, mumbling softly in his ear. Hardly noticeable at first, but with increasing strength, his tail starts to wag and I nudge Katie.

"Atta boy, Blue. You gotta stay another night, but tomorrow we'll come get you, okay? And you'd better get prepared to live in a house, 'cause I'm not letting you go."

The slow lift of an eyelid reveals a watery and rather red-rimmed signature blue eye, catching Katie straight on. I'll be damned. Fucking dog. Katie leans in and kisses that dirty mutt right on the nose before turning to me, "Let's go."

With the agreement we'll call first thing tomorrow morning to confirm his pick up for noon, and the assurance that Katie can call to check on him as much as she wants, we head out to the Tahoe. I'm about to lift her into the cab when she throws her arms around me and kisses me full on the lips. I lean into the kiss before suddenly pulling back.

"Hey! You just kissed that dirty mutt with those lips."

"Yeah, but he's part of the family now, so deal."

Eyes sparkling, smile on her face, the disappointment of a few moments ago gone, I feel I've got it all, and I want to give it all back.

"About that..." I start, "I've been trying to find the bitch who was supposed be looking after you—your adoptive mother? I may have found something."

The surprised look on Katie's face is quickly replaced with a darker one. Not the look I was going for.

"Was meaning to talk to you about that," she bites off, "but as usual, shit got in the way. Tell me."

How the hell did she find out? Neil. That little fuckface. Fine. All or nothing.

"Asked a buddy who served with me to look into it. Former Ranger who works from Denver tracking missing people. Denver, 'cause Neil told me that is the last place there is any official record of her. Phil, my buddy, took her latest DMV picture to the streets and got a hit. She was known as Cora and hung around the Pearl Street Mall for a few years but hadn't been seen the last two. When he checked deeper, he discovered that during an extreme cold spell in 2013, in total three homeless people had died due to exposure. One still only identified as Jane Doe."

Realization spreads over Katie's face and I wrap my arms around her and quickly lift her up into the cab before she falls down. Cupping her face in my hands, I look in her eyes. "You okay, sweets?"

Nodding, she motions for me to go on; her lips firmly pressed together.

"Phil took her particulars, the information he got from the streets and his suspicions to the coroner's office and we are waiting for confirmation, but he's pretty sure it's her."

The sob that escapes her lips has me second-guess my decision to tell her. *Christ*. Did I fuck up again? Did I just break her heart even more?

"I'm sorry," I mumble in her hair as I wrap her in my arms. Idiot. But then I feel her hands pushing me back so I move.

Her eyes wet with yet more tears, she scowls at me. "Be sorry for going behind my back, Caleb Whitetail; however well-intended, but don't be sorry for what karma decided to dole out. I wouldn't wish a death like that on anyone and I am sorry her life ended like that, but hers consisted of a series of self-destructive choices that not only carried consequences for her, but my dad and me as well."

Wiping her nose on her sleeve she continues, "I'm emotional because that's all I seem to be these days and it is fucking driving me insane!" Her voice goes up in frustration as a stubborn tear manages to escape her tightly squeezed eyelids.

I sweep her hair off her forehead and lean mine against it. "I just wanted to give you a chance for the family you deserve, Katie," I tell her, a rasp to my voice.

Her hands come up to hold my cheeks and her luminescent green eyes look straight into my dark ones.

"Silly man, I already have all the family I need right here."

CHAPTER TWENTY-SEVEN

It's mid-afternoon when we walk in the door and the house is bustling with activity. Hell, it's a Saturday and still Clint has his crew working non-stop. Okay, they'd had the Thursday off, but that was almost negligible with the damage that was done to their work that day.

"Hey Clint!" I yell from the bottom of the stairs.

"Little lady," his smiling face appears in the opening above me.

"Didn't think you guys would come in today?"

"Actually just finishing up a few loose ends. I'm putting the crew on a new project next week and it'll just be me here from time to time, to see what your man needs assistance with. He's determined to do the rest himself."

I turn to look at Caleb's smiling face. He seems happy – relaxed almost – and we're still neck deep in shit with this case, but it doesn't seem to dampen his mood. He wants to wield a hammer and get dirty; he can be my guest. I might be willing to pick up a paintbrush, but that's about as far as I'll go. Now outside, that's a different ballgame altogether. I can't wait to get Seb's little sister Faith over here and start working on a garden for the summer.

Leaving the men to talk about plumbing, scheduling the elevator delivery and other mind-numbing stuff, I hoist the bags of stuff Caleb brought in over to the kitchen table and start unpacking. A little pang when I pull out the gigantic dog bed we bought Blue, reminds me that we've had to leave him behind, but it makes me feel better to find a place for it beside the couch; not too far from the fireplace. The vet mentioned he would have the appropriate food ready for him, so we never bothered picking that up; I assume we'll get it tomorrow - and the two giant metal bowls to hold his kibble and water are beside the island on the floor. Whether or not Blue would decide to stay with us, I don't know, but if and when he does, I'm gonna make damn sure he is at home.

The next bag I take into the bedroom, closing the door behind me.

The slight tilt of the bed startles me and I find Caleb sitting on the edge of the bed beside me. I must've dozed off.

"I can't believe how small they are."

His fingers toy with the little socks I am clutching in my hand. I can't help but smile. His hand looks ridiculously huge in comparison.

Lifting my eyes to his, I see a hint of concern on his beautiful face.

"We haven't really talked about this yet, have we?" he says, his fingers now lazily tracing my hairline. I simply shake my head.

"I..." he stops, runs his hand through his hair and starts again, "I realize everything about us has gone into fast-forward for you, and that this may not have been how you envisioned your future, but Katie, it's everything I've lived and breathed for for the past four years. Fuck, it's more. The first time I touched you was the last time I ever touched another woman. This baby... I'm gonna be an old asshat of a father, but I so want this baby... with you."

Scooting back in the bed, I tug on his arm until he lays down beside me and I can crawl up on his chest and look down in his face.

"You listen and listen carefully. If I had known any of this was even remotely possible for me. If I had known this kind of thing existed, I wouldn't have wasted four years on something I thought I was only good for. I recognized you for the man you are four years ago, Caleb, and all I knew was that what you deserved was not in me to give. You have the most beautiful soul of anyone I know and why you have chosen to save it all these years... to save yourself for me, I'll never understand, but I won't question it. Not anymore. I love you, and if someone like you can love me. Hell, that must mean I'm loveable too. Building a family together? God, you've handed me the world on a platter."

My face is wet with tears that have been streaming down my cheeks since Caleb started talking and when his strong arms crush me to his chest and his hand presses my face in his neck I can feel his face is wet too. Fuck, we're a mess.

"You gut me, *Yázhí*," he chokes on his words.

My eyes are gritty as my eyelids slowly open up to Katie draped over my chest sleeping deeply, the receding light of the day throwing a hazy light over the room. Another buzz from the vicinity of my hip reminds me what woke me up in the first place and I shift her body slightly to fish my phone out of my pocket.

"Yeah," I croak, my voice still rusty from sleep and lingering emotion as I try to slide out from under my warm wrap, but her eyes blink open at the disturbance, looking straight at me.

I sit up and hold her gaze while listening to Gus's update, struggling to keep my focus.

"What time is it now?" I ask him.

"Okay, give us an hour to clear some stuff up and then meet us there."

Sitting up now, Katie's eyebrows are raised in question.

"That was Gus with some news. Joe spoke with Teva from Grand Junction and they picked up Larchwood's facility director."

"Holman?" The confusion is clear on Katie's face.

"One and the same. Rolf Baird, the man now sans package, finally decided to sing when he found out he was being linked to one of the large Mexican cartels. That was apparently a bit too rich for his blood and he spilled that Director Holman had contacted him through a 'mutual acquaintance' and given him fifteen grand to, in his words, "take you out.""

"Holman?" Katie repeats, the look of incredulity still firmly in place.

"That's him."

"But why?"

"My guess, and apparently Sergeant Teva's also, is that Holman was well aware of who your old neighbor was and was paid handsomely to keep his possible indiscretions due to his mental confusion under tight wraps. You mentioned Sue had her suspicions already and had tried looking into his files but was caught by Holman himself, right? So he must've been spooked when he saw her talking to you. Especially after the scene in your room with Ernesto. I'm guessing the older Duarte brother was none too pleased his father was able to fraternize with other residents so freely and called Holman out on it. It may well have been Holman responsible for killing Sue and it appears he is now trying to clean up all loose ends by taking care of you too."

"Huh. What do you know? Never liked that douchebag. Always seemed too much like a politician to me. All smooth and slimy."

"Anyway, that puts a bit of a new light on our possible interactions with the cartel and is something we have to talk over with Mal. Gus wants us to all meet, but I want you to meet him first."

A small smile ghosts over her lips.

"Okay, but why keep him hidden in the first place? I never questioned it because... well, you know, your family and all that."

I lean in and kiss her hard, leaving my lips on hers when I say, "yours too. Sorry to say he's a bit of an asswipe though."

Katie giggles at that. First fucking time I've ever heard her giggle. Such a girlish sound to come from her, so I just stare.

"Stop gawking at me and let's get cleaned up." Blushing and suddenly all business, she's off the bed and in her wheelchair before I can even say a word.

"That was cute."

"What?" She pretends not to know what I'm talking about.

"The giggle thing. Cute."

Pulling off my shirt to get into a fresh one, one at least a little dryer, I catch the look she throws me over her shoulder. And the smile shining in her eyes.

It being a Saturday at dinnertime, the parking lot at the diner is full up in front of the building, which suits me just fine. I pull around the back and park beside the new stairway to the second floor apartment and the dumpsters flanking the kitchen entrance.

"He's here?" Katie looks around as if he is about to come walking out of the woods and I chuckle.

"Upstairs, sweets. Seb's known, although how he has been able to keep it from Arlene, I have no idea. Mal is very good at being extremely quiet, I can attest to that, but when Arlene finds out Seb's been keeping a secret, all hell's gonna break loose."

"Would love to be a fly on the wall," she snickers, "Although, Seb does have a way with her. He's the ultimate 'Arlene-whisperer'. As bristly and sharp as she can get, one touch or word from him and you can just see her melt. Kinda endearing, really."

"Reminds me of someone I know," I say in a low voice right by her ear, earning me a well-aimed punch to my bicep. *Fuck.* Forgot how lethal those little fists can be.

"*Not* me," she huffs, opening the door and letting herself out.

I scramble to get to the other side, but Seb apparently saw us pull in from the kitchen window, because he's already hugging her when I come around the trunk.

"Coming in or going up?" he wants to know.

"In," I say at the same time as Katie resolutely states, "up!"

I hang my head and shake it, Seb chuckling in the background.

"Fine. Up it is." I hand Katie her crutches, which she uses more and more on short treks. She grabs them and with a triumphant smirk turns around and heads for the stairs. Behind me I hear Seb laughing, "didn't take her long to get you on her leash."

"Fuck off. Go check on your own hellion."

"I embrace my leash, buddy. You will too. Give it time."

He walks back in the kitchen chuckling. Bastard.

I hustle to follow Katie who is already one third up the stairs.

"Babe. Not a sprint. Give me a chance to introduce you."

"Then get your old butt in gear, honey, or eat my dust," she says, laughing all the way up the stairs, her competitive streak coming out to play.

"That ass is gonna be red tonight, little one. Count on it." I growl and the deep raspy laugh that rolls down the steps only serves to fire up the lust that is making my blood pool in my already rigid cock. Fuck me.

When I reach the top I adjust myself, but not before my brother's rumbling chuckle comes from the open doorway. My hand in the small of her back, I guide Katie inside, where the idiot stands grinning from ear to ear.

"Can't blame ya, Jefe. I like her already."

Smartass.

"Jefe?" Katie picks up on that of course, but I ignore it, introducing them instead.

"Katie, this is my brother, Malachi. Mal, meet Katie, and behave." I add as an afterthought when I see the glint in his eyes. Always a hit with the ladies, Malachi knows how to play up his Navajo roots by leaving his hair long and wearing it loose most of the time. For some reason chicks go nuts over it. To me, it was always a pain in the ass, and as soon as I enlisted I was required to shave it. Katie sticks out a hand to shake but Mal, in true player fashion, only uses it to pull her closer and wraps her in a big hug. Wiggling his eyebrows at my over her shoulder.

Asshole. But then he takes it a step too far when he lets his hands wander too low, and too close to Katie's ass.

I simply step back with my arms crossed over my chest and a smirk on my face, because my little brother just fucked up good. Still hamming it up to me, he has no idea what my little hellcat has in store for him.

The moment his hands touch her butt, I see his facial expression change and he jumps back with a yelp, slapping his hands over his nipples.

"Ouch! That fucking hurt!"

"It's called a nipple twist. Very effective for both women and men alike. Especially gropy douche bags who don't know how to keep their hands off their brother's woman."

Oh, this is fun. My girl is in full swing now.

"For the record, you might have success with some big-boobed, small-assed, pea-brained bitches, flaunting those pearly whites and that luscious shiny black hair, Bubba, but when you approach a regular woman with a brain and some self-respect, you better ask permission first before you feel her up!"

By now I'm bent over laughing so hard I have tears running down my face. About fucking time someone got in that cocky bastard's face. And who better to do it than my little one. Man, she's something.

On impulse, I tap her shoulder and she whips around, biting off, "what?"

"May I?" I ask politely, before bending her over my arm and kissing the breath out of her. Right. There.

I have to pull back before I make a spectacle out of us in front of my brother, but not before I mumble against her ear,

"That was fucking hot," and leave her wiping the hair out of her eyes with a smile on her face.

Stupid Malachi just stands there with a grin on his face.

"Yup, like I said, liking her already."

"Jury's still out on you, Bubba. So far you're not scoring any brownie points," Katie huffs as she manages to work her way past him into the apartment.

I hold him back when he tries to go in after her.

"Hold up, man. You disrespect my woman again and we have problems. She can take care of herself, as you can see, but that doesn't mean I'll stand by and let that happen. Just so we're clear. And another thing you should know is that that woman in there is smarter, faster, and has more courage in her pinkie finger than you and I put together. Do. Not. Underestimate. Her." I underscore every word with a forefinger poked in his chest. Something I know he absolutely hates and has since we were kids. But this has to be clear right now.

"Brother, I had my fun. I'm done. I swear. I'm not blind to a good woman. Don't make the mistake of underestimating me either. I know you've seen me as one thing for years and I can't blame you, I've done the same to you. Enough now though. Enough."

With a hand to my neck he draws me into an embrace and for the second time that day I find myself choked up.

Pussy.

We have about half an hour of surprisingly comfortable conversation. Katie warms up to Mal, even laughing at his jokes before we hear two pairs of footsteps coming up the outside stairway and just like that the entire room is buzzing with an alert energy. Katie has her gun in hand and is on her knees beside the coffee table, Mal is against the wall at the door opening to the little foyer and I'm at the ready by the peephole in the apartment door.

When I see Gus's dark hair appear, I let the breath I was holding slowly escape and shake my head in Mal's direction. Gus's voice outside only confirms it and when I crank the door, I see Neil standing behind him with that big goofy grin on his face.

"The fuck did you guys come from? We didn't hear the truck?"

"Hello to you too," Gus pushes past me to face off with Mal who has stepped into the foyer behind me. "We had dinner first, figured we'd give you a minute for the family reunion. Truck's in front, we came through the kitchen and Seb's got the door on a stop. Hotter than hell in there."

Noticing the way the two are staring each other down, I make quick work of introductions, but from the 'barely-there' chin lifts and lack of handshake I'd say there's not gonna be a lot of love lost between Malachi and Gus. Neil, however, does not seem to have any compunction about pumping Mal's hand and slapping him on the shoulder like some long lost relative. Kid is fucking nuts.

A squeal from inside tells me Katie has caught sight of Neil. He walks with a distinct limp and I realize he must still be sore, but you wouldn't know it to look at him. Points for the kid.

By the time I follow everyone is inside, Katie is hanging off Neil's neck, smiling huge and making him blush—something that propels me to walk over, snag her around the waist and tuck her to my side, effectively pulling her arms from around his neck, and that apparently is because for everyone in the room to burst out laughing. Fuckers.

CHAPTER TWENTY-EIGHT

"So what is our next move?"

Caleb is deferring to Gus, once the tension-breaking hilarity has settled down and everyone has found a place to sit. Caleb's arm still firmly around me, anchoring me to his hip on the couch in an ongoing show of ownership that makes me chuckle inwardly.

"Joe is in constant communication with the GJPD getting updates on their investigation of Holman and it looks like the case against him is tightening up nicely. The only loose thread is the presence of one Ernesto Duarte at, and the disappearance of Juan Duarte from Larchwood around the same time the murder took place. I spoke with my FBI contact to pass on this latest information and the feds aren't too happy that they may not be able to use this murder to put the nail in the cartel's coffin. Passed on Teva's digits to them so they can confirm the case details with her, but as far as the murder goes; unless Holman fingers Ernesto, which is highly unlikely given the cartel's reach, he is off the hook."

"So one way or another, we need to talk to Duarte," Neil offers, earning a nod from Gus.

"Right. The only way to clear up this mess is to convince him he has a loose cannon among his own men, in order to get the target off Malachi's back and the heat off Katie. She's still the only one who can put him in Grand Junction at the time of the murder but that is almost a moot point with the murderer behind bars. I recorded my conversation with the FBI contact I can play him, in hopes that might help show our goodwill. As for Malachi's situation–" Gus is interrupted when Mal holds up his hand.

"I'll meet with him–"

"No! He'll shoot you on sight," Caleb shoots up from his seat, "I won't let that happen. He won't stop to listen or ask questions. Can't do it, brother."

I can see the struggle to keep his composure as his nostrils flare and I reach my hand to grab his, squeezing it hard.

"Caleb, sit and listen. First, let Mal finish," I urge him quietly.

For a minute I don't think he's going to react, but then he lets out a harsh breath, drops his chin and turns his eyes to me, worry shining through. A light tug on the hand I'm holding in mine and he drops back down beside me.

"I'll meet with him..." Malachi persists, "after Gus has made contact. The only way for me to ever walk away from this is to face the man head on. I need out of this life. I've had enough, and unless I can convince him of that, there is no moving forward. I'll be too busy looking over my shoulder."

With a pained expression on his face, Mal turns to face Caleb who is keeping his eyes to the floor. "Shínaí, I spent days in the kiva thinking of different possibilities. Even before you came and found me; before we had a name to give to him, I knew this was the way. The *only* way."

Slowly Caleb lifts his eyes and simply nods his understanding.

It's quiet in the room, everyone weighed down with the possible implications of Mal's plans, but no one able to argue its merits. 'Lost his way', something Caleb said to me at some point about his brother suddenly was more evident than ever. This was a man struggling to find his way back. Hell. Willing to face down a possible death squad to get there.

With a framework in place, what is left is hammering out the details, and the next hour or so is spent doing just that. Gus will wait until tomorrow around noon to contact Ernesto, hoping to learn as much as he can from Sergeant Teva in Grand Junction and Manny in Farmington who is still in the process of getting details from Benjamin Chee. Getting a hand on the stolen drugs would go a long way to pacifying the cartel, but hopes that Guzman hadn't moved them as soon as his partner was picked up seem moot.

Locating Guzman himself would of course be the cherry on the cake, but for all we know he is safely tucked away outside of our reach and under the protection of the unsuspecting cartel. The man is a ghost.

Finally Gus gets up and slaps his hands on his thighs.

"I'm starving. I'm heading out. Neil, you coming?"

"Thought we just had dinner?" Neil says, slightly perplexed.

"Who said anything about dinner? I said I'm starving. I have a hot-blooded little redhead waiting at home. I'll be in touch with you lot tomorrow. And you, get your gimpy ass in gear," he directs at a groaning Neil on his way to the door.

"Fucking like bunnies here in Cedar Tree, I swear!" We hear him grumble after his boss, leaving us chuckling at their antics.

"Hungry?" I ask the two guys. None of us have eaten yet.

"I could eat," comes from Caleb.

I turn to Mal. "How about you? Are you able to come down for a bite?"

He shrugs his shoulders and turns to his brother. "Think the crowd has died down enough if we sneak in through the kitchen?"

"It's after seven, we should be ok. Let's go."

Caleb grabs my hand and pulls me up from the couch before handing me my crutches.

"Wanna tackle the stairs yourself or can I hurry shit up and carry you?"

Craving a bit of his body heat I smile, "Heave away, caveman."

"Let me see you"

Caleb has me pinned up against the headboard, his big body wedged between my legs with my hoodie over my head, and trapping my arms. Holding me blinded and immobile with one hand he uses the other to trace the lightly calloused fingertips over my exposed body. The light abrasion of his touch on my skin and the promise of his hot breath following closely behind becomes my entire focus. Near breathless in need, I don't have to see or touch him to feel the reverence with which he adores all of me; tracing, then licking and nipping at every bump and valley; turning the most common of places into erogenous zones.

When he finally lets go of my arms to slide down inch by inch, I can't even bring myself to move. Don't want to do anything to disrupt my utter bliss. Never have I been sexually passive, but giving myself over this completely, feels delicious.

"Gonna prep you babe," he mumbles with his lips buried in the short curls of my pubic hair.

Too busy feeling, I only faintly register his intent, but when he spreads my legs up, wide and completely open, and licks me very thoroughly from the very base of my spine to my clitoris, leaving a wet trail in his wake. I'm starting to get a clearer picture. While his lips and tongue are working that little button, his fingers are teasing my perineum, dragging the wetness from my pussy to my ass, until - finally - he gently inserts a finger causing my spine to arch of the bed. *Oh my God.* That is intense. The firm pumping motion of Caleb's digit paired with the rhythmic sucking on my clit has the entire area between my legs pulsing. Still blind and bound, my hips buck against the deep penetrating finger and his mouth working my pussy - my movements mindless and greedy for release. The sharp hiss at the bite of burning when he inserts a second finger is quickly replaced with a deep guttural groan as I experience the most incredible sensation of fullness. Faster and faster I try to fuck against Caleb plunging in me, and with a sharp sting of his teeth when he bites my clit, Caleb sends me over.

Beautiful.

Her body ripe with my child, in total submission with her hands voluntarily kept over her head, eyes closed - and a light sheen of sweet covering her flushed skin. Fucking gorgeous. It's all I can do not to take her as she lies there, soft and pliable, but I have other plans.

I kiss my way up her body and remove the hoodie tangled around her arms and head. Her short hair is stuck to her flushed face and her eyes are heavy and thick with the remnants of her climax. My Katie.

"You're delicious," I tell her, my mouth covering her lips. "Your flavor is changing, richer and a tad spicier with pregnancy. I like it."

Her mouth twitches under mine as she mumbles, "That's a good thing, 'cause the way you like my pussy, it'd be a long fucking nine months otherwise."

"Not just your pussy, little one..." I pull back and find her bright green eyes darkening with renewed interest. "You liked me playing with your ass."

It's a statement, not so much a question, since the results were obvious from the way she ground herself into my fingers. Holy shit, I had a hard time not coming right there and then. When she started coming, the muscle contractions on my fingers just about cut off all circulation and all I could think about was plunging my cock in. There is no way I'm going to let her deny she loved having me there, so I hold her chin and tell her again, forcing her to look at me.

"You enjoyed my fingers in your ass, didn't you?"

She nods, a slight blush tingeing her cheeks. "I did. It felt amazing," she admits.

"Fuck, baby. I want you so much. You have no idea how much I want to have my cock buried there, feeling your ass tighten around me as you come." My heart is pounding in my chest and my control is hanging on by a thread.

And then she asks, "did you happen to get lube?" and I almost roll off the bed groaning.

"Katie, babe. I'm barely hanging on here, sweets. I'm prepared—been prepared for–" I don't get a chance to say more, which is a good thing because how do explain away buying a bottle of lube 'just in case'? Well I did, but thank fuck Katie is keeping my mouth occupied so I don't have to say another word. Enough talking. My hand finds its way over to my nightstand and pulls out the brand-new purchase and a condom, tucking both under the pillow, ready for grabs. Her eyes have followed my every move and have darkened even more. Her hands come up to pull my head down and she attacks my mouth with lips and tongue. My little hellcat. She twists her fingers in the short strands and the pinch almost brings tears to my eyes, but only stirs up my need for her. My hips nestled between her legs I grind my cock against her heat; the evidence of her earlier release soaking through the thin barrier of my boxers. Perhaps the only thing holding me back from shooting my load here and now. Grabbing both of her arms I stretch them over her head and hold them down with one hand while the other plumps one of her ripe breasts. The arch of her back pushes the pert nipple in my palm and my lips go in search of its mate. Down the generous slope of her chest to the hard little peak that feels like heaven on my tongue. Her moans and mumbled encouragements tell me she is more than ready for me, but I take my time tasting and teasing her twitching body. When I suddenly sit back on my heels, needing to regain some control, a soft whimper leaves her lips and she watches me from between heavy lidded eyes as I shove down my boxers and kick them off. My dick, hard and seeping pre-cum from the crown sits hot against my stomach, and when Katie bites her bottom lip I spring into action. Grabbing a bunch of pillows, I shove them under her lower back, lifting her hips up high.

"You don't want me on my stomach?" she asks, confused.

276

"I need to see your face, *Yázhí*. Your arms are stronger than your legs, hold behind your knees and pull back."

In this position with her ass high and legs high and pulled way back, her luscious pussy is on full display and my hips are perfectly lined up with the dark rose of her puckered hole just below. I quickly roll on the condom, snatch up the tube and flip off the cap, squirting the cool lube liberally around her anus, and then more on my fingers. Sitting back on my heels, I watch my middle finger disappear without problem inside her and I twist and turn, stretching her tissues as I do. Flicking my eyes to her I see her mouth as fallen open as she is lightly panting with the invasion, her eyes glittering from between her eyelids, never leaving mine.

"That feel good, little one?"

"MmmHmm," she groans as I pump my finger a few times and add a second, pulling and stretching as I go.

"Ahhh... Caleb. I need more... That feels so good...," she moans out.

With my left thumb I start playing with her clit, rubbing it lightly.

"Adding one more finger, babe. Don't fight me, just push back on me."

Tightly grouped together and with firm pressure I push through the already loosened ring of muscle before finding my fingers finally sliding in further quite easily.

The sight of her splayed out in front of me, is almost too much and I quickly use my left hand to squirt some lube on my cock, making sure it is nice and slick.

Moving my hips in closer, I slowly pull out my fingers and hear Katie complain at the loss. And before the muscle ring has a chance to fully tighten itself again, I carefully line myself up and work my way into that dark, hot and very tight hole.

"Fuuuuuuuck yesssss." The feeling is indescribable and I have to pause to control the impulse to pound myself balls deep into her.

"Baby, you ok?"

"So good, but Caleb? You gotta move."

No patience with my cautious moves, Katie bites out, "harder" a few times until I'm pumping so hard you can hear the sound of flesh slapping together.

The hitches in Katie's breath tell me she's close and I slip two fingers in her pussy and push down on her clit. The tight muscle contractions of her orgasm around my cock jumpstart my own and I power myself inside the tight channel, once, twice, three times more before my eye almost roll out of my head with the force of my climax. Just as she finishes yelling my name, I bellow out hers when my release bursts free and I allow myself to slide out and slump down on her body.

When I open my eyes, I find her studying me intently.

"Does it feel as decadently unbelievable to you as it does to me?" she wants to know and I chuckle.

"I think I actually blacked out for a moment. Never experienced anything quite like that in my life," I admit, noticing a small smile form on her lips.

I lift myself off her body and head to the bathroom to dispose of the condom and get something to clean us up.

After I quickly wash up and rinse a washcloth with warm water, I head back to find Katie rolled over on her side.

"You sore, little one?"

"A little, but a good sore," she snickers, "like after a good work out."

"Roll back for a minute so I can clean you up."

"I can do that," a small voice of protest comes from the pillow where she is hiding her face, but I'm ignoring it.

"Well aware of that," I say as I firmly roll her on her back and proceed to wipe any remaining lube from between her butt cheeks and around her vaginal area, "but in this case, it is my pleasure to take care of you. And you're gonna let me."

"It's a tad embarrassing," she huffs.

"Nothing embarrassing between us," I lean into her, touching my nose to hers, "not a thing. Not ever. You and I? We can and have and will share the most intimate moments together, and I will treasure every one of them. There is no shame in that. I've never wanted to share with anyone what I share with you."

A tap on her nose before I toss the washcloth in a corner and pull her up on my chest, where she plants a wet kiss before settling in with her arm around my waist.

Why today it was important for me to lay claim to all of her—to imprint myself on every possible part of her. I don't know. Maybe it has to do with her meeting Mal, or maybe it's the lack of control we have of this fucking case we find ourselves in the middle of. No idea. All I know is that part of me that had never quite wanted to settle down, this inner 'caveman' as Katie calls it, suddenly seems to have quieted down.

I press a kiss to her hair when she snuggles deeper in my arms, mumbling, "So glad you were my first..."

For a long time I lie awake with the implication of those innocent words settling into my heart, and my awareness.

CHAPTER TWENTY-NINE

"More coffee?"

Caleb is waving the pot in front of me, since I obviously missed the first time he's asked. My eyes have been glued to Blue who's been sleeping quite peacefully in the massive dog bed beside the couch since we brought him home this morning. The vet said he did fine through the night and although would need to be watched and finish his round of antibiotics, he should be well on the road to recovery. I haven't been able to move away from his side though and Caleb is chuckling at my obsessive fussing.

"Stop laughing at me. The vet said we had to keep an eye on him, so that's what I'm doing," I pout.

Setting the pot on the table, he drops on the couch beside me putting his chin on my shoulder to have a look at Blue himself.

"Not exactly laughing at you, little one. Just enjoying this new side of you—this protective, nurturing side. Figure I'll be seeing a lot more of that."

He slides his hand over my as yet unchanged belly meaningfully. Ah yes. Would it be pregnancy hormones already?

"So how about that coffee, little one? Before it gets cold?"

"Okay fine, but decaf really doesn't put a dent in it, I'll have you know."

A smiling Caleb gets up and fills my mug. "I know," he says, amusement clear in his voice.

I'm enjoying the quiet puttering around this morning, still tender both physically and emotionally from last night, but in a very good, albeit exposed way. Not much was said, but so much learned. I could see the change in Caleb right away; the edge of whatever it was he had been hanging on to was gone this morning. The intensity mellowed some. As for me; for the first time since I've been able to think for myself, I have completely surrendered to a feeling. No reservations, no little voices of caution, no self-doubts or questions of any kind, just an odd sense of letting go of yourself and handing it all to another. Knowing they're as vulnerable to you as you are to them. I always thought it would make you weaker, but it doesn't; it makes you whole.

The ring of a cell phone shakes me out of my musings.

"Can you get that, babe? Just got my hands in suds," Caleb calls out from the kitchen and I grab his phone from the coffee table.

"Hello?"

"Ah, the lovely Ms. Acker, no? It is a surprise, but a very pleasant one I must say."

"Mr. Duarte. To what do we owe the pleasure?" I try to maintain my cool, but I have goose bumps all over my skin at the sound of the smarmy thick Mexican accent. Heavy footsteps approaching alert me Caleb has heard and fast clued in.

"I was hoping to speak with Mr. Whitetail about the whereabouts of his brother, since I had the most interesting conversation with Mr. Flemming just moments ago which has left me with a few questions you perhaps can clear up, now that I have you on the phone."

Caleb tries to grab the phone from my hand, but pulls back at my hard shake no. Instead, I lift the phone away from my ear a little so he can hear both sides of our conversation.

"By all means. I will answer whatever I can."

"It has been brought to my attention that the person responsible for the death of that poor nurse at Larchwood Inns has been caught—"

A shiver runs down my spine at the cold, arrogant and mildly amused tone of his voice, but I answer evenly, "That is as I understand it."

"And that any witnesses concede my perceived presence at the facility would have been likely to collect my ailing father, and bring him back to attend a family tragedy?"

"That would be a very likely assumption," I respond, swallowing hard.

"Very well. One or two more questions, my dear, and I will be, how does one say, '*Out of your hair*'." The almost breathless chuckle is bone chilling, as much as his faux endearments and cold politeness is.

"It appears I may have an employee who has taken a few too many liberties. One who seems to have made it a habit to be a tad overzealous, resulting in the unfortunate demise of an innocent woman, I hear."

Caleb's body freezes next to me and I put a calming hand on his knee. Fucking monster doesn't give a rat's ass and I'll bet he knows damn well Caleb is listening.

"This employee was also instructed to pass on a message from me to you, Ms. Acker. One of a rather urgent nature, but at the insistence of my father, who seems to have taken quite a shine to you. There was to be absolutely no violence involved."

I can't help the snort that escapes me. No violence. The man ran me off the road and tried to shoot me.

"Very well. I believe I have my answer. One last question; Was he alone?"

"No, I couldn't see in the truck very well, but someone else was driving; Guzman was doing the shooting."

Duarte hadn't mentioned his name yet, but he doesn't deny it either, simply thanks me and asks to speak with Caleb. I hand over the phone, sit back and let the conversation replay in my head while listening to Caleb's monosyllabic responses.

A knock on the door interrupts and I grab my crutches, which I've opted for in the house. The unmistakable shape of Gus outside the small glass pane in the front door has me unlocking and opening the door right away.

"Couldn't get through," he says as he steps in.

"My phone must be out of juice and we've been busy on Caleb's with one Ernesto Duarte, but you probably already guessed that?" I offer quietly, not wanting to disturb Caleb's conversation, indicating my head in his direction on the couch.

Following my motion, Gus notices Caleb. "I see. Coffee?"

"Kitchen. Only decaf though."

Eyebrow raised pointedly, he shrugs off his coat and heads in that direction to grab a cup.

"You will hear from me within the next two hours." I hear Caleb say as I take my place next to him on the couch. A low growl from beside me has me look over the armrest to see Blue's head up and eyes open. He looks past me at Gus who slowly approaches.

"S'Okay, buddy. Just Gus. He's good people," I coo, stroking his fur with my fingertips.

"The pooch is back. How's he doing?" Gus wants to know, sitting down in the big club chair on the other side of the coffee table.

"Better," Caleb answers for me, "infection's under control and he should be fine. I'm guessing you're here to warn me about Duarte?"

"Guess he got to you before I could."

"Yup. Had some words for Katie first and then wanted to discuss Malachi. Took all of me not to fucking rip his throat out through the phone."

"Coldest bastard I've every had to deal with, but he loves his family."

"How's that?" I ask Gus.

"That plane crash that got us involved? The one that killed his younger brother? Turns out there was originally twice as much meth in that shipment. Looks like it may not have been an accident. Someone set that plane to go down and exactly where it did too. All arranged to point in the direction of Malachi. Only problem is, the only thing they do know from the investigation into the crash is that it wasn't shot down. That would have been a pretty easy tell. And Mal wouldn't have had access to the plane before take off in Mexico, so whoever it was had to be closely connected to Duarte himself. That little bit of insight is what ultimately convinced our friend Ernesto that he is barking up the wrong tree and needs to look closer to home. All I know is I don't want to be Guzman when Duarte gets his hands on him. He's been known to keep his enemies alive for months while killing them."

Gus takes a sip of his coffee, and with a grimace plunks his mug back on the table before turning to Caleb.

"This tastes like horse pee. You on a new health kick?" He asks him, making me snicker, which turns both guys' eyes on me. Oops. Little too much of the attention, making me very uncomfortable. Especially since Gus's eyes have that calculating gleam when he moves them between Caleb and I.

Thank God, Caleb breaks the tension, by ignoring Gus completely and moving right along.

"Duarte basically wanted Katie to confirm Guzman's insubordination to him, but the son of a bitch is not ready yet to let go of Mal. He may be a family man, but he's an even bigger businessman. He doesn't want to lose the gateway for his drugs into the states. He thinks Mal and the Klesh is it. Wouldn't listen when I said Mal was out unless I promise him we'll deliver Guzman. He seems to think a trap with Malachi as the bait will draw Guzman out from under whatever rock he is hiding to salvage his hide and his stash. Duarte wants his drugs back and he wants his pound of flesh, and he wants us to deliver."

Caleb leans his head back against the couch and closes his eyes.

"Okay," Gus says after a minute of silence, "here's what we do."

The rest of the afternoon is spent plotting and planning, and when five o'clock rolls around Gus gets up and slides his phone, which has been in constant use the past few hours, in his back pocket.

"All set. I'm heading home, and Neil is on his way to the diner to pick up some grub and Malachi with his gear. They'll be here within the next forty-five minutes with extra hardware. Joe's gonna keep an eye out on access routes with as little fanfare as possible. Don't want to draw any attention, and you two keep your phones charged at all times. I'll be in touch."

And with that Katie and I are alone again. Well, and the dog, which has been sleeping on and off all afternoon barely moving.

"You think he needs to go out?" I ask her.

"Probably not a bad idea, seeing as the last time he did anything must've been at the vet's."

Grumpy and a little wobbly, Blue lets himself be guided out the sliding doors and off the back deck where he stands nose in the air, his ears perked and attentive, before ambling off to the nearest sagebrush. Sniffing around for a minute he goes to lift his leg, but thinks better of it at the last minute, opting instead to sag through his haunches. Too much weight to carry on his front for now, I guess, but I can't resist teasing.

"Anyone tell you you piss like a girl?"

The ice blue glare in my direction tells me the mutt is not amused at my interference, turning his head back to look straight ahead as he continues to void what is a load of fucking epic proportions. When Katie sticks her head out to see if he's ok I tell her, "Your dog's a fucking camel."

"How so?" she asks, hobbling up beside me on her crutches, and for the first time I notice how small she is compared to me. The top of her head barely reaches my chin and her shoulder fits perfectly under my arm, which is where I tuck her tightly as we watch our dog take his massive piss. Romantic.

288

"He's been emptying the tank for five minutes straight."

Chuckling she elbows my ribs. "The drugs will do that to you. Believe me I know. Poor puppy."

Finally done, Blue gingerly straightens his legs and slowly ambles back over to where we're standing. For a while we just stand there, looking out at the receding sun over the mountains in the distance. It's peaceful, with my family tucked against my side, my fingers trailing through the coarse mane of the ugly mutt who's slowly burrowing himself under my skin, and the beginnings of a dream home behind me. I manage to stay in the moment, not allowing the nagging worries and fears around the arrangements and potential dangers for the coming hours and days to spoil this moment right here. First the twitching of his ears and then the low growl emanating from Blue is the early alert that someone is coming up the drive. The crunch of wheels on the gravel is next.

Reluctantly I turn to Katie, lift up her chin and brush my lips over hers.

"Love you, Katie."

"I know honey," she whispers back, "and I love you." Pulling back she straightens herself on her crutches and moves inside. "You coming? The cavalry is here."

By the time I have Blue introduced to Malachi who, surprisingly take to each other right away, Katie and Neil are chatting away in the kitchen pulling out plates and setting out the food Neil picked us up.

"Drinks?" Katie calls out.

"Beer for me. Mal?"

"Sure."

Back in her chair so she can have her hands free, Katie rolls to the table with bottles and napkins in her lap. She looks so... at home. The hint of a smile plays on her lips when she hands out drinks and when she hands me mine I grab her hand and pull her in for a kiss.

"What's that for?" she asks when I let her up for air.

I give a little shrug of my shoulders and try to ignore Neil who is spouting his nonsense to Malachi.

"You know it might not be a bad idea; moving here? Every time I fucking turn around, these people are going at it. Must be something in the water. They screw like rabbits, I swear. Gus and Emma are the same way, and so are Seb and Arlene, it'd be almost sickening if I weren't craving some affection myself, *if* you know what I mean."

For a minute Mal says nothing and just looks at Neil, before responding.

"Well you better not be fucking looking in my direction, pal. I don't do dick."

In the seconds of absolute silence that follow, Neil's mouth drops open, his face hits every shade of red and purple before losing all color completely and I can't hold back anymore and burst out laughing.

"I can't fucking believe your brother thought I was swinging the other way."

Neil is furiously scrubbing the few plates we dirtied while I dry and put them away. We managed to get through dinner although it was clear Neil's usual large appetite had diminished some.

"You run off at the mouth sometimes, Kid. Some of what comes out sounds a little fucked up sometimes. Get over it. Besides, you are kinda pretty," I tease him

I just managed to twist away from his elbow only to have it land in my kidney instead of my gut. *Ouch.*

"You had some hardware?"

"Yeah. Lockbox in the bed of my truck. Let's grab it."

Grabbing his keys from the counter, he leads the way out the door.

When everything is inside piled on the dining table, I can see there are not just ammunition and additional firearms but a bunch of Neil's electronic gadgetry as well.

"That gonna keep him out?" Malachi nods at the table.

"I think the idea is not so much to keep him out, but to let us know when he gets in."

Katie enlightens him from her perch on the couch, her fingers back to stroking Blue beside her.

Smart woman.

CHAPTER THIRTY

"Hey little lady! Whatcha doin' out there?"

It's been a quiet few days since we put our plan to draw Guzman out into the open in place. The guys have been upstairs most of the time, working hard to finish framing in the bedrooms and bathrooms, putting drywall and cement board up and the entire house is constantly covered in a thin layer of dust, despite the heavy duty plastic sheeting we have hanging in the stairwell.

I'm on the deck with Blue and a sketchpad on my lap planning out where I want my garden to go in. It's funny how easily my mind has accepted this as my home as much as it is Caleb's. We haven't even talked about money and finances; how those should be divided or joined, but even that doesn't seem to give me any anxiety. I somehow sense that it will all work itself out once we have our way to the future clear.

A future. One I had never pictured myself in, but so oddly right.

"Clint! How are ya?" I greet the big burly man whose redneck upbringing and bluster no longer hides the kind and solid heart underneath from me. The innocuous little beep of the alarm Neil had installed at the turn-off on the main road had alerted to a visitor, and the lack of follow up a little further down the drive in the form of an obscured camera had reassured me after the first few seconds that whoever was coming up the drive was not a threat. Either Neil or Gus were manning the visuals from the GFI offices only five or so minutes down the road and would sound a different alarm if they saw anything suspicious. Despite the building tension, looking from the outside in, life had all the appearances of going on as usual.

"Just coming to see if you're ready for that elevator yet? The weekend Caleb told me to hold off a few days, but I haven't heard so I thought I'd check in."

He peeks over my shoulder at my doodles and then out into the yard.

"Is that what they call abstract? 'Cause I'm not seeing it."

"That's 'cause it's not there yet. Planning the garden. I want it in as soon as possible. Thought I'd plan it out first, makes it easier once we get going," I smile at him. "If you're looking to talk to Caleb, just follow the sound of drilling and prepare to get dusty. They're in the ensuite bathroom this morning I think." Pointing with my pencil over my shoulder I add, "and there's fresh coffee in the pot, but it's decaf I warn you."

Grumbling about idiots on health kicks, Clint ambles off inside, leaving me back to envisioning this summer and fall's bounty.

"How are you doing? Kendra says you've missed a few sessions so I thought I'd check in. Everything alright?"

"Hey. Yes everything is fine, we've just been really busy with Caleb's brother in town and work on the barn. I've been keeping up with exercises though, and been walking on crutches as much as I can, but mostly in the house."

I can't tell Naomi the real reasons I haven't been in Cortez all week. I feel bad for lying to her but there's no use in involving her in any way.

"What about the pregnancy? Any issues? Morning sickness, extra sensitivity, any other complaints? I assume it's still being kept quiet?"

"Jeeze, you're full of questions," I chuckle at her staccato inquiries.

"No, no, no, no and yes, to answer them all and trust me. I'd be on the phone to you so fast, your head would spin. I have no experience with this, never had a sister or girlfriend who went through this and am gonna need to do some serious reading up at some point, but for now I'm counting on you to guide me through."

"Okay, okay. I'm just checking up."

"Look; as soon as this drywall shit is done and the dust has settled, literally, you're gonna have to come over and have a visit, okay? I just spent the morning planning my vegetable garden."

"Can't wait, and don't be a stranger," Naomi responds before she hangs up.

The moment I put down the phone two arms slide around me from behind and a deep voice rumbles in my ear.

"What's that you've got there?"

"Sandwiches. Was just gonna call you guys down when Naomi called."

"That who that was?"

"Yeah, just checking in since I've skipped a few sessions at Kendra."

A wet slide of lips at the juncture of my neck and shoulder sends a little shiver down to the tips of my breasts, perking up enthusiastically.

And then Clint walks in the kitchen.

"Lunch! Awesome, I'm starving."

And the moment is gone. From the groan behind me, Caleb can feel the loss of it as much as I do.

With Mal not far behind, I deduct it is time to feed the animals and shove the plate with sandwiches in Caleb's hands to take to the table, which he does after planting a quick hard one on my lips. I open the fridge door, but before I have a chance to ask around for drinks, Mal is beside me with his arm around my shoulders.

"Go sit down, little sister," he tells me softly, kissing the side of my head, "I've got this."

Not having had much direct interaction with Mal since he moved in and has been camping out on our couch on Sunday, this move touches me. I have sensed a person much different from the one he likes to portray underneath the surface; one who doesn't trust easily, and he at times has reminded me much of Blue. Observant, distant, threatening and all bluster; intended to hide a fear of trust. Thick, thick layers of self-protection that I've just seen crack a little. Not trusting myself to speak, I simply nod and with a firm hold on my crutches I do as I'm told, blinking my eyes to clear my vision.

"Why do we need the elevator at all?"

I've listened to Clint and Caleb go back and forth about the stupid elevator contractor not being able to wait any longer before he is needed on another job. They stop and look at me.

"Babe, the shaft is built already."

"I get that, but seriously—"

"Seriously," Caleb interrupts me, earning him a glare, which only makes him smile, "since it is already there, it might as well go in as planned. You never know when it comes in handy. Life is funny, right little one?" He looks at me from under his heavyset eyebrows and makes me think. I hate when he makes me think and trying to get a point across. I hate it even more that I'm getting it. We're getting an elevator. Crud.

"But," he continues to Clint, "I do agree with Katie that the urgency we had isn't there anymore, so you can tell the contractor to handle the other job and not wait around for us to be ready. He can contact me when he has a spot in his schedule and we'll work something out."

Clint nods, "that'll do."

Not long after when there are nothing but crumbs left on the plate, Clint is gone to look in on his crew working in Cortez somewhere, and Caleb and Mal are back to screwing in drywall. I settle in on the couch, flip up my laptop and soon lose myself in the wonders of nine months of gestation.

"Hey, little one." The soft hum of Caleb's lips against the shell of my ear wakes me up. Once again I've dozed off without intending to, something that seems to happen from time to time lately. Blinking the sleep from my eyes, I see his stern face leaning over me, but his eyes hold all the tenderness I need. Over his shoulder, Mal is sitting at the kitchen island, a beer in hand, wearing a smile.

"Hey," I yawn; my eyes back to Caleb, who watches through squinting eyes as I stretch. "I fell asleep," I state the obvious.

"Noticed that," he says as he sits down and pulls me on his lap burying his face in my neck, "and if you stick your tits out any further, I can't promise I'll hold back even with my brother looking on," he growls in a low voice I hope not loud enough for Mal to overhear.

"Caleb!" I try to push off him, but he has me locked tight in his arms. Sneaking a peek at his brother whose shaking shoulders are clear evidence he hasn't missed a word, my embarrassment is complete. Fuck my life and being surrounded by all these grunting Neanderthals. Can't a person have a little nap around here?

"Settle down, sweets. We've run out of the right size drywall screws, so I have to run into Cortez. I just wanted to let you know. We're almost done the last of it before we can do the taping, which I'd really love to start tomorrow."

"Can't someone else pick it up?" My embarrassment quickly forgotten I frame his face in my hands and kiss his lips, mumbling, "please?"

"Appearances have to be as normal, *Yázhí*, you know that. I've called Gus who is going to 'drop in' here with some food from the diner, which is not unusual since we're in the middle of construction, and we'll time it so you'll always have that extra man. Besides, when I talked to Joe earlier he said there had been no movement whatsoever. No flags have gone up anywhere. I wouldn't be surprised if the coward's in South America somewhere with his stash, living it up."

There is nothing to say, because of course he is right and I'm impatient for this to be over. So I stick my lip out. It works about as well as it did last time 'cause Caleb chuckles, "Doing that mopey thing again? Cute."

I'm fighting it but I lose. The smile wins. I can be *such* a girl sometimes. It's horrible, but the guys seem to think it's hilarious.

"Go fucking buy your screws, okay?" I manage to crawl off his lap and shoo him away with my hands, my cheeks sore from the big grin I'm trying to suppress.

I love how I'm being an idiot and still this man can make me feel special and safe. Not only that, but even Malachi's laughter at my expense feels more like a comfortable and loving tease than a hurtful mockery. Amazing how one moment you realize it isn't so much how people treat you that holds the power, but how you interpret and react to the treatment.

A few minutes later, Caleb is on his way to the hardware store, and Mal drops down beside me on the couch.

"How far along?"

"Sorry?"

"Had my eyes on you for a few days now, the way you drop off to sleep, the emotional swings, on the dog that hovers around you. The way Caleb handles you. How pregnant are you?"

My mouth drops open in stunned disbelief. How. The. Fuck?

"Emotional swings?" is what actually leaves my mouth. Not any of the other very insightful stuff he brings up, but that specifically.

Throwing back his head he laughs out loud and suddenly I see the beauty in Mal that I can always see in Caleb. "How would you know to recognize any of that shit anyway?"

The moment I say that, the smile disappears from his face and it's as if shutters drop over his eyes.

"I had a friend..." But he stops right there, and I don't push. It's enough to hear the pinch of pain in those four words. Instead I grab his hand and tell him.

"Only very early. At most four weeks, so we are trying to keep it quiet. Also 'cause... well, you know. This whole thing is still hanging over our heads, and we have barely had a chance to be together."

"I'm glad for you. Both of you. He deserves a family again."

I don't have anything to say to that. I agree, we both deserve a family and I'll happily take Mal as part of mine; he looks so lost.

The muted beep breaks through the silence in the room and has Mal jump up and grab the gun from the small of his back. Blue growls softly from his bed beside the couch, ready to spring into action, but the lack of a second warning is once again reassuring.

By the time Gus pulls up to the barn, Mal is already opening the door.

"Sorry it took me a bit," he says as he walks in, putting two bags filled with containers on the kitchen island. "I walked in on a bit of drama with Beth all up in Clint's face." He chuckles, "should've seen the man; I've never seen anyone look so stumped."

"Clint? He left here a while ago, saying he was heading to Cortez must've changed his mind."

"Well he's on his way there now, I'm sure. He left the diner muttering something about never understanding women and why he ever thought '*this one*' was any different. I had to call Seb from the kitchen to give me a hand, 'cause all the girls followed a crying Beth into the washrooms."

When I open my mouth to ask him the first of the many questions bubbling to the surface, he sticks up his hand, "Don't ask me. I don't know the scoop. I don't *want* to know the scoop, and I'm sure if you can wait until tomorrow, the *scoop* will come to you, whether you want to hear it or not. Probably in the form of that mouthy redhead of mine."

I snicker at Gus's show of exasperation when he talks about Emma, because that's all it is; show. I know as well as he does that anything that woman does is born of concern for others and not out any malicious intent to gossip. If anything is going on with Beth and Clint, she'll likely want to feel me out to see if Clint has dropped any hints about Beth and I really, I'll have nothing to give her. Nothing but suspicions that is.

Mal is digging through the bags, "Fuck that smells good, what is it?"

"I brought a little bit of everything. Seb had something called Bouillabaisse, some kind of fish soup as a special, but given Katie's condition, I wasn't sure if she could have it, so I brought some other stuff too."

Once again, I am stupefied and look at Gus with my mouth hanging open. I can hear Malachi chuckle in the background.

"Excuse me?" I manage to get out.

"Come on, Katie. I'm not blind or stupid. And apparently I'm not the only who guessed either, by the sound of your brother in law's snickering."

"But... but does everyone know?"

This is not how I had envisioned this going. I did not want the entire world to find out without having a chance to tell anyone myself.

"Can't say for sure, but I doubt it. Only one who has seen much of you recently is Neil and he's usually got his head up his ass so far he's staring at his own tonsils. Not for me to tell anyone else, that's up to you, but a word of warning. Don't hold off too long. My Emma has a sixth sense better developed than anyone's I know."

Wrapping his long arms around me, he tucks me under his chin, the shape of him now only a familiar comfort.

"So happy for you. This is what you've always deserved," his voice rumbles from his chest.

Hauling my fist back I punch him in the side.

"Fuck! Ouch, what was that for?" he asks, rubbing his side as I worm out of his grip.

"For making me all emotional and slobbery. Quit saying nice stuff already."

"Fine. I gotta head out anyway. Caleb should be here shortly and I don't wanna overstay my welcome," he says throwing a teasing look my way. My response is to stick out my tongue at him. Very mature.

The moment he's gone, I find Malachi looking at me.

"What?"

"You are one weird bird," he says slowly shaking his head.

I snort and tell him, "And you wouldn't be the first one to say that."

We just have the food on the table when the first beep announces Caleb's return. Despite knowing it's him, Mal still finds his spot behind the door with his hand on his gun, but as soon as Caleb's car drives up, he tucks it away.

"It's him."

"Okay," I call back from the kitchen, but when after a few minutes I still don't hear anything I look to the front to see Mal intently staring out the little window. "What's up?"

"Dunno. He's just sitting in the car. I think he must be talking on the hands-free."

"Well come sit down. He'll come in when he's done," I suggest.

Shrugging his shoulders, Mal turns away from the little window and comes to sit down across from me, and starts to pile food on his plate.

When finally the front door opens I immediately call out, "Hi honey, dinner's on the table," and only then notice the frozen expression on Mal's face across from me. He is watching the doorway behind me and I finally hear the increasingly loud growl of the dog at my feet. My eyes flick to the reflection in the sliding doors behind Mal and I can clearly see the outline of a second shadow behind Caleb. *Fuck.*

Aware there is no way to get my gun from the coffee table unnoticed, I feel the edge of the little wooden knife that came in the cutlery set with the diner food under my fingers on the table, and slip it in my sleeve. You never know.

"Well, well, well..."

CHAPTER THIRTY-ONE

"I need the longer ones; the ceiling screws," I tell the young clerk at the hardware store who has pulled out every type of drywall screw except the right size so far. Diving back behind the counter and pulling at the large number of small drawers again, he comes back with another three samples for me to pick from. Been here too long already and I'm getting antsy. I wasn't happy about leaving Katie and Mal home alone to start with, but finding the regular old geezer who owns the place out on an errand and having to deal with this young kid left in charge of the store is seriously testing my patience.

Luckily this last trio of screws has one that looks close enough. I hold it up.

"This one. Give me about a hundred of these. Just to be on the safe side."

Then the counting starts. Sweet Jesus. I don't think the kid's finished elementary school. Every time he reaches twenty, he gets flustered and has to start again. Finally I take the drawer from his hands and say, "Count with me, okay?"

Hearing the irritation in my voice, he simply nods his head. I figure since he only seems able to get to twenty, I count out five piles of twenty and just to make sure he gets it, I clarify that five times twenty makes one hundred. From the fervent nodding of his head and the fact he is shoving them all in a brown paper bag, I'm thinking he's with the program. Thank fuck. I don't think I could've taken much more of this.

Bag in one hand, bought and paid for and my keys in the other, I walk up to the Tahoe on the far end of the parking lot. I click the remote lock and open the door to toss the bag on the passenger seat when I feel the cold steel of a barrel behind my ear. *Damn.* I wasn't paying attention and somehow walked right into this one.

"Take your gun out between thumb and index finger," I hear behind me, "drop it to the ground and kick it under the truck."

When I hesitate, my mind going a mile a minute he leans in and hisses, "Do it *now* and don't try anything or you won't be the only one with a bullet hole, *esé*. Promise."

Looking around me at the relatively busy strip mall I'm at, I know I can't take any chances and do as he says.

When I slide in my seat, my eyes immediately go to the rear-view mirror and I get my first glimpse of Gorge Guzman.

"Eyes forward, *pendejo*. Let's go."

Feigning ignorance I shrug and say, "Go where?"

"Don't play me. Bring me to your *pedazo de mierda* brother," Guzman spits out with venom.

I remind myself that although this is not the scenario we had counted on, there may still be a way to turn it around. That is if Gus is still at the house. So I turn the keys in the ignition and start driving toward Cedar Tree.

A few times during the drive I try to pull Guzman into conversation, but each time he cuts me off, getting more and more agitated. I strongly suspect he may be heavily into the shit he peddles from the sweat on his face and the constant twitching of his eyes. Finally giving up I spend the rest of the time working through all different scenarios—most of those involve Gus's presence at the bar. So when I pull into my driveway and I see his Yukon drive towards me on his way out, my heart sinks. I feel the barrel of Guzman's gun sliding between the top of my seat and the headrest and his voice quietly states, "don't even think about it or she suffers."

"I have to acknowledge him," I say, at same time lifting my hand off the wheel in a risky and very uncharacteristic move. I hope Gus catches on, and as if it is the most natural thing in the world, I give him a military salute as his car passes mine on the narrow drive.

"The fuck was that?" Guzman is losing his cool in the back seat, jabbing the barrel in my skull and I'm having a hard time not reacting. "Did you just signal him?"

"Are you a moron? Check behind you. Does it look like he's turning around? Chill out man, if I'd have let him drive by without a wave he would've been suspicious."

I stop in front of the barn and keep half an eye on the door, willing it to stay closed. I hope to be able to avoid going into the house, but I need for Gus to clue in for that. He's taking a fucking long time.

"What are you on?"

"On? The hell are you talking about? I'm not *on* anything. Shut up, you mother-fucker! You don't know nothin'."

"Come on, man. You're twitching all over the place. What is it meth? Your boss know this? Ernesto aware you're testing the goods?"

A sharp hit with the butt of the gun against the side of my skull has black dots dancing in front of my eyes. Fucking hell. That hurts, but I have to keep him distracted and out here.

"*Basta. Dentro...* inside, now!"

I think about it; about trying to take him down and damn the risk for me, but knowing the people most important to me are inside and possibly completely unaware holds me back. I can't protect them if I'm dead and even if I manage to take out Guzman, there will always be the threat of Duarte who expects a delivery. No. This can only end one way.

I push the door open and the first thing I hear is the dog's low growl. Katie has her back to me, apparently unaware we have company, but Malachi freezes in place. I just look at him and tell him with my eyes to stay calm. No sudden moves. This fucker is so wired and unpredictable we have to wait for the right moment.

I can tell the moment Katie recognizes the situation, her back goes ramrod straight and she suddenly barely moves an inch. My eyes try to catch hers in the reflection on the sliding doors.

"Well, well, well..." Guzman drawls, eager to play the big man. "Just in time for dinner you say?"

I start moving forward, but he suddenly grabs my shoulder.

"Where the fuck is that dog, I can hear him. That dog comes anywhere near me, he's dead, and your woman too. You! Bitch, put that thing outside. Now."

Katie doesn't move, she just sits there not reacting. In fact, not acknowledging at all. Good girl.

"She can't walk. You that dumb you don't know that?"

Another knock over my head, this one brings me down to my knees and the growling gets louder when the hammer on the gun cocks loudly against my head.

"Get that fucking dog outside now!"

Malachi raises his hands in a defensive gesture, palms out and slowly gets up from the table, walking backwards until he hits the glass door. With one hand groping behind him he finds the handle and slowly slides the door open.

"Blue, come."

The damn dog won't go. Won't leave Katie's side but I can't have her move and turn into a target.

"Go on Blue. See Mal." I can hear her voice coax the dog softly.

Reluctantly and with the bristles on his neck standing straight up, Blue comes out from under the table almost crab walking to the back door slowly, his eyes never leaving Guzman and he never once stops the insistent growling. The moment he slips outside, Mal closes the door and Guzman directs him away from the glass.

"Come this way, slowly."

There is blood running down my face and stinging my eyes and I'm fighting to keep my them open and my wits about me. Bastard must've torn the skin. Dropping down to all fours, I create distance between the barrel and my skull. Swearing, Guzman hauls back his big boot and plants it firmly in my ribs bringing me down all the way.

Jesus.

Takes everything out of me to stay sitting and pretend I can't get up, but it's killing me. When that son of a bitch kicks Caleb, I can hear the crack of ribs as he drops down.

In the next moment everything starts happening at once; Malachi is advancing on Guzman who swings his gun on him and fires, stopping him mid-stride and dropping him to the ground. He then turns to me. I'm halfway out of my seat, but Guzman is faster and wraps an arm around my waist.

"Where are you going little *puta?* No big boys to protect you now. All this blood makes me hungry for some pussy."

With his gun under my chin, his hot rancid breath on my cheek and one hand now groping my breast, he starts grinding a hard-on into my ass. Fucking gross. I try to ignore his animalistic grunts and carefully let my secret weapon slide from my sleeve into the palm of my hand. Almost gagging, I make sure I time his grinding rhythm right, knowing I'll likely have one chance, and the next time he rubs his package on me, I twist and pull away a little, plunging the little knife in his groin.

Howling he releases me and makes a grab for his balls, blood starting to run down his legs.

"Jesus, Katie. What'd you do? Castrate him?" Gus walks in gun drawn, with Neil closely behind him. Ignoring him I drop on all fours and crawl to where Caleb is laying blood coating his beautiful face. I'm about to lift his head in my lap when Neil says, "Better leave him the way he is in case of a concussion or spinal damage, honey."

Right.

"Mal?" I ask Neil who is checking him out, while Gus is handling the debilitated Guzman.

"Chest shot, but high close to the shoulder. Alive but struggling."

"Anybody seen Blue?"

As it turns out, Blue and I were the only ones without a scrape. For once.

Neil had been able to drag the dog away from the front door, where he was apparently trying to claw his way in, getting nipped in the process. I never heard a thing, too preoccupied with what was happening inside to worry about any sounds from out there. Safely locked in Gus' truck to make sure he couldn't get in the way, the guys finally were able to make their way in.

Malachi is airlifted to Durango, hanging on and Caleb... Caleb is refusing to go anywhere but follow his brother to the hospital. I can't blame him, but I try to convince him to get checked out first.

"Baby, please," I plead, holding his battered face in my hands. "I promise I'll get you signed out of there as soon as is possible and on your way to Durango, but for me… for us, let them have a quick look at you." I shamelessly grab his hand and place it on my abdomen. I'm not beyond emotional blackmail if it the situation warrants it.

"You don't play fair, little one," he croaks on a sigh, rubbing his fingers slightly over the swell of my stomach.

Bending over the gurney I kiss him gently and with my mouth still on his, say; "I'm sorry," But I'm really not. I'll do whatever it takes.

With a squeeze to his hand and a nod to the EMT's I move back so they can load him up. Gus steps up behind me and puts an arm around my shoulder.

"You ok, honey?"

I nod, keeping my eyes on Caleb.

"What happened with Guzman?" I need to know.

"He's being transported to Durango by ambulance, since his injuries are not life-threatening but he requires specialized surgery. I just got off the phone with Duarte. He knows. It's out of our hands, Katie. Go with your man, Neil and I will take care of things here, look after your mutt."

With a nod, I move to get into the ambulance with Caleb, getting a hand up from Gus, who closes the doors behind me.

Caleb grabs for my hand as soon as I sit down beside him and ignoring the EMT who is scribbling on his clipboard beside me, we focus only on each other.

"Did he hurt you?" Caleb growls beside me.

"Who, Guzman? No, he tried to, but was too hopped up on whatever he had in his system to think straight. I managed to take him down quite easily with Arlene's picnic cutlery," I chuckle.

"What?" Confusion is stamped across his face and I'm reminded he was likely out for much if not all of my confrontation with the creep.

"The only thing within reach was the wooden take out knife that came with the diner order Gus had just dropped off. I waited my chance, and well, I may have castrated him," I tell him matter of factly.

A loud clatter has me turn to look where the EMT has just dropped his clipboard and pen to the floor, his eyes nearly bulging out of his head as he stares at me in fascinated horror, causing both Caleb and I to burst out laughing. Not so great for Caleb who winces and grabs for his ribs, saying between clenched teeth to the poor paramedic, "Better watch it, her aim's been off for a while now. This is the second man she's maimed for life in as many weeks."

Three fucking broken ribs and a concussion. I wish I could've killed the bastard. Not fighting back had taken every ounce of restraint out of me, but I knew doing so would've been too big a risk. Too much at stake with Duarte waiting to have this man delivered to him alive. I expected to feel some guilt over sacrificing a human being to what was sure to be inhuman torture awaiting him, but I felt little. Not even a twinge of remorse over circumventing the FBI in our dealings with Duarte, since they were more than willing to sacrifice my brother for the sake of their investigations into the cartel. Nothing but frustration remains at being bound to a bed, with Katie sleeping in a chair beside me, waiting to be released so I can go and be with my brother.

"Hey–" Gus's low voice comes from the doorway. "Okay if I come in?"

"Please."

He must've just come from the barn and looks like shit. I'm eager to get a status on my brother's condition and have about a million questions for him.

Pulling up a second chair from against the wall, he sits on the other side of my bed, running a hand over his face.

"Long day."

"Can say that again," I agree.

"Have you heard–" I start.

"Malachi–" he begins at the same time. I nod for him to go on. "is out of surgery. The bullet hit him between the first and second rib, piercing his lung on the left side and nicking an artery, but missing the heart. By the time he got to the hospital his lung had collapsed and he was losing blood in his chest cavity, making it difficult for his heart to pump. They got him to the OR right away where they managed to stop the bleeding, repair the artery and the lung, and retrieve the bullet intact from where it was lodged in the trapezius muscle in the back. Aside from an initial rough patch in the OR, he's expected to pull through. He was lucky, my friend."

Choking back emotion, I swallow hard before I force out a shaky "Thank you" to Gus.

The small fingers lacing through mine on the bedspread tell me Katie is awake and heard every word.

"Hey," her soft voice whispers against my ear.

"Sorry to wake you," Gus apologizes.

"Not at all; we needed to know. As soon as we can get out of here, we'll be on our way."

My little one. For someone who grew up without knowing what family means, she has come in and taken hold of this one like it's all she knows.

"Neil volunteered to drive you, 'cause as far as I know the Rav is still at the shop, right?"

At my nod and Katie's 'yes', he continues. "Before they come kick me out let me quickly update you. First off; Blue is fine, albeit a little whiny. Neil is staying at the barn with him, since he went ballistic when we tried to drive off with him in the truck. He won't budge. It also gives Neil a chance to do a bit of clean up. It's a bit of a mess. Next the Feds swarmed in as soon as the calls went out on the airwaves, so be prepared for a visit at some point. The paperwork on this may follow us for a bit to come, but what else is new," he chuckles, but then sobers immediately and takes a deep breath. "Finally there's Guzman; he never arrived in Durango. A call came in to Joe about an hour and a half after they left that a state patrol car had spotted the ambulance just past the 140 turnoff at Hesperus on a dirt road maybe 100 yards from the highway. Both EMT's and the guard were tied up and duct-taped, but otherwise unharmed, in the back of the ambulance. No sign of Guzman."

CHAPTER THIRTY-TWO

"Blue! Where are you! Blue?"

"Sweets, he'll come when he's good and ready."

"Yeah but what if he doesn't come back?"

I chuckle when I spot her pouty lip again; something she's taken to doing from time to time and I can't quite figure out whether she does it on purpose 'cause I think it's cute, or whether pregnancy hormones have brought out some new and unusual behaviors. Doesn't matter to me, I'll take it either way; it's still cute as hell. Especially on hard-nosed, ball-busting Katie Acker.

Last night she let Blue out and he hasn't been back since. I say he's got a bitch lined up somewhere he goes to visit every now and then, but Katie is convinced he's hurt or caught in a trap somewhere or something. She's been protective as a mother hen over all of us, Blue, me and even Malachi ever since his release from the hospital. I thought she'd cry when he announced he was going back to the apartment over the diner instead of staying with us. His reasons were clear, and apologetic when he saw Katie's disappointment, but he just didn't want our house to be overrun with law-enforcement day in and day out. They have been relentless in their pursuit of answers from him, but there just haven't been many to give and there is little concrete that can be pinned on him other than suspicions and conjecture. Guzman is still in the wind without a trace and none of us knows where the hell he is, although some of us have a pretty good idea who might.

Mal figures at least when the FBI visit him at the diner, Arlene and Seb might get a few extra customers out of it from time to time. With his stairway next to the kitchen vent, there's no way anyone can walk out of there without getting a good whiff off Seb's cooking. And that is not easy to walk away from.

Other than that life has been fairly calm in the past three weeks. By the time I got out of the hospital, Clint was already back at the barn with his crew finishing up the drywall Mal and I had started. I reluctantly let him finish since my main interest was the woodwork anyway. The guys stayed on for a week; enough time to tape, mud a few layers and paint. They even tiled and installed the hardware in the bathrooms. Including a surprise I have for Katie in the en-suite upstairs, but I haven't let her go up there yet. I have a plan for that.

Katie's been busy getting her garden in the ground. It's been a labour of love, with help from Faith, Seb's little sister who has the mental development of an eight-year-old, but when it comes to growing vegetables, she is like a living encyclopaedia. She's spent a few afternoons here, going over Katie's sketches and plans and giggling like a little girl at Blue's nuzzles and licks. Damn mutt seems to have a thing for women. Well... and Malachi. He loves Malachi. Only seems to tolerate me because Katie loves me.

And she does love me.

Looking up at me from where she is digging in the soil, her short hair starting to grow out a little again and dirt streaking her face, she is the most beautiful thing I've ever seen. I'd rather bite my tongue and swallow it than tell her, but since she got pregnant she is filling out even more and I am loving all the swells and dips it creates on her luscious body. There is something so wholesome about a strong, plump and feisty woman, this one in particular.

I get up from the lounger and stalk over to where she is on hands and knees planting seeds, my shadow covering her.

"Watcha doing?" She peeks over her shoulder up at me, a knowing gleam in her eyes.

I drop down on my knees behind her in the dirt and wrapping my arms around her, haul her up so her back is flush against my front and she can feel the steel of my arousal firmly lodged between our bodies.

"God, Caleb. It's been so long," she moans. My lips taste the salt from the skin of her exposed neck. It's been too fucking long. Other than curling herself around me carefully every night and giving me some much needed relief between her delicious lips, Katie has refused to let me fuck her, or make love to her since the doc said to take it easy.

"I need you, little one. Need inside you."

"But the doctor said–"

"Fuck him. I'm fine. Been three weeks, baby. Three fucking weeks without this," I mumble against her ear as I slide my hand inside her pants, straight down to her pussy, already slick with her want. "Fuck you're so wet for me, sweets. So juicy. Slide your pants off."

"Here? Outside?"

"Right fucking here. Our house, our yard, right here."

A few quick moves has her pants down to her knees and I help pull one leg free and drape it over my lap so she sits, spread wide on my knees, her back against my chest. It takes even less time to undo the few buttons that hold down my straining cock and once free, it stands up straining and full. An arm around her waist and a hand under her leg, I help her lift herself over and torturously slow onto my erection.

"Ah fuck, babe. Nothing better. Nothing fucking better than being inside you. Put your hands on my knees and let me do all the work."

Katie leans forward, grabbing my knees and I push up her shirt in the back to get a view of that glorious white ass. With one hand sliding between her legs and the other behind me for leverage, I start slowly at first; lifting my hips and pushing into her. Watching my cock disappear into her tight channel and then pull out, slippery with her juices is the most erotic fucking thing I've ever seen. My finger on her clit is rubbing circles and my movements increase as the light breeze that picks up over the fields only adds to heighten the experience. Exposed, wet, hard—the soft grunts from her throat every time my cock bottoms out inside of her. The wet slide of my fingers through her curls and over her nerve centre brings out my own groans.It's everything, and not enough. In one move I have her under me, still lodged firmly with my body wrapped around hers, one arm holding her hips up and the other hand working her clit furiously, while I pump into her.

Hips pistoning, I can feel the walls of her vagina start to contract around me and a tingle starts at the base of my spine. With her hands clawing the soil, she is panting with her mouth hanging open.

"Fuck. Caleb, now. Coming nowww..." Arching her body and throwing her head back, Katie screams out her release, and I follow closely behind. Curved over her body, my cock planted as deep as it'll go I can feel my hot seed spill inside her.

"Holy hell," is all I manage to formulate before I roll on my back, taking Katie with me, turning her in my arms.

Holy hell is right.

I can hear Caleb's heart racing under my ear and my own isn't doing much better. Both of us are pretty much covered in the rich black soil I had dumped in last week to give the garden a good start, and suddenly a fit of giggles overcomes me. We're fucking near middle-aged, kid on the way and we are literally fucking like bunnies in the vegetable garden? If only Neil could see us now.

"What's funny?" Caleb's voice rumbles from his chest.

"Us," I snicker, "lying in the dirt, half-naked. All we need now is Neil coming around back."

"Oh hell no." And just like Caleb is sitting in front of me, struggling to get my foot back in my pant leg. "Come on Katie, cooperate."

All I can do is laugh harder, especially when he leans in, his nose touching mine and growls, "Not. Helping." Now I'm almost rolling on the ground with hilarity until I hear a distant bark and just like that the giggles are gone.

"Blue! Come 'ere boy!"

Suddenly cooperating fully, my pants are on and in place in seconds and Caleb is tucked in and buttoned up.

Good thing too, because Blue comes bounding around the side of the barn, Malachi following closely behind. Mal takes one look at me and then Caleb, no doubt noticing the black dirt all over us and simply shakes his head.

"Neil is right. Fucking bunnies." Which of course sets me off again, this time with my arms around Blue's neck who has cuddled up against me.

"Where've you been, buddy? Been looking for you."

"Showed up at the diner. Actually, he was sitting out back by the stairs. Funny dog. Turns out Seb's sister, Faith, was visiting and in the kitchen. Guess between the two us of we have just enough attraction to beat you out, little sister."

"Silly dog. You wanted to go for a visit?"

I don't mind him going over to visit Mal. I like it actually, I'm just a little worried about the road, and I guess I wouldn't want him to try and get to Cortez to visit Faith, but for a stray, he's been very faithful to me and to the barn.

"Just came by to drop him back off and to see if you guys want to come grab a bite at the diner tonight? Something I want to discuss."

"Sure," is my automatic response, but I see Caleb eying his brother with concern.

"Everything alright, Mal?" he asks.

"Yeah. Good. Everything's good," Mal says with a curt nod.

"Alright. Yeah, we'll see you later. Have an appointment in Cortez first, but we'll be there. Six?"

A nod and a hand wave is all we get for confirmation as he disappears around the corner as stealth as he appeared.

CHAPTER THIRTY-THREE

By the time we walk into the diner, it looks like the entire crew is assembled, including Joe. Malachi, Neil, Gus, Emma and Joe were all sitting at the far end of the diner, where three smaller tables were pushed together to make room for everyone. I help Katie in a chair beside Mal and sit on her other side.

"Quite a crowd," I notice.

"I invited everyone, since it affects everyone. Arlene and Seb will sit down when they can." Mal starts, for all appearances calm and collected, but I know the telltale signs of nerves on my brother. The rubbing of the pad of his thumb of his knuckles is something he's done since he was a little boy.

Arlene pulls up a chair and sits. "Sorry, had to finish serving someone. Seb is bringing out a pot of goulash soon. We'll serve at the table if that's okay with everyone?"

Everyone nods or voices their acknowledgement, while my eyes seek out Malachi's and hold over the table. I see insecurity there, but also resolve and I give him what I hope is a reassuring smile, conveying without words that whatever it is he needs, I will be there for him. The smallest of nods ends our wordless conversation and he turns to the rest of the table, clearing his throat.

"There are no words sufficient to thank all of you for how you have taken me on; taken me in over the past weeks and even before I came back from Durango. Actually, probably especially for that time. I don't have much I can share with you to show my gratitude, but in the family I grew up in, which was a very long time ago, that family believed in sharing a meal to celebrate and give thanks."

"Perfect! See Gus? There is a damn good reason I'm always cooking," Emma elbows Gus in the ribs, who only shakes his head smiling. Apparently a subject often revisited.

"I'm hoping to stay here, in Cedar Tree."

I can barely hear his voice over the discussion that has emerged between Emma and Arlene, but with his eyes focused on me I know exactly what he is saying. And apparently so does Katie, because she about climbs in his lap to hug him.

"We would love that!" She grabs his face and kisses his cheek. The little ass just lets her with a big, shit-eating grin on his face. Leaning over I grab her by the waist and pull her back.

"That's my brother you're mauling."

"Oh hush. It is your *brother* I'm mauling. We're gonna have a total family here in Cedar Tree. Uncle Malachi!"

The dead silence that follows is deafening, until Arlene of course is the first one to break it.

"Pregnant? You're fucking pregnant? Holy shit. That's some fast work, my friend." She punches me in the arm and has a big wobbly smile on her face. "Happy for ya."

I grab Arlene around the neck and pull her into a hug. "Thank you, girl. Thank you so much."

When I turn back to the table hugs and kisses are flying and Emma is grabbing extra napkins to staunch her flow of tears. She seems to be elated.

I have one arm around my Katie, never to let go and the other around Arlene, keeping her close until Seb can get here; feeling on top of the fucking world.

It isn't long before Seb comes out with a steaming pot, followed by Beth with a tray of bowls and fresh bread. With a glance my way he puts the pot on the table, taking his place beside Arlene, and I release her in his care.

A raucous and celebratory two hours later Emma, Gus, Katie and I stand outside saying our goodbyes, the women still chatting about pregnancy, when Gus turns to me.

"Your brother any good as a tracker?"

I can't help but smile at the memory of the way he bested me out at Arches National Park not that long ago. "Might be. Might even be better than I am. What's on your mind?"

"I may be interested in sitting down with him sometime. See if he's interested in trying to walk this side of the law. How would you feel about that?"

I consider it for a minute. Any reservations I thought I might've felt are simply not there. Even without too many words, simply by watching my brother interact with people and respond to his environment, without the garbage of our past cluttering the space between us. I've been able to get a much better picture of the man that is and not the man I thought I knew.

"No problem whatsoever," I can wholeheartedly respond.

Gus nods, turning back to the women.

I notice Katie looking toward the Tahoe.

"Caleb?"

"Hmmm?"

"What's that on your windshield?"

"Stay here," Gus orders Emma and Katie, following me across the parking lot. Of course I immediately hear the sound of Katie's crutches and Emma's walker following. These are not women you order around.

The envelope stuck under my wiper is a regular manila color and letter sized. Katie's name is printed in bold on the front. When Katie, who has drawn up beside me, reaches out to grab it, I hold her back.

"Wait up, little one. Let's get Neil and his gadgets out here first, okay? Just to be on the safe side?"

I just nod numbly at Caleb. I don't know what I was thinking, reaching for that envelope like that. I know better—been trained better. Pregnancy hormones are really taking a toll on my brainpower.

Behind me Gus and Emma are bickering whether or not Emma should go back into the diner for safety and it sounds like Emma is winning, insisting that if Gus thinks she will sit safely inside to see the love of her life potentially be blown to bits by what could be a bomb or something, he's got another thing coming. Mumbling and swearing, Gus stomps off inside to fetch Neil.

Despite the surreal feel of this situation, I can't help but smile at the love between them, evident in the things they choose to argue about. Caleb and I are much the same, I realize, and I slide an arm around his waist, leaning in to him.

Neil comes running out and makes a beeline for his truck without saying a word. Gus follows behind at a slower pace, and sidles up to Emma, who doesn't say anything but snuggles in when he pulls her in close.

Eager like a puppy with a bone, Neil comes back with some kind of scanner in his hand. Running it over the surface of the envelope the excitement on his face slowly falls.

"What? What is it?" I ask him.

"It's a fucking envelope. Not a single electronic component; no wire, nothing metal, nothing. I was so looking forward to practice my rusty demolition skills."

Caleb and I look at each other with eyebrows raised. *Bomb demolition?* So much we still don't know about *the kid.*

"Let Katie be the only one to handle the envelope, Neil, in case we need to print. Less to eliminate?" Gus suggests when Neil is about to grab the envelope from under the wiper.

"All yours, babe." Caleb urges me on in a low voice and I reach up to pull the envelope toward me.

Opening the flap I shake out the contents on the hood of the Tahoe. A few loose documents and "What the fuck?"

"Is that...?"

"Ziploc baggie, Neil."

"Don't tell me that's the knife?" Emma exclaims, "Eeewww. That's so fucking gross."

On top of the papers is a little wooden knife, completely stained a dark rusty brown. I'm sure the blood of one Gorge Guzman. Neil has a baggie inside out and picks up the knife and seals the bag, holding up for a good look.

"Geeze Neil, put that thing away. What does the note say, Katie?" Emma wants to know.

Right. A note. Aside from some official looking papers in what appears to be Spanish, there is a handwritten note on lined paper.

"It says: Dear Ms. Acker, I am returning to you something you may have lost. I was able to salvage it from a pile of garbage brought to me a few weeks ago. You'll be happy to know it is the only salvageable item remaining. The rest of the garbage was appropriately disposed of."

A chill runs down my back when I think what could be done to a human body in the timespan of three weeks, but then something in the next paragraph catches my eye.

"It goes on to say: My father regrettably passed away two weeks ago. He left detailed instructions on how he wanted his affairs handled. Your name was on an envelope left with his will. I trust you will forgive me; due to the nature of our business I had no choice but to open and screen the contents of the envelope and found myself as shocked as I am sure you will be. Signed; *Su hermano?*"

The note flutters from my hand and the last I remember is Caleb's voice; "Jesus, Katie!"

And then nothing.

"Baby, wake up. Come on, little one."

Forcing my eyes open, I find myself on the couch back home at the barn. Blue whimpering by my side. As I look around at the concerned faces of Caleb and Malachi, the last conscious memory comes back with a gasp.

"Easy, *Yázhí*. Mal made some hot tea, drink some first and we'll talk."

Caleb helps me sit up, sliding behind me, and with shaking hands I accept the mug Mal gives me. He sits down on the floor next to Blue and strokes his head, while keeping one hand on my foot, which feels icy cold.

"You have to stay calm or I promised Naomi I would bring you in."

"You talked to Naomi?"

My voice sounds shrill to my own ears.

"Just to tell her you had a shock and fainted, nothing more. She gave me a choice to bring you in or take you to familiar surroundings but that if you didn't come to quickly or if you weren't able to stay calm, to bring you in. For peanut's safety."

The last words sink in and my hand slides down to rest on my abdomen. My god.

"We left straight from the parking lot and only Malachi saw you fall. He drove us home. We were gone before anyone noticed. Gus, Neil, Emma, Mal and the two of us, Katie. No one else. Do you understand? No one. We are your family. Always will be. Now, Gus took the papers and with Neil is working on verifying at them. They were a birth certificate and a death certificate. He and Emma will be over shortly, if that is ok with you."

All I can do is nod, too numb to do much more. The men in my life trying to infuse my chilled body with heat.

I don't know how long we sit there, almost drowning in the silence, when the perking of Blue's ears and then the crunch of the driveway gravel alerts the arrival of Gus and Emma.

"Hey darlin'," from Gus, who bends down and kisses my head, while Emma scoots on the couch beside me and grabs my hands in hers.

"Gus, honey, can you see if there is a blanket you can grab from the bedroom?"

In no time, I'm tucked under a quilt wedged between Emma and Caleb, and while Gus is building a fire, Mal is fetching drinks for everyone. If I didn't know any better I'd think we were settling in for a cozy evening with friends.

Having had some time with my turbulent thoughts, I am slowly coming out of my shock and find I want to know more.

"What did you find out?" I direct my question at Gus, surprising everyone in the room.

"You sure?" he wants to know and I nod firmly. "Okay. The birth certificate is for one Ekatarina Creemore-Duarte, mother Diana Creemore, father Juan Duarte. It's the real thing. The death certificate is Diana Creemore, dated 3 days after the birth certificate."

A sharp pain slices through my chest and I can't help the involuntary gasp that escapes me. My mother – my birthmother – is dead. Been dead my entire life.

"I hope you don't mind, I didn't think you'd want to so I called Ernesto. Told him it was a big shock, that you had no idea. He spent the last few weeks doing a little research and found out from his aunt, Juan's sister, that Diana had been a vacationing American tourist Juan had fallen in love with. At the time he was married to Ernesto's mother who was pregnant with the youngest of the Duarte brothers. He tried to keep Diana a secret, as his mistress but when she ended up pregnant with you, he started spending more and more time with her and his wife found out. Shortly after Diana gave birth to you she died from complications and although he tried to take you home, his wife convinced him you would be better of in the US with a good adoptive family.

According to the sister, that was a decision he regretted his entire life and had tried to track you down. When he started losing some of his cognitive functioning and his sons took over the daily workings of the cartel, Juan spent his lucid time putting out feelers and was surprised when he was contacted by an adoption lawyer who had been contacted by a woman who fit the general age and description, looking for information on her birth parents. The name he was given was yours, Katie. He didn't end up in Larchwood by accident, Ernesto says he requested to go there, even asked that specific room, claiming to need the exact southern exposure it had. Ernesto says he rarely ever questioned his father's whims and I guess it fit his own plans just fine."

"Oh my God," I'm so overwhelmed with a barrage of feelings. Most of them pretty freaky but some of it feels good. "Juan looked me up, to get to know me? Why didn't he ever tell me?"

"Babe," Caleb rumbles behind me, "from what I recall, he was quite confused a lot of the time. And besides, if I put myself in his shoes for a minute, I would perhaps want a chance to get to know my daughter, but I wouldn't necessarily want my daughter to get to know me, given my history."

Right. There's that.

"The odds of this are... out of this world," Emma points out and I start laughing.

"What's funny?" she turns to me and I smile.

"I used to believe all odds were against me, but I'm starting to think I'm luckier than I ever could have imagined."

"How in hell do you figure that?"

"Think about it? What do think the 'odds' would be of the cartel coming after any of you, my loved ones, my family, ever again? Their sister? Their own blood? In a disturbing and sick kind of way, I think I've never been safer before in my life."

The stunned looks on the faces around me quickly break out in laughter when Malachi deadpans, "Like I said, you are one weird bird."

I'm laying on my side in bed, my head propped up on my hand, looking at Katie beside me, who has taken on much the same position.

"You are the most refreshing, remarkable and resilient woman I have ever met," I tell her, my finger tracing the middle of her forehead, down to the tip of her nose to her full lips and finally her chin, which I tip up so I can reach her mouth with mine.

"I need you to sit up." I tell her, sliding my hand under the pillow to retrieve what I placed there earlier.

Katie pushes up and sits as naked as the day she was born, not an ounce of shame, beautiful and smiling before me. I grab the blanket Mal found for me and place it around her shoulders, while she looks on mildly amused.

"I was originally going to wait until the upstairs was done, but today seems a very good day."

Tucking the ends of the blanket around her I pull her in for another kiss before I go on; "Traditionally a Navajo wedding is a simple one, without a lot of fanfare. Often arranged between the groom and the bride's parents, but even these days, you find couples that prefer the traditional ways. From what I can recall, the couple feeds each other a corn paste, which I don't have. I could've fed you creamed corn from a can, but that seems almost sacrilegious. But what stands out most in my memory is the way the groom wraps his wife to be in a blanket. That simple gesture of comfort and protection is his vow to her. Once that wordless promise is made, they're man and wife..." I pause for a moment before adding "Mrs. Whitetail." And laugh when her eyes shoot open and my feisty Katie comes out.

"Oh no you don't! You don't get to marry me and not let me in on it!" She pushes me back on the bed and straddles me with the blanket still wrapped around her shoulders, looking like the fierce warrior woman she is.

"Truth is, I have belonged to you for years, *Yázhí*. Been yours in heart, body and spirit even before you were aware. From the moment you gave yours to me, I've considered you my wife— my other half. A legal paper is likely needed to have you share my last name, but the only truth my heart needs is your blessing."

"I am honoured to call you my husband, and my life has already been blessed beyond my imagination with what you've brought me," she smiles at me, "I don't need anything more than this."

I carefully take her left hand and slide the turquoise band I've been hiding in my palm around her fourth finger.

EPILOGUE

"You coming?"

Caleb's been calling from upstairs for the past few minutes, but I just wanted to finish planting my seedlings in my new mini-greenhouse. Quickly washing my hands at the sink, I grab my crutches and make my way to the stairs.

"Coming!"

"Take the elevator!"

The elevator was just installed last week and Caleb had been using it all week to make sure it was working properly. I had not yet been upstairs, per his insistence, so no matter how eager I was to see, I wasn't above making him wait for me a little for a change.

"I'll just take the stairs," I answer.

"Elevator!" Comes the response.

Too excited to argue, I push the button and find the car already there. The ride up is smooth and uneventful, but when I push the door open the sight stops me in my tracks. Gorgeous gleaming wood floors span the walkway that runs from the bedrooms and bathroom at the front of the house to the master suite in the back and a trail is laid out in tea light candles leading to the master bedroom. I follow it into a massive space spanning the full width of the barn directly over the kitchen and dining areas. The broad board wood flooring continues, but is broken up with an occasional throw rug. A massive bed is centred in the space, facing a huge window with a view of the mountains. That will make for some fantastic mornings in bed. Caleb is chuckling as I'm taking it all in; the sheer size, the beautiful ceiling beams, the wood detailing on the framework and the phenomenal bed.

"You do this?" I want to know.

"With Mal. We learned young, before my father lost control he loved working with wood and we enjoyed spending time in his shop with him. Guess you never quite lose that."

"It's stunning." I run my fingers along the smooth surface of the solid headboard. It has a slight incline, which will make it so comfortable leaning back against to enjoy the view.

"It's huge."

That makes Caleb laugh. "I'm not exactly small and I like room to move around," he says, an eyebrow raised. Right. "Also, when this little peanut gets here," he says walking up behind me and sliding his hands around my stomach, "and whatever other children we might end up having, we will all fit."

I turn around and tilt my head, looking into his eyes. "You want our children to sleep in our bed?"

"Fuck no. That would seriously cramp my style, but after my morning sex with their beautiful mother..." He is nuzzling my neck when I notice the glass block wall on the right.

"Is that the bathroom?"

Without waiting for an answer I carefully move my crutches around the candles dotting the floor, and walk into the bathroom where the sound of running water draws my eye immediately to the most amazing shower. A waterfall, about two feet in width is raining down from the back wall of the natural stone shower, with several other showerheads at a variety of heights and angles adding to the rush of water. A wide ledge juts out from the tiled walls and runs underneath the waterfall and along the length of the stall, which is substantial; almost large enough for an average family. On the other side is the tall-edged claw foot tub I saw them carry in last week. A wide trough-like sink in the same stone of the shower sits along the wall beside the tub with two separate taps and mirrors. A door on the opposite side is cracked open to reveal the toilet.

"Holy crud, Caleb. This is decadent!"

I'm practically salivating over the rustic luxury in this room.

"Remember the shower at the guesthouse? The one you *enjoyed* so much?" Caleb is right behind me once more and I can feel his warm breath tickling the hair by my ear when I nod.

"I designed this shower with that experience in mind."

This time when I turn around and see his eyes, they're a burning dark hazel and my body instantly reacts.

"Show me," I challenge him.

In no time at all he has made fast work of our clothes and I find myself standing naked under the delicious spray of water, where Caleb proceeds to show me every last benefit of his innovative design.

"Blue! Where are ya boy? Blue?"

"He take off again?"

Katie's on the back deck yelling for that damn mutt, who seems to take off every couple of weeks for a day or two. Drives her crazy. Sometimes he shows up at the diner and Malachi brings him back and sometimes he just shows up here, a bit dirty but otherwise none the worse for wear.

I look at my wife, something we made legal on a quick getaway weekend in Vegas without telling anyone months ago, and am struck by how much she has changed since I first met her. Her face once almost gaunt and reserved is now fuller and open, her body before was perfectly toned and strengthened and now was richly curved and blossoming with her eight-month pregnancy. She doesn't look much like the hard-nosed, ball-busting security specialist anymore; more like a warm-hearted earth mother. But that woman is still a force to be reckoned with and if I had to pick a partner to have my back in any situation, she'd be at the top of my list.

We've got the whole gang coming over for a Fall cookout. The weather's been surprisingly mild so late in the year and after a hot summer spent mostly indoors in cold, but canned air, it'll be nice to hang out outside. Even if we have to do it with sweaters on.

We picked Monday so Seb, Arlene, Beth and Julie could be here too. Seb said he'd be bringing sides and Emma will take care of desserts, not that we had to ask, it's a given.

Mal's been here since early this morning, stoking the fire out by what was the vegetable garden where we've got a pig roasting. Mal's idea, so I told him since it was his, he was welcome to execute it too. The moment Neil heard about an open fire, he volunteered to help. Kids.

I'm surprised, now that I think about it, that with the mouth-watering smell of that roasting pig, the dog hasn't turned up yet. But before I can even mention anything to Katie, she's already waddling to the door to let the first visitors in. Her walking was fine until she hit the seventh month of her pregnancy. Suddenly her gait changed and Mal tortures her mercilessly. My little one just shrugs it off, though. She is still so grateful to be walking at all. Waddling or otherwise. She's not going waste time worrying about mundane things like that, not anymore. We've all learned some lessons and the most important one is; Life won't wait.

That damn dog. It's such a great day with everyone here. We finally get to enjoy the space and location of the barn and the grounds and of course Blue picks today to disappear. Better be careful not to stand too much today, I can already feel it in my back. Damn. I'll be glad when this kid is out. Pregnancy is fun and all when you have a cute little belly, but once you turn into a whale the fun is done.

We have a nursery set up upstairs, but I guess Caleb thought it might be a little too far from the master bedroom at first, so he put a bassinet in our bedroom with a room divider. Damn room is big enough, we could probably sleep a football team in there. I have a feeling Caleb might be a pretty protective father, regardless of whether our baby is a boy or a girl. We've chosen not to find out the sex and just wait till nature sees fit to tell us. Naomi was funny. She said that she wouldn't want to do the ultrasounds anymore then, just in case she spotted the genitals. She wants to be as surprised as we are.

Naomi has become a great friend, one I can really show the back of my tongue to. Emma will always have a special spot in my heart, but feels more like a peer. Even if she's had her hand up my twat more times than I want to remember. That is freaking weird, but I guess it happens when your doctor becomes your friend and also the person who will be delivering your baby.

I'm happy to see she brought her son out for this, even though he doesn't seem too thrilled to be here. Mal seems to be taking him under his wing though. Good. Mal probably knows all about troubled youth and the problems they can get into. I don't envy Naomi and the path she's had to walk on her own. Still does. Stupid Joe. Where is he anyway? He was supposed to show up as well.

Damn my back aches.

"Hey, little one. You okay?"

"Just a sore back, gonna be on the couch putting my feet up for a bit. You gonna be ok to handle this crowd?"

"We're good. Why don't you just take the elevator upstairs and lay down for a bit. I'll check on you in a little."

A sweet kiss on my lips and a shove in the direction of the front hallway and he's off outside.

Must've been sleeping for a bit because the sun is pretty low in the sky when I open my eyes and look at the mountains. At the same time I feel the pain in my back returning, but much more intense, and moving into my lower abdomen. Oh fuck, this is a contraction. Relax and it will go away.

I manage to breathe through the intense sensation but before I have a chance to get up and find Caleb, another one hits, this one even stronger then before. It's a fucking battle not to grit my teeth but I know any added tension will only make it worse. Breathe through it. Another one builds before the last one is even gone, and part of me is starting to panic. I can't seem to move.

It's ok, I tell myself. This takes hours. I can handle pain. Someone will come upstairs.

One after another, the storm of contractions become so overwhelming, I'm barely thinking straight. When at the height of another one a flood of water gushes between my legs, I can't help it, I cry out loudly. Within seconds I hear Caleb shouting, "Mal! Get Naomi and come up here." Then his voice turns soothing in my ear. "You'll be ok, *Yázhí.* All your people are here. We can do this."

If it wasn't for the stupid mutt showing up just when he did, and bugging me to let him inside the house, I might not have heard Katie cry out from upstairs.

One look at her and the state of the bed and my guess was this baby was going to be born right here—at home, whether we liked it or not. First person I think of to call is my brother; I need him here and Naomi of course. Christ what a stroke of luck to have Naomi here.

Katie is barely registering her surroundings, she's already so drawn into herself. With Naomi and Mal's footsteps coming up the stairs, I start pulling off her sopping wet pants and underwear. Mal moves in behind Katie and starts whispering to her while Naomi slides in beside me and quickly starts shooting off instructions.

"Look," she says, at the peak of the next contraction when a little patch of ink black hair becomes visible between her stretched labia. "We're having this baby in the next few minutes"

"Will it be ok?"

"Thirty-seven weeks, Caleb. Technically it's considered full term."

"You take her, I'll grab what we need," Mal says and I take his place, pulling my wife up between my legs.

I can't remember much of the next minutes until Naomi tells both Katie and I to slide our hands around the slippery little body between Katie's legs and lift it up on her belly. Time stands still to engrave that moment in our memories for eternity. My hands cover Katie's as we pull our son up, where he is warm and nestled between his mother's chest and the warmth of our hands.

"Caleb, want to cut the cord?"

I'm about to answer, when Katie puts a hand on mine.

"I'd like Malachi to cut the cord. Mal? Would you?" Katie asks in a soft voice.

My brother simply nods and takes the sterilized scissors from Naomi.

I bury my face in my little one's neck and count my blessings.

----THE END----

ABOUT THE AUTHOR

Freya Barker inspires with her stories about 'real' people, perhaps less than perfect, each struggling to find their own slice of happy, but just as deserving of romance, thrills and chills, and some hot, sizzling sex in their lives.

Recipient of the RomCon "Reader's Choice" Award for best first book, "Slim To None," Freya has hit the ground running. She loves nothing more than to meet and mingle with her readers, whether it be online or in person at one of the signings she attends.

Freya spins story after story with an endless supply of bruised and dented characters, vying for attention!

Freya

Stay in touch!

https://www.freyabarker.com

https://www.goodreads.com/FreyaBarker

https://www.facebook.com/FreyaBarkerWrites

https://twitter.com/freya_barker

or sign up for my newsletter:

http://bit.ly/1DmiBub

ACKNOWLEDGEMENTS

A bunch of big thank you's!

To my family…. ALL of them.

My hubs who has been more patient than any other person I know; staring at the back-end of a computer while I work and am being a-social; keeping the fridge full and the household running while I have my head buried deep in my fictional characters – and all with silent acceptance.

My amazing kids who are equal parts proud and mortified with what I do… From their relentless 'porn'-teasing over dinner to their frequent interest in my radically changed life.

To my parents who are awesome; my mom who at almost ninety has read each book and my dad who is just happy when I'm happy.

To my big sister, who would be cheering me on if I'd decided to make a career of pole-dancing. She's that amazing.

My brothers; big burly men – all four of them, and I know they have watched, they have supported and yes… they've even read.

Three wonderful sisters in law who are so much more than their title implies, and a great bunch of amazing nieces and nephews; all of them 'adults' now, who are absolutely wonderful!

I am so blessed with my big crazy family.

I also want to thank a group of women, most of whom I have not had the pleasure of meeting face to face yet, but who are tireless in their support of me and relentless in their promotion of my books: Catherine Scott, Nancy Huddleston, Deb Blake, Pam Buchanan, Kerry-Ann Bell, Linda Funk, Aimee Shannon, Tracy Meighan, Lena Gaitanou, Bonnie Trujillo, Nicole Mccurdy, and last but certainly not least, my brand spanking new PA, Leanne Hawkes, who is working her buns off to keep me organized. I love you B&B's!

A special mention to Pam Buchanan and Deb Blake, who have taken over my former blog Ripe For Reader, and are doing a phenomenal job. I am so proud of you girls!

In this industry you don't get anywhere by yourself. I am so incredibly fortunate to have a group of amazing author friends who motivate, encourage, correct, and support me. You all make me so grateful!

Ava Manello is one of those authors and her friendship, intelligence, industry knowledge and insight have helped me out more often than I can recall. Love you big time, honey!

And finally all you amazing readers – you wonderful people who have taken, or are taking a chance on me. The stories I write are ones that I would like to read myself. I write them for me – so the thought that these books that are meaningful to me, might mean something to you too still boggles my mind.

Thank you from the bottom of my humble heart.

Also by Freya Barker

Cedar Tree Series

Book #1

SLIM TO NONE

Book #2

HUNDRED TO ONE

Book #3

AGAINST

Book #4

CLEAN LINES

Book #5

UPPER HAND

Book #6

LIKE ARROWS

Book #7

HEAD START

Portland ME Novels

Book #1

FROM DUST

Book #2

CRUEL WATER

Book #3

THROUGH FIRE

Book #4

STILL WATER